CHAPTER 1

"Good morning, kids," Dr. Rebecca Miller said in greeting to the two dogs and three cats who were currently residing in the intensive care unit of the Animal Friends Veterinary Clinic. Dr. Miller was the clinic's owner and its only veterinarian. She typically arrived at the clinic about an hour before the rest of her staff to check on her patients.

Rebecca stood a little over five feet tall. She had an athletic build that attested to her active lifestyle. She kept her medium-length brown hair pulled away from her face more from necessity than preference. She was all about practicality and keeping her hair pulled back prevented it from getting in her way while she worked. On more than one occasion, she had thought about cutting it all off, but she hadn't been able to bring herself to do it.

"How's everyone feeling this morning?" Dr. Miller's habit of talking to the animals, as if they understood every word she said, was a constant source of amusement to her staff as well as her patients' owners. It was also one of the reasons she had a reputation for being an excellent veterinarian. Dr. Miller loved animals, and it showed. In fact, she felt much more comfortable talking to them than she did their owners. She had never been much of a people person. Oftentimes, she barely even noticed the person standing in the exam room. Instead, her focus was centered entirely on her patient. Occasionally, a client would approach her at a public place, and Rebecca would have no idea who they were until they mentioned their pet.

"Looks like you got your IV all twisted up again, Harvey," she said reproachfully, addressing the red and white Boxer who sat in the wire cage at the far end of the small room that served as the ICU. Harvey looked up at her through large brown eyes, the wrinkles on his face adding to his guilty expression. He wagged his stubbed tail enthusiastically as she approached him. Rebecca opened the cage door and crawled part way inside. She reached for Harvey's leg and pulled it toward her in order to flush the catheter with heparinized saline. Harvey bumped his muzzle into Rebecca's shoulder, knocking her to one side.

"Hey, watch it, you big oaf," she chided as she righted herself.

Harvey let out an apologetic whimper.

"I forgive you," Rebecca chuckled, reaching out to rub Harvey on the ears. He moaned softly and leaned into her hand. "Like that, do ya?" she asked as she continued to massage his ear. "I think you're looking good enough to go home this morning, big guy. How about you don't eat any more of your mom's clothes, okay?"

To the embarrassment of Harvey's owner, Rebecca had removed three socks and two pairs of lacy underwear from Harvey's stomach two days previously. Rebecca had been relieved that the underwear had indeed belonged to Mrs. Johnston. The last time she had removed underwear from one of her patient's digestive tracts it had turned out not to belong to the dog's owner, but instead had belonged to her husband's mistress. That was a scene Rebecca was happy not to repeat.

She backed out of Harvey's cage and went to check on her other patients. They occupied the bank of stainless steel cages that were pushed up against the room's north wall. The bank was arranged so that four small cages rested on top of two larger ones. Rebecca's short frame made it difficult for her to reach the patients in the top cages. She pulled up a step ladder and climbed onto it, raising herself up high enough to peer into one of the upper cages.

A low growl emanated from the cage. Rebecca smiled at the gray tomcat who sat hunched in the back corner of the

4

cage. The strong ammonia-laced scent of cat urine filled her nostrils. She wrinkled her nose and said, "It smells awful in there, but I'm glad to see you're urinating, Mr. Jenkins."

He was brought into the clinic two days previously with a blocked urethra. Dr. Miller passed a urinary catheter to clear the blockage. She had pulled the catheter the night before in the hope that Mr. Jenkins would be able to urinate on his own.

The cat glared at her and let out another low, threatening growl. He twitched his tail in agitation. "I don't blame you. I'd be upset too, if I'd been put through the indignities you've had to suffer for the last two days," Rebecca said in a soft soothing tone. "Easy does it, I'm just gonna reach in there and pull out that stinky towel. You know, it would've been more pleasant for everyone, if you had used the litter box."

Mr. Jenkins continued to growl threateningly as Rebecca gingerly reached into his cage and pulled out the urine soaked towel. "You are a contrary one, aren't you? Don't worry, I'm sending you home today. You won't have to spend another night in a room full of dogs."

Just then, Rebecca heard someone knocking on the front door. She stood and hurried toward the front of the clinic. She knew that someone banging on the door at that time in the morning meant they had an emergency, or at least they thought they did. Pet owners were funny. There were the owners who completely overreacted to a mild symptom and rushed their pet in to see her, and then there were the owners who would wait until it was too late for her to help the pet before they brought it in. She really never knew which one she was going to get.

As she entered the waiting room, she saw a woman with a panicked look on her face peering through the window. Rebecca pulled the door open. Before she could say anything, the woman blurted out, "I just ran over my dog. He's in the car. He's bleeding. Please help him."

"How big is he? Do I need to get a stretcher?" Rebecca asked.

"He's only about 20 pounds. I was afraid to move him, so I left him in the car," the woman answered, casting a worried glance toward the Jeep that was parked in front of the clinic.

"Okay, let me take a look at him," Rebecca said as she walked toward the woman's vehicle.

The woman hurried ahead of her and opened the left rear door. Rebecca leaned inside. A brown and white mixed breed with wiry hair was lying on a blanket. He was taking quick, shallow breaths. Rebecca could see blood oozing out of his nose. His right rear leg hung at an awkward angle. Rebecca wrapped the blanket around the dog and gently lifted him into her arms. As she turned to move toward the clinic, she asked, "What's his name?"

"Benson," answered the woman.

Rebecca took Benson into one of the exam rooms. When she placed him on the stainless steel table that took up the center of the small room, he lifted his head and wagged his tail at her.

"Aren't you a sweetheart?" Rebecca cooed. "I know you're hurting and yet you still managed a tail wag for me."

She continued to talk to him while she performed her examination. She listened to his heart and lungs, palpated his abdomen, and looked for any external injuries. Benson's owner stood on the opposite side of the table nervously wringing her hands. When Rebecca finished, she looked up and said, "His lungs sound like he has a contusion on the right side. He is also showing signs of shock, and his right rear leg is broken. I need to get him started on an IV to stabilize him. Then I'd like to take some radiographs to see how badly the leg is broken and to look for any other broken bones."

"All right," the woman answered. "Please do whatever he needs. I feel terrible. I didn't even know he was outside. My husband let him out of the front door right as I was backing out of the garage."

The bell over the front door jingled as someone entered the clinic. "Good morning, Rebecca," the new arrival called.

"Good morning, June," Rebecca responded. A moment later, a large-boned, older woman with short gray hair poked her head into the room. Her round face was smooth despite her age. Her blue eyes sparkled with intelligence and good humor.

"Who do you have there?" she asked.

"This is Benson. He's been hit by a car and is in shock. Could you please give me a hand getting an IV started?"

"Sure thing. Let me just put my stuff away, and I'll be right there."

June Montgomery had been Rebecca's receptionist since she had opened Animal Friends five years ago. Rebecca had hit the jackpot when she had hired June. She was friendly, efficient, and caring, all the qualities needed in a good receptionist. She and June had immediately bonded. She relied heavily on June to handle the duties of smoothing the ruffled feathers of unhappy clients as well as collecting overdue payments. Rebecca knew the place wouldn't run nearly as efficiently without June there to handle the front office.

She nodded in response to June. Then she said to Benson's owner, "Make sure he doesn't decide to leap off the table while I go get the supplies I need to place the IV."

A few minutes later, she had the IV running. She and June shot the radiographs. Then she carried them into the exam room to show Benson's owner. "Benson's right tibia and fibula are broken. Those are the bones in the lower half of the leg," she said, pointing to the break on the radiograph. "The good news is that the break was clean.

He'll need to be in a cast for 4-6 weeks, but the leg will be good as new. Nothing else seems to be broken." She pointed to the chest radiograph and said, "The lungs should be black. Air doesn't show up on a radiograph. However, you can see all this cloudy, white stuff here." She pointed to the spot on the radiograph. "That's the contusion I was talking about. It will heal with the help of some medication. Bottom line, with a little TLC, Benson is going to be fine."

The woman sighed with relief and said, "Thank you so much. When can I take him home?"

"He'll need to stay here today to get more fluids. He should be able to go home tomorrow. It'll just take me a few minutes to put a cast on that leg. Once we've got him all set up in a cage in the ICU, you'll be welcome to go back and see him before you leave," Rebecca answered.

June assisted Rebecca as she placed a cast on Benson's leg. Then Rebecca took Benson's owner back to visit him. Silent tears ran down her cheeks as she opened Benson's cage door and gently ran her hands over his head. "I'm so sorry, Benson," she whispered. "I love you. You're such a wonderful dog." Then she said to Rebecca, "I really need to get to work. I'll call later this afternoon to check on him." She closed the cage and hurried out of the room. Benson whimpered softly.

"Don't worry, Benson. She'll be back," Rebecca soothed.

After the woman left, Rebecca finished checking on her other patients. Lobo, a young Blue Heeler mix, had broken his leg and had a large section of his skin torn off of his hip and thigh when he fell out of the back of his owner's pickup. Rebecca had given Lobo's owner an ear full on the importance of making sure his dog was secure when riding in the back of a truck. The man had been shocked, and a little angry, but Rebecca hadn't cared. She was usually very even-tempered. However, dogs riding unsecured in the back of pickups was one issue that could get her fired up quickly. She had been embarrassed by her outburst after the man left, but whenever she looked at Lobo's leg, her irritation returned. She would have to wait for Jimmy, her technician, to arrive to help her clean and dress his wounds.

The two kittens, one male and one female, in the other top cage were litter mates. They had been brought in to be neutered and spayed. Their owner had asked to leave them overnight due to her late work schedule. They would be going home first thing this morning.

A few minutes later, Jimmy sauntered into the clinic. "Morning, Doc," he greeted. Just out of high school, Jimmy still had the acned face of a teenager. He was tall and lean with sandy blond hair that fell across his hazel eyes. He wore a faded T-shirt and jeans with rips in the knees.

Three months ago, Jillian, her previous technician, had suddenly eloped leaving Rebecca in a jam. Jimmy had walked in two days later asking for a job. Rebecca had been certain he wouldn't last, but he had been very persuasive during his interview, and she had decided to give him a chance. Since that time, he had proven himself to be a hard worker and a fast learner. He had not given Rebecca any reason to regret her decision.

"Good morning, Jimmy," Rebecca returned.

"Who's the new arrival?" Jimmy asked.

"That's Benson. His owner accidentally ran over him with her Jeep this morning."

"Bummer for him," Jimmy responded.

"Yeah," Rebecca agreed, "Thankfully, he wasn't hurt too badly. Grab Lobo while I get some bandaging material, and we'll see how his wound looks today."

A few moments later, Jimmy laid Lobo down on the grated table in the middle of the treatment area that ran behind the two exam rooms. "Man, you sure tore into that dude yesterday. I've never seen you so mad," he said, grinning at Rebecca while she carefully removed Lobo's bandage.

"Yeah, well, you can see what his negligence did to his dog," grumbled Rebecca defensively.

"I didn't say he didn't deserve it," replied Jimmy. "I just didn't know you had it in you. The guy outweighed you by 100 pounds, and you intimidated him. It was fun to watch."

Wanting to change the subject, Rebecca said, "It looks really good." She ran warm water over the wound to clean it and to stimulate blood flow to the area.

Understanding Dr. Miller's desire steer the subject away from what happened yesterday, Jimmy let it drop and replied, "Sure does. You think it'll leave much of a scar?"

"No, once it's all healed, it will barely be noticeable."

The rest of the day passed like most days in a busy veterinary practice. Dr. Miller spent the morning performing spays, neuters, and other minor surgical procedures. She spent the afternoon seeing patients. She administered vaccines, treated ear infections, and gave several lectures on the importance of dental hygiene. By the end of the day, she was exhausted.

As Rebecca was locking up for the night, she felt a spurt of satisfaction. She loved being a veterinarian. It was all she had ever wanted to do. She had set her goal on becoming a vet while she was still in elementary school and had never wavered from it.

Rebecca drove the short distance to her home at the end of a cul-de-sac in an older subdivision. The house had belonged to her grandmother. Rebecca inherited it when her grandmother had passed away a year ago. It was a red-brick home built in the 1970s. It still had all the trimmings inside typical of houses from that era, including orange Formica countertops, wood-paneled walls, and green shag carpet. All of her savings had gone into building and starting up Animal Friends, so there hadn't been any money left to remodel the house. Now that the clinic was finally making a profit, she intended to start fixing up the place.

The green shag was definitely going to be the first thing to go.

Rebecca pulled her blue Camry into the driveway on the left side of the house and parked under the carport. It was early spring, and a light rain had begun to fall. She was grateful for the carport's protective covering as she stepped out of her car. She hurried across the open space between the carport and her front door. As soon as she stepped inside the house, she was greeted by a large Golden Retriever holding a tennis ball in his mouth.

"Hi, Captain," she greeted warmly as she came down to her knees to wrap her arms around the dog's neck. "How's my boy?" Captain leaned into her embrace. His feet danced beneath him as his enthusiastic tail wagging rocked his big body back and forth. Rebecca chuckled and said, "I missed you, too."

She straightened and moved toward the back door. Captain padded softly along beside her. "Sorry, buddy, but you're gonna get a little wet out there," she said as she opened the door to let Captain outside. The big dog trotted across the porch and leaped off of it, bypassing the stairs. Her back yard was enclosed by a privacy fence, so she didn't need to worry about Captain wandering out of the yard. Rebecca closed the door and moved toward the kitchen to see what she could rummage up to eat for dinner.

Half an hour later, she and Captain were curled up on the sofa watching television when her cell phone rang. Rebecca reached for the phone and saw that the call was from her mother, Barbara Miller.

"Hi, Mom," she answered.

"Hello, Rebecca. How was work today?" her mother asked.

"Good," Rebecca replied. "It was a pretty ordinary day."

"Did you meet anyone interesting?"

Rebecca sighed. By 'interesting', her mother meant had she met anyone who would make prospective marriage material. Recently, getting Rebecca married had become Barbara's number one priority. Ever since Rebecca had graduated veterinary school, Barbara had made sure to remind Rebecca about the need to find a good man. However, since Rebecca's 30th birthday three months ago, Barbara had changed her game plan and made it an almost daily topic of conversation.

"No, Mom. I didn't meet anyone interesting," answered Rebecca in a 'you're stretching my patience' tone.

"You're not getting any younger, Rebecca. You need to start taking finding a husband more seriously. You need a man in your life, honey."

"I have Captain. He's good enough for me," Rebecca said, reaching out to rub Captain's shoulder as he lay snuggled against her.

"Dogs aren't men, Rebecca," Barbara said in exasperation. "And Captain certainly isn't going to be able to give me any grandchildren."

"Mom, we've been through all of this before," Rebecca said, trying to hold on to her patience. "It's not like men are lining up at my door, and I'm turning them away. Men just don't seem to notice me."

"Poppycock. Men notice you all the time. You're the one who doesn't notice them. You need to take off your blinders, Rebecca."

Rebecca let out another big sigh and said tiredly, "Mom, it's been a really long day, and I'm tired. Can we have this conversation some other time?"

"Will you at least promise me to try to be more open to the possibility of finding someone?" Barbara asked, a note of pleading in her voice.

"Yes, I promise," Rebecca said reluctantly.

"All right. That's all I'm asking. I'll talk to you later. I love you."

"I love you, too, Mom," Rebecca answered as she ended the call. Rebecca heaved another big sigh. It wasn't as if she didn't want a man in her life. She had dated a few times, but nothing serious. During veterinary school, she was too focused on her studies. Then, for the last few years, all her energy had been devoted to getting Animal Friends off the ground. When Rebecca added the knowledge that she wasn't going to win any beauty contests to the fact that she was 30 years old, she concluded her chances of finding someone anytime soon were slim to none. She also knew that her mom didn't see it that way and therefore, wouldn't stop hounding her about finding a husband.

"Like I said to her, Captain, you're the man in my life," she said, giving him a good belly scratch. He moaned his pleasure. Her mother's words echoed through her mind. 'Dogs aren't men, Rebecca.' *She's right about that. Dogs are a lot easier to please. Captain doesn't care that I'm plain and old.*

CHAPTER 2

Rebecca pulled a patient's folder out of the plastic bin that hung on the back of the exam room door. The Animal Friends Veterinary Clinic had two examination rooms. Typically, while she saw one patient, June would get the next one settled into the other exam room. Then June would place the folder in the bin to let Rebecca know that someone was in the room and ready to see her. Rebecca always skimmed over the patient information before entering the room. This file indicated the patient was an eight-week-old orange tabby named Buster. He was there for his first set of vaccines. The owner's name was Barry Hays. Rebecca noted that he had filled out a new client card, which meant this was his first visit to the clinic.

Rebecca pushed open the exam room door and stepped into the room. Her eyes widened in surprise as she got her first look at Barry Hays. He stood on the opposite side of the exam table. He was tall and barrel-chested. He wore a black leather vest over a tight black T-shirt. Both of his arms were covered with an assortment of tattoos. The lower half of his face was hidden by a thick gray beard that hung to the middle of his chest. Long gray hair, parted down the middle, flowed to well past his shoulders. His skin had the leathered appearance of someone who had lived a rough life. A thin, jagged scar started under his left eye and ran down his cheek disappearing into his beard. Rebecca felt mildly intimidated by the man's rough appearance.

"Good morning, Mr. Hays" she greeted as she glanced around the small room looking for a kitten. She felt a little confused when she didn't see any sign of one. *Did June give me the wrong file?* she wondered.

"Morning." His voice was deep and gruff.

Rebecca took another quick glance around the room. "So, Buster's here to get his first shots, huh?" she asked, hoping to prompt the man into producing the kitten.

"Yep," he replied. He didn't move. He only stared at her as if he expected her to do something. Rebecca was getting more confused by the second.

"Okay, then, let's get started," Rebecca said, eyeing the man expectantly.

Just then, the exam room door opened, and Jimmy stuck his head inside. "Need any help in here, Doc?" he asked.

Rebecca turned toward him and answered, "No, we're fine. I think Oscar's here for his monthly nail trim. Go ahead and take care of him."

Jimmy nodded and shut the door. Rebecca turned toward Mr. Hays. Just as he came into her view, his beard moved. Rebecca's eyes widened in surprise. A moment later, a small orange head popped out from between the strands of the big man's hair. Large golden eyes peered curiously around the room. Rebecca smiled. *So, there you are,* she thought. *I couldn't see you through all that hair.*

"Hi, Buster," she said, reaching out for the kitten. "Let me take a look at you." The kitten quickly retreated back into his hiding place.

Mr. Hays chuckled and reached up to pluck the kitten off his shoulder. He gently placed him on the table. The kitten purred loudly. Mr. Hays' eyes twinkled as he smiled fondly down at the little ball of orange fur.

Buster's got him wrapped around his little paw, Rebecca thought with amusement. *He doesn't seem nearly as intimidating now.*

Mr. Hays glanced up and said, "I found 'im at a truck stop about a week ago. I went inside to take a shower and get something to eat. When I came back out to the truck, he was sitting on top of one of my tires like he was king of the world. He didn't even flinch when I picked 'im up. He started purrin' like a locomotive. I couldn't just leave 'im there. He was lucky I spotted 'im, but he might not get so lucky the next time. I set him on the seat next to me. Next thing I knew, he climbed up on the back of the seat and then right onto my shoulder. He's pretty much made that his permanent spot. He's turnin' out to be a great travelin' buddy."

Rebecca grinned up at the big man. It wasn't often that she was surprised by someone. She certainly hadn't expected such a rough looking man to be so fond of a tiny orange kitten. She proceeded to examine Buster. The kitten purred loudly through the entire process.

"He looks like a healthy kitten," she stated once she finished her examination.

Mr. Hays grinned widely. "That's good. I'm awfully attached to the little guy." He picked Buster up and placed him back on his shoulder.

Rebecca filled out the rest of her paperwork and took it to June. She didn't have any other patients waiting, so she stayed up front as June checked Mr. Hays out. As the front door shut behind him, June turned to Rebecca. Her eyes shone with the moisture of unshed tears. "Wasn't that the cutest thing? Seeing that big old truck driver being so sweet to a little orange kitten just made my day."

Rebecca smiled and teased, "You get all teary-eyed over the funniest things, but I agree, it was pretty sweet. When I first walked into the exam room, I was confused. I didn't see Buster perched on Mr. Hays' shoulder. I thought you must have given me the wrong file. I kept subtly glancing around the room trying to figure out where Buster was."

June chuckled and said, "I guess I should've warned ya."

Rebecca smiled and said, "It would've definitely saved me some confusion. What else do we have today?"

"Mr. Stockton is bringing Sandy in for another heartworm and flea treatment," answered June. Her cheeks took on a slight flush of pink.

Rebecca grinned and teased, "When do you think the old guy will get up the nerve to ask you out? You know he only comes in here once a month, so he can visit with you. He's perfectly capable of treating Sandy himself. She's such a sweet dog."

"He isn't coming in here just to see me," June answered defensively. "He enjoys visiting with you, too."

Jimmy had walked up to them just as June finished speaking. "Are ya talkin' about old Mr. Stockton?" he asked.

"Yes," answered Rebecca.

"Yep, that old dude's got a serious crush on you, June. It's as plain as day," Jimmy said matter-of-factly.

June's cheeks now burned a bright red. "You two cut it out. We're too old to have crushes."

Jimmy laughed and said, "You like flirting with him, and you know it. You light up like a Christmas tree every time he comes in."

June reached out and batted Jimmy on the arm. "Don't you have some work to do, young man?"

Jimmy's laughter echoed down the hallway as he headed back to check on the animals in the ICU.

Thirty minutes later, the bell over the front door chimed as Mr. Stockton walked in leading Sandy. He was a spry little man who looked to be in his late 60s. The wrinkles at the corners of his eyes and the laugh lines running down the sides of his face gave testament to his good humor. He wore a bright-red ball cap, a blue shirt, and red suspenders. As he stepped to the front counter, he reached up and pulled off the hat, causing thin white strands of hair to stick out wildly. He swiped his hand over his head in an attempt to smooth it.

"Hello, June," he greeted. "You're looking lovely today."

"Hello, Walter. How's Sandy?" responded June.

"She's doin' fine. We took a long walk through the park this morning. She got to chase a few squirrels."

Jimmy and Rebecca were huddled together peeking around the corner to spy on June and Walter Stockton.

"How long should we let them visit before I go get Sandy?" Jimmy whispered.

"Oh, let's give them a few minutes. We don't have any other patients waiting," Rebecca responded. *Jimmy's right,* she thought. *June does light up like a Christmas tree when she's talking with Mr. Stockton.*

June's husband of 30 years died a little over a year ago from a heart attack. June was normally a very happy and optimistic person. However, for the first few months following Cal's death, June's spirits were crushed. She had done what was needed to get through each day, but there had not been any joy in her work. She had gradually regained her vibrancy, but Rebecca could still see the remnants of pain in her eyes. She thought that maybe Walter Stockton would be the answer to healing June's broken heart.

"We really shouldn't spy on them," she said to Jimmy.

"So, do you think he's ever gonna get up the nerve to take her to dinner?" Jimmy asked in response.

"I hope so," answered Rebecca. Then she stepped around the corner. Walter and June both turned to watch her approach.

"Hi, Mr. Stockton. It's good to see you again," greeted Rebecca. She walked up to Sandy and knelt down beside her. Sandy was a liver and white Brittany Spaniel. Unlike most of the dogs of her breed, Sandy had a very calm disposition. She wagged her tail softly as Rebecca knelt beside her.

"Hello, pretty girl," Rebecca cooed. "I'm glad you came to see me today." Rebecca reached out and ran her hand across the top of Sandy's head down to her tail in a long firm stroke. Sandy's tail wagged a little harder.

"Why don't I take her back and weigh her for you, Mr. Stockton? It looks like she may have put on a few pounds," Rebecca commented.

Walter chuckled and said, "I know I'm not supposed to feed her table scraps, but she looks at me with those big brown eyes, and I just can't refuse."

"Walter," June chastised. "You know people food's bad for dogs. Don't you want Sandy to live to be a ripe old age?"

"Of course, I do," he replied.

"Well, then, stop feeding her table scraps," June said sternly.

"Come on, Sandy," Rebecca whispered in the dog's ear. "Let's leave June to set Walter straight."

The two older people barely noticed as she stood and led Sandy to the back. Rebecca could hear June continue to lecture Walter on the dangers of feeding dogs people food. Rebecca was sure that June would have Walter duly chastised by the time she returned Sandy to him.

"Sorry, Sandy. Looks like you've enjoyed your last non-dog food meal," she said.

"What's got June all riled up?" Jimmy asked as he stepped out of the ICU room.

"Walter confessed to feeding Sandy table scraps. June's giving him a piece of her mind about it," Rebecca answered.

"Well, I guess he won't be asking her out today then," responded Jimmy.

Rebecca laughed and said, "You're probably right about that."

A few minutes later, Rebecca returned Sandy to Walter. "Looks like Sandy's gained three pounds since your last visit," she said as she handed Sandy's leash to Walter.

"Hear that, Sandy?" he asked. "It's just plain old kibble for you from this point on. June has set me straight about that."

Grinning to herself, Rebecca left to give the couple a few more minutes to talk. A little while later, she heard the bell above the front door jingle. She went back up front to talk with June. At the sound of her approach, June turned to look toward her. She wore a stunned expression on her face.

"I guess you and Jimmy were right," she said, her voice flustered. "Walter invited me to go to dinner with him tomorrow night. Can you believe it? After I finished lecturing him, he said 'I like a passionate woman', and then he invited me to dinner."

Rebecca threw her head back and laughed. "Jimmy and I weren't completely right. We thought you blew your chance of getting a date when you started lecturing him."

"He asked her out?" Jimmy asked as he walked up to them.

"Yes," Rebecca replied. "He told her he liked passionate women."

Jimmy chuckled and said, "He's got a point there. You said 'yes' didn't ya?"

June nodded and said, "My love life's really not any of your business, you know."

"Ah, come on, June, you know we're gonna want to know all the juicy details," he teased.

"There aren't going to be any 'juicy' details," she said, blushing with embarrassment.

~

Later that night, Rebecca smiled to herself as she remembered her friend's response to Jimmy's teasing. "Well, Captain, it looks like even June has better luck with men than I do. I think my mother should kiss her thoughts of grandchildren good-bye."

Just then, her phone rang. "Speak of the devil," she mumbled as she picked up the phone.

"Hi, Mom. What's up?"

"Now, don't say 'no' until you hear what I have to say," Barbara started.

What now? Rebecca thought apprehensively, afraid to hear what would come next.

"I was at the beauty shop getting my hair done, and I started talking to this really nice lady. Naturally, our conversation turned to our children."

"Naturally," Rebecca said dryly.

"Anyway, she told me that her son is a doctor. He works in the ER at St. Luke's. She told me that he's 35 and single. What do you think of that?"

"What am I supposed to think?" asked Rebecca. "Do you want me to drive over to St. Luke's tonight and see if I can bump into him?"

"Don't be sarcastic," replied Barbara. "His mother told me that she would tell him about you. I gave her your number."

Rebecca rolled her eyes toward the ceiling and took a deep breath before she spoke. "Mom, I don't want you passing out my phone number to strangers."

Ignoring the statement, Barbara continued, "I just wanted you to know in case he calls. You'll say 'yes' if he asks you out, won't you?"

"He's not going to call, Mom. And if he did, I'd probably think he was a nutcase. What kind of guy would call the number of a strange woman his mother had gotten from a lady in a beauty shop?"

"Well, when you put it that way, it does sound pretty unlikely. Anyway, how's everything else going?"

"Great. I really wish you'd stop worrying about me so much. I'm honestly pretty happy."

They spoke for a few more minutes before ending the call. Rebecca spent the rest of the evening curled up on the sofa with Captain watching television. *I really am happy,* she thought. *I'm not sure having a man in my life would make me any happier.*

CHAPTER 3

"Come on, Mitch, show me what you've got," Derrick taunted. Derrick Peterson and his friend, Mitch Holt, faced each other at the foul line of the Spring Valley Community Center's basketball court. It had been their routine to meet for a game of one-on-one every Saturday morning since high school. The only reason they ever missed was if one of them got called into work on an emergency. He worked as a physician in the emergency room of St. Luke's Regional Hospital. Mitch was a detective with the Spring Valley Police Department.

"How about this?" Mitch asked as he threw an elbow into Derrick's midsection and drove around him for an easy lay-up.

Derrick laughed good naturedly as he caught the ball coming through the net. Their games were notoriously rough. They were best friends, but they were also very competitive. Both men gave and took their fair share of elbows over the course of a game.

Derrick and Mitch had been friends since first grade. They were both athletic, intelligent, and devoted to their jobs, but that was where their similarities ended.

Derrick had a serious, no-nonsense personality. He was quiet and preferred spending most of his time alone. He had a long, lean body with sharp angular features. He kept his black hair cut short and neat. His typical attire consisted of a pressed dress shirt, dark slacks, and a power tie.

Mitch was a few inches shorter than Derrick and had a stocky build. He tended to wear brightly-colored polo shirts and khakis that went well with his light blonde features. His wavy hair fell over his ears, brushing the top of his collar. Other than his job, Mitch rarely took anything seriously. He had an easy-going, gregarious personality.

"3-2, you lead," Derrick commented as he tossed the ball back to Mitch, who stood waiting at the top of the key.

"You're getting slow in your old age," Mitch teased.

"We're the same age, idiot."

"Yeah, but I'm holding up better than you," responded Mitch.

Derrick settled into a defensive position in front of Mitch. Mitch took a quick jab step to the right and then a hard dribble to the left. He pulled up at the left elbow and shot a fade-away jump shot.

Derrick didn't fall for the fake, so he was perfectly positioned when Mitch took the shot. He leaped high into the air and swatted the ball away. It flew across the court and bounced into the third row of the bleachers.

"How's that for old?" Derrick asked with a note of satisfaction.

Mitch chuckled and said, "Not bad. Out of bounds on you. It's still my ball."

Derrick grinned in response and trotted toward the bleachers to retrieve the errant ball. Just as he bent to pick it up, his cell phone started ringing. The phone was in the side pocket of his gym bag, which rested on the bottom row of the bleachers. He unzipped the bag, dug into the pocket, and pulled out the phone. "Dr. Peterson," he answered.

Knowing that the call meant the game was over, Mitch trotted over to join Derrick. He saw a slip of paper fall out of Derrick's bag as he pulled out his phone. He picked it up and saw a woman's name and phone number scrawled on it.

"Be there in 15 minutes," Derrick said, ending the call.

"Gotta go," he said to Mitch as he turned to gather his things. "Car accident. One of the cars involved was a passenger van carrying eight kids."

"What's this?" Mitch asked, holding up the slip of paper.

"What?" asked Derrick, turning back to Mitch with his bag slung over his shoulder. He saw the paper in Mitch's hand. "Oh, Stella gave me that number a few weeks ago. Some woman she met in the beauty shop gave it to her. I think it's her daughter's number," he answered as he started to move toward the showers. Stella was Derrick's step mom. They had never been close, but she had taken it on as her personal mission to get Derrick married.

"You plan on calling it?" Mitch asked.

"No," Derrick answered.

Mitch wasn't surprised. Women had thrown themselves into Derrick's path since they were boys. They were attracted to his dark, brooding nature, but he rarely gave them the time of day. He hated the whole flirting, giggling scene most women displayed when they were around him. Oh, he'd dated over the years, but never anything serious and certainly not someone his stepmother had found for him in a beauty shop. When Derrick did date, it was usually someone sophisticated and beautiful.

Mitch, on the other hand, loved women. He thought they were fascinating, and he enjoyed their attention. It wasn't unusual for him to date two or three different women a week.

"You mind if I call her?" he asked as he hurried alongside Derrick.

"No, go right ahead," answered Derrick, shrugging his shoulder dismissively.

They reached the end of the bleachers. Derrick turned sharply around the corner toward the locker rooms. As he rounded the corner, he plowed into a small woman. Derrick grunted as they made contact. The woman took the brunt of the impact and fell backwards, landing hard on her backside.

"I'm sorry. I didn't see you," said Derrick, reaching out a hand to help the woman to her feet.

Mitch rounded the corner. "Are you okay?" he asked, his voice filled with concern.

Rebecca sat in stunned silence. She looked up at the two men staring down at her. Her cheeks burned with embarrassment.

"I'm fine," she finally answered, reaching out to accept the outstretched hand of the man who had bumped into her. He grasped her hand firmly in his and effortlessly pulled her to her feet. Rebecca was surprised by the tingling sensation that ran up her arm as their hands joined. Her gaze flew to his face. He was strikingly handsome. His eyes were hazel with flecks of gold that stood out against his darkly tanned skin. He had a wide, strong jaw. She knew she was staring, but she couldn't seem to look away. She racked her brain for something to say, but it had gone completely blank. She felt her face growing warmer by the millisecond.

His voice brought her out of her momentary stupor. "I apologize again." He gave a brief nod and moved past her. Rebecca watched as he hurried down the hallway.

"He's an ER doctor. There's an emergency at the hospital."

"I understand," replied Rebecca, turning her gaze to the man speaking to her. He gave her a dazzling smile. His blue eyes twinkled with an easy charm. Rebecca recognized the confidence of a man used to the attention of women. Although Rebecca preferred the sharp, angular features of his friend, she was sure that most women would find him very attractive.

"Are you sure you're okay?" he asked.

"Yes, I'm fine," answered Rebecca. After a brief pause, she said, "Well, that group of girls standing over there staring at us is my team. I had better join them before they die of curiosity."

Rebecca stepped around Mitch and hurried toward the group of ten-year-old girls huddled together on the opposite side of the gym. Rebecca had been their basketball coach since they were eight. Despite her short stature, she loved the game. Marilyn, her best friend, had talked her into coaching her daughter's team when their first coach had quit unexpectedly in the middle of the season. She fell in love with the group of girls and had decided to remain their coach even after the season ended.

"Who were those hunks?" Kristen, the most outspoken girl on the team, asked as soon as she joined them.

"I have no idea," Rebecca answered. "One of them bumped into me and knocked me down. They were just helping me up and making sure I wasn't hurt."

"I wouldn't have minded him bumping into me," said Marilyn from her spot on the bench just behind the girls.

Marilyn's daughter, Emma, rolled her eyes and said, "Mom, you're married. You're not supposed to say things like that."

Marilyn laughed at her daughter's exasperated expression. "Being married isn't the same as being blind. I still notice cute guys, and that was one good-looking man. They both were."

Rebecca grinned at this exchange between mother and daughter. Then said, "Time for practice, girls. We've only got two more weeks before our first game. Give me two laps."

The girls moaned in unison and then began the trip around the gym.

"You have to agree, they were really hot," Marilyn said.

"I was too embarrassed to notice," Rebecca hedged. She knew she'd never hear the end of it if she admitted to Marilyn how attractive she had found the man who had knocked her down. Marilyn hounded her about finding a man almost as mercilessly as her mother. Besides she would probably never see them again.

~

Two hours later, Rebecca and Captain were in the car on their way to St. Luke's Regional Hospital. Every Saturday afternoon, Rebecca took Captain to visit the kids in the children's wing. Three years ago, Rebecca found Captain in a ditch on the side of Highway 50. He'd been hit by a car. His left femur had been broken, and he had several bruises and lacerations. She immediately fell in love with his warm and gentle nature. She knew that he would make a great therapy dog. Once his wounds had healed, she took him through the required training. She had been right, Captain was a natural. The patients loved him, and he loved them.

Rebecca glanced over and felt her heart swell with affection for the big golden dog sitting beside her. He sat up tall in the seat, a wide grin on his face. His eyes were shining with happiness. She reached over and rubbed his ear. He thumped his tail in appreciation.

Rebecca pulled into the hospital parking lot. She and Captain walked into the lobby, and she pressed the elevator button. A few seconds later, the doors opened, and they stepped inside. Just as the doors were closing, a large male hand shot through the opening. The elevator doors immediately reversed direction. Rebecca's eyes widened in recognition as the man entered.

"Sorry," Derrick mumbled as he reached to push the button for the third floor. He was tired and needed a shot of caffeine. The nurses in the ER made coffee that could almost pass for tea it was so weak. He had to go to the cafeteria to get coffee that had any bite to it.

None of the car accident victims were seriously injured, but he'd had to bandage and stitch several lacerations, set a few broken bones, and calm a number of distraught parents. The morning had taken its toll. He leaned heavily against the elevator wall. He glanced over at the woman and therapy dog who shared the elevator with him. The woman looked at him with that expectant look of someone who was waiting for you to remember that you knew her.

Derrick looked at her closely but didn't recognize her. He offered a polite smile.

He doesn't recognize me, thought Rebecca. She wasn't sure whether to feel relieved or offended. *Should I say something or just pretend like this morning never happened?*

The elevator signal sounded as it stopped on the third floor. Rebecca sagged with relief when Derrick exited the elevator. She was glad she had not said anything. *Well, that was further proof that men don't notice me. The man ran me over a few hours ago, and he still didn't recognize me.*

A few seconds later, she and Captain reached their floor. As they stepped off the elevator, they were warmly greeted by Allison, the pretty nurse who usually worked the Saturday afternoon shift in the children's wing.

"Good afternoon, Dr. Miller. How's Mr. Handsome today?" she asked as she came down to her knees and rubbed Captain's head.

Captain wagged his tail and leaned into her. She laughed and rubbed him a little harder.

"Who are we visiting today?" Rebecca asked.

"I thought we would try Robby. He's an eight-year-old who came in on Monday. He was diagnosed with kidney failure. He's on a dialysis machine and needs a transplant. He was adopted, so neither of his parents is a match. He's been very depressed. I talked with his mother, and she agreed that Captain may be just the thing to cheer him up."

Rebecca's heart constricted in sympathy for the boy. "Okay," she said. "Lead the way."

They stopped in the doorway to room 412. "Mrs. Adams," Allison said to the petite, dark-haired woman who sat near the hospital bed. "May we come in?"

The woman smiled when she spotted Rebecca and Captain standing behind Allison. "Yes, please," she replied.

Allison moved further into the room. Rebecca and Captain moved in behind her. Robby looked so small and frail sitting up in the large hospital bed. His face lit up at the sight of Captain. He looked questioningly at his mother.

She smiled at the look on his face and said, "This is Dr. Miller and her dog, Captain. They wanted very much to meet you today."

"Really?" Robby asked in surprise.

"Yes," Rebecca answered. "Captain loves visiting children. Would you like to pet him?"

Robby nodded his head enthusiastically. Rebecca released Captain, and he moved immediately to the side of the bed. He rose up on his hind legs and placed his paws on the mattress. Then he dropped his big head onto them and looked up at Robby through his large brown eyes.

"Hi, Captain," Robby said as he reached out and rubbed Captain on the top of the head. Captain nuzzled Robby's hand. The boy laughed and said, "I love dogs. I'm really glad you came to see me." Captain's tail wagged gently as Robby continued to talk to him.

Mrs. Adams caught Rebecca's eye and mouthed, "Thank you." Moisture shimmered in her eyes.

"You're welcome," Rebecca mouthed back. This was what she loved about her and Captain's visits to the hospital. She knew they were making a difference in the lives of the patients who were there as well as their families.

They stayed with Robby for several minutes. He chatted to Captain almost non-stop. He told Captain all about how he needed new kidneys and how scared he was.

Silent tears ran down Mrs. Adams cheeks as she listened to the exchange. She motioned Rebecca to join her in the hallway.

"I can't thank you enough," she said. "This is the first time Robby has talked to anyone about what he was feeling."

"Captain is a good listener," Rebecca responded. "He loves visiting the kids."

Robby was very disappointed when it was time to say good-bye.

"Can Captain come see me again?" he asked Rebecca.

"Well, I hope you're outta here by the time we come back next Saturday, but if you're not, then we will certainly be happy to visit you again," she answered.

"Thank you," he said. Then he turned to Captain and said, "Bye, Captain. Thanks for coming to see me." He reached out to give Captain one more ear rubbing.

"Say good-bye, Captain," said Rebecca.

Captain gave a short bark and lifted his paw. Robby looked at her quizzically.

"He wants to shake your hand," Rebecca said.

Robby giggled and reached out to grab Captain's paw. When he let go, Captain trotted over to Rebecca. Robby turned to his mom and said, "Captain's really smart, isn't he, Mom?"

"He sure is," she answered, reaching out to ruffle her son's hair.

Rebecca and Captain visited two more kids before they left the hospital. "You did really well, buddy," she praised Captain on the trip home. "You're such a good dog."

Later that evening, Rebecca's cell phone rang. She didn't recognize the name on the caller ID.

"Hello."

"Hi," a deep male voice that was mildly familiar answered. "Is this Rebecca Miller?"

"Yes," she answered.

"My name's Mitch Holt. A friend of mine gave me your number. I was hoping we could have dinner on Friday."

Rebecca was completely taken off-guard by the question. Then she remembered the conversation she'd had with her mother a few days before. *I wonder if this is the guy she was telling me about.*

"I'm sorry, I don't date men I don't know," she finally answered.

"How about if I invite a couple of friends of mine along?" Mitch asked.

Rebecca started to refuse. Then her mother's voice popped into her head. 'Dogs aren't men, honey. You need a man in your life.' Surprising herself, she answered, "Well, I guess if we make it a double, then I'd be happy to go."

"Great," Mitch replied. "Do you know a place called O'Malley's?"

"Yes," Rebecca answered. O'Malley's was a karaoke bar that also had an extensive menu. She had been there once before to celebrate Marilyn's 30th birthday.

"How about we meet you there at around 6:30?" Mitch suggested.

"Okay, see you Friday," answered Rebecca. As soon as she ended the call, she regretted her decision. *What did I just do? I can't believe I said 'yes', and I didn't get his number, so I can't back out. What kind of desperate guy calls a woman out of the blue like that? There's got to be something seriously wrong with him.*

CHAPTER 4

Derrick's alarm buzzed incessantly on the nightstand beside his bed. He groaned and reached out to shut it off. It was 5:30 Monday morning. He sat up and swung his legs over the edge of his bed. He took a deep breath and gave himself the mental pep talk necessary to convince him that jogging was good for him.

Come on, old man. Time to get your ass out of bed and moving. You don't want to start getting that middle-aged gut.

He groaned as he stood and dressed. Once he started running, he was glad he had won the mental struggle. It felt great to give his muscles a workout. He ran for about a mile and then turned a corner to begin the trip back home. Immediately after turning, a small dark shape moved into his path. Surprised, Derrick took a short hop to the side. His foot caught on the edge of the sidewalk, and he went airborne. He landed in the grass a few feet away. *What the hell was that?* he thought in aggravation, sitting up to look around.

The creature scurried toward him. Derrick could barely make out the animal's shape in the dim, pre-dawn light. *Is that a skunk?* His heartbeat quickened at the thought. He knew if a skunk was running toward him, then it must be rabid. Plus, he had no desire to be sprayed with its disgusting scent. He scrambled backwards trying to stand. A moment later, the creature reached his side. Derrick sucked in his breath. Then he chuckled with relief when he realized it was a black puppy with a white stripe on its chest and not a skunk. It stopped about a foot from him.

The puppy cocked her head to one side and looked at him quizzically.

"What are you doing out here all by yourself?" Derrick asked.

The puppy took the question as an invitation and quickly closed the gap between them. She placed her paws on Derrick's left leg and wagged her tail furiously.

Derrick smiled and reached out to rub the puppy on the head. "Are you lost?" he asked. She scrambled the rest of the way onto Derrick's lap, jumped up, and licked him across the face.

"No you don't," Derrick said, placing the puppy on the grass. He stood up and looked around. None of the houses had any signs of life coming from them. *Now what?* he thought. *She's got to belong to someone around here.* He convinced himself that it was okay to leave the puppy there. He was certain she would go back to wherever she belonged as soon as he left.

He started to move away, and the puppy fell into step beside him. "Stay," Derrick commanded.

The puppy sat and looked up at him. Derrick turned and continued jogging down the street. He looked down and saw her running right along beside him. He stopped and said sternly, "Go home."

The puppy continued to follow him. *She'll get tired soon*, Derrick thought. He picked up his pace. To his annoyance, the puppy followed him all the way to his house. Derrick jogged up the steps of his porch. She stopped at the bottom and gave a questioning yip.

"Well, come on in," Derrick said as he pushed open his front door. She bounded up the steps and into the house. Derrick walked to the kitchen and filled a glass of water. As he tilted the glass up, he saw the puppy looking up at him longingly. Derrick pulled out a shallow dish and filled it with water. As soon as he set it down, she started lapping it up. Now that Derrick got a good look at her, he could see that she was very thin. He could count every rib.

Derrick leaned against the counter and pondered what to do next. He needed to be at work in an hour. He decided to take her to the nearest vet clinic. He could drop her off and let them know where he'd found her. Maybe they would know who she belonged to. Sure that the vet clinic would be closed this early in the morning, he moved down the hall to take a shower and get dressed for work.

After he finished, he looked up the address of the nearest animal hospital. Not wanting to give them a chance to tell him they wouldn't take her, he decided to drive straight to the clinic without calling first.

~

Rebecca heard the bell over the front door jingle announcing June's arrival. Eager to hear all about her date with Walter Stockton, she hurried toward the front. As soon as she saw her friend, she knew it must have gone well. The old sparkle was back in her eyes.

"By the look on your face, I'm guessing you enjoyed your date with Walter."

June smiled broadly. Her cheeks turned a rosy hue. "Yes, we had a great time. He took me dancing. Can you believe it? He's an excellent dancer."

Rebecca chuckled. "I certainly wouldn't have guessed that. So, did you make plans to see each other again?"

"I'm cooking dinner for him tomorrow night," answered June.

"So soon? I'd say things must have gone very well indeed."

The bell over the door jingled again. Rebecca and June both glanced up. Rebecca's eyes widened when she saw Derrick step into the clinic. He was carrying a black puppy in his arms. He strode purposefully up to the counter.

"This puppy followed me home this morning while I was out jogging. She first started following me at the corner of

Baker and Olive. I'd like to leave her with you. I thought her owner might check for her here." He had addressed his comments to June, who sat behind the reception desk. He'd barely glanced toward Rebecca.

"Based on how skinny she is, I'd say she probably doesn't have an owner. But it sounds to me like she's picked you," said Rebecca.

Derrick turned to look at her. She felt a spurt of annoyance when he didn't seem to recognize her. *Am I that forgettable?* she thought.

Derrick suddenly felt put on the spot. The woman's eyes held a challenge in them, as if daring him to turn his back on the puppy. "Well, um, I don't really have time for a dog," Derrick said lamely.

Rebecca's eyes narrowed in agitation. "So, you're just going to dump her here?"

Just then, Jimmy shouted from the back, "Ralph's out!"

A moment later, a large brown dog ran into the waiting room. He stopped a few feet from Derrick. The hair on the back of his neck stood on end. His lips were pulled back in a snarl. A low, threatening growl emanated from his throat.

Derrick's heart pounded in his chest. He stared wide-eyed at the angry dog standing before him. The puppy in his arms began to squirm. It gave a little yelp. Derrick hadn't been aware of how tightly he was squeezing her. He willed the muscles in his arms to relax. He felt a bead of cold sweat slowly trickle down his back.

"Open the first exam room, Jimmy. Then come back and stand behind him," Rebecca said calmly. Jimmy backed up and went around to open the door from inside the room.

As soon as Jimmy was back in place behind Ralph, Rebecca took a step toward the dog. *Smack!* Both Ralph and Derrick jumped at the sound of Rebecca suddenly clapping her hands together. Ralph saw the open exam room door and darted toward it. Rebecca moved swiftly to pull the door shut behind him. A second later, the door banged against its frame as the big dog slammed his body into it.

"I'm going to go take care of Ralph. See if you can talk him into keeping the puppy," Rebecca said, motioning toward Derrick.

As she moved toward the door, Derrick snapped out of his momentary trance. Staring at the exam room door, he asked incredulously, "You're going in there?" He could hear Ralph growling angrily from the other side. "Do you want to get yourself killed?"

Rebecca gave him an exasperated look. "I have no intention of getting myself killed," she replied, just as the dog slammed himself into the door once more. "Now, if you'll excuse me, I really need to calm him down before he hurts himself."

Derrick watched in slack-jawed amazement as Rebecca opened the door and quickly stepped inside.

"Don't worry. She knows what she's doing," June said from behind the desk.

"Yeah," Jimmy agreed. "She'll have him calmed down in no time."

Derrick looked from June to Jimmy and back to June again. "Are you people crazy? She just locked herself in a room with a man-eater, and you're not worried about her?"

"Like we just told you," June said calmly. "She knows what she's doing. Now, what have you decided to do about the puppy?"

"The puppy?" Derrick asked in confusion. He was starting to think he might be having a bizarre dream.

"You can leave her here today while you're at work. Dr. Miller will give her a thorough exam. By the time you come back for her, we'll have her all fixed up for you. If you'd like, we can put up a sign saying where you found her, but I agree with Rebecca, she looks like a stray."

Derrick glanced down at the puppy he still held in his arms. She looked up at him adoringly. He lifted his eyes back to June. She smiled knowingly back at him.

"Okay," he heard himself agree. "I'll be back for her around 6:00."

"Perfect," said June. "Jimmy will put her in the back while you fill out this paperwork." June pointed to the clipboard resting on top of the receptionist's counter. Derrick nodded numbly as he handed the puppy to Jimmy and picked up the pen that was lying beside the clipboard.

He realized that he wasn't hearing any sounds coming from the exam room. *I wonder if Ralph's eaten her*, he thought, glancing toward the door.

Seeing his worried look, June said in an amused tone, "Quiet is good. If she was being eaten, we'd hear it."

Derrick turned his gaze back to June. "Good point," he conceded.

As he backed out of the parking lot, he realized that he had agreed to keep the puppy. He shook his head in dismay and sighed. *I guess I had better get some supplies before I pick her up.*

~

Rebecca stepped quickly into the room. Ralph stood on the opposite side of the exam table. He snarled angrily at her.

"It's okay, Ralph. I know you're scared. I'm not going to hurt you," Rebecca said soothingly. Ralph looked around nervously.

Rebecca slid to the floor and rested her back against the door. "It's really not worth getting so worked up. I'd like for us to be friends."

Ralph was brought in the previous day by his owner for vaccines. Rebecca convinced her to leave him overnight, so that he could be neutered as well. Ralph's owner was an older woman who hadn't socialized him. This was the first time since he was a small puppy he'd been away from her and around other people. Rebecca knew he was reacting out of fear, not aggression.

Ralph continued to growl at Rebecca, but his stance had relaxed slightly. The hair on his neck no longer stood on end. Rebecca smiled and said softly, "That's it, boy. Why don't you come on over here and let me pet you a little?"

Rebecca got to her knees and slowly inched toward the scared dog. He eyed her warily, but he didn't move away. She stopped when she was within a foot of him. She sat cross-legged on the floor and continued to talk softly. After a few more moments, she held out her hand. Ralph sniffed it, but didn't budge.

Rebecca closed the rest of the gap. She reached out and rested her palm on Ralph's shoulder. His muscles twitched beneath her hand.

"Good boy," she cooed as she began slowly moving her hand down the side of his body. She could feel the tension leave him as she continued to rub him with long, slow strokes. Finally, with a big sigh, he lay down and placed his head in her lap. Rebecca chuckled. "See, isn't this better?"

A few moments later, a soft knock sounded on the door. "Everything okay in there, Doc?" Jimmy asked.

"Yes, Ralph and I are just getting to know each other. We'll be out in a minute. Go ahead and get the anesthetic ready for him."

~

After Derrick left work, he pulled into the parking lot of Happy Pets, the large pet store located a few blocks from St Luke's. As he stepped through the sliding glass doors, his eyes widened in surprise. Several long aisles filled with an assortment of pet supplies ran the length of the store's interior. Derrick didn't know where to begin. He hadn't owned a dog since he was a small boy. He stood just inside the entrance.

"May I help you?"

Startled, Derrick jerked his head toward the sound. A teenage boy wearing a name tag that read, "Joey" stood to his right.

"I have a new puppy," Derrick said. "I need to get her some things, but I'm not sure what she needs."

"No problem," Joey said. "Follow me and I'll get you all fixed up."

Joey grabbed a shopping cart and headed down the first aisle. Derrick followed along in a daze as Joey filled his cart with bowls, a collar, a leash, a crate, a dog bed, an assortment of toys, and food. By the time they finished, the cart was full.

The cashier rang him up and gave him his total. His eyes widened in shock, "You're kidding me, right?"

The girl looked at him in amusement and shook her head.

Sighing, Derrick pulled out his credit card and paid the bill. *I don't even know how long I'll have her,* he thought in aggravation as he wheeled his cart outside.

A few minutes later, he arrived at Animal Friends. "Hello," June greeted warmly.

Dr. Miller stepped around the corner and said, "I wasn't sure if we'd see you again."

Derrick felt insulted by her remark. "I said I'd be back for her," he said gruffly.

June smiled. "Yes, you did," she agreed.

"I'll go get her for you," Rebecca said, feeling a little guilty for her remark. Even if it is what she'd been thinking, she shouldn't have said it to him. *I guess I'm still annoyed that he didn't recognize me this morning. I'm not sure why it bothers me so much.*

She reached into the cage and pulled out the happy puppy. Rebecca smiled as she tried to lick her face. "Oh, no you don't," she chuckled, moving her head to avoid the kiss.

When she reached the waiting room, she handed the puppy to Derrick. The puppy's whole body shook with excitement. She let out a happy little yip and started licking him all over the face. Derrick struggled to maintain his hold on her and at the same time avoid her kisses.

Rebecca laughed and said, "She's crazy about you already. Why don't we go into the exam room? She can run around on the floor while we talk," Rebecca suggested.

Derrick nodded in agreement and followed Rebecca into the room. As soon as the door closed behind him, he set the puppy on the floor.

"She looks to be about eight weeks old. Overall, she's pretty healthy. She does have worms, but I gave her a dewormer. She also got her first set of vaccines. She'll need to come back in 3-4 weeks to get her next set. Then she'll need to come back for one more set after that. I suggest we spay her on that last visit."

"I don't think I'll still have her by then," Derrick said, holding on to the thought that this was just a temporary situation.

Rebecca grinned. "Well, just in case, you can go ahead and schedule the next visit with June when you check out. I also suggest you pick up some flea and tick prevention. I'm done for the day, so I can keep her company while you visit with June."

"Okay, thanks," Derrick said. He left the room and walked to the receptionist's counter.

"Have you thought of a name for her?" June asked.

"No," replied Derrick. "Do you have any suggestions?"

"Give it a few days. I bet something will come to you," June replied. "When would you like to bring her back?"

"How about the same time on the Monday three weeks from now?" Derrick suggested.

June checked the calendar and said, "Looks good. I'll pencil you in for Monday, March 31 at 5:00."

"Dr. Miller suggested I pick up some flea prevention, too."

June grabbed a package of flea prevention, handed it to him, and told him his total bill.

Derrick shook his head in consternation as he paid the bill. *How much is this dog going to cost me?* he wondered as he returned to the exam room. When he opened the door, his annoyance faded. Rebecca sat cross-legged in the middle of the floor with a large smile on her face as she watched the puppy pounce on a toy she had just tossed. Derrick was struck by how pretty she looked. *Her whole face lights up when she smiles,* he thought.

She looked up at him and asked, "All set?"

"Looks that way," he answered.

She scooped the puppy into her arms and handed her to Derrick.

"I'll see you in a couple of weeks then," she said.

As Derrick drove toward home, the picture of Rebecca sitting on the floor flashed through his mind. He was surprised by his reaction to her. She was definitely not his usual type. Blonde bombshells were more to his liking, but there was something strangely appealing about the petite doctor.

Just then his cell phone rang. "Dr. Peterson," he answered.

"I've got a favor to ask of you," Mitch said by way of greeting.

"What kind of favor?" Derrick asked suspiciously.

"I need a wing man. Remember that phone number you gave me on Saturday? I called it, and she agreed to go out with me on Friday, but only if we make it a double," Mitch answered. "We're going to O'Malley's. I've already asked Ginger to come. You remember her?"

Derrick definitely remembered Ginger. Now, she was more his type. She was tall, blond, and very well endowed. "I remember," Derrick answered.

"So, you'll come?" Mitch asked.

"All right," Derrick agreed. It had been a while since he'd been out. He figured he could use a little fun. "What time?"

"6:30."

"I'll be there," Derrick said.

"Thanks, buddy," answered Mitch. "I owe ya one."

CHAPTER 5

"5:30," Rebecca grumbled to herself as she locked the clinic door on Friday night. "That only leaves me an hour." She'd been nervous and jumpy all day. June had asked her about it, but Rebecca had sidestepped the question. She didn't want to admit that she had agreed to this blind date. Her nervousness had also been sensed by some of her patients making them much less cooperative than usual. Rebecca's patience had been stretched to the breaking point.

She made the drive between Animal Friends and her house in record time. As soon as she parked her car, she jumped out and hurried toward her front door. When she stepped inside the house, Captain greeted her with his favorite tennis ball in his mouth.

"Sorry, buddy, I'm in a hurry," Rebecca said as she walked briskly through the house to open the back door for him.

She checked her watch. *5:50, just enough time for a quick shower,* she thought. Ten minutes later she was tearing through her closet trying to find something to wear. *Too sexy. Too casual. Too ugly,* she thought, her frustration mounting as she rejected one outfit after another. Finally, she settled on a pair of dark designer jeans and a pale sapphire silk blouse. The top enhanced the blue color of her eyes. She chose a pair of black boots with a moderate heel to round out the outfit. She checked her watch again. *Crap, is it 6:15 already?* O'Malley's was a twenty-minute drive from her house.

Rebecca hurried to the back door to let Captain back inside. Then she grabbed her purse and keys and flew out the door. *What am I doing?* she asked herself as she drove to the bar. *This is crazy. He's probably either a nutcase or someone looking for a one-night stand.*

She pulled into the parking lot at 6:35. She hurried through the entrance door. *Now what?* she wondered as she scanned the dark interior. There were several round tables spread out across a large open area. The far wall and the wall to the right of the entrance were lined with circular booths that faced a small wooden stage to the left of the entrance. Currently, a large, dark-haired woman was on stage belting out a poor rendition of the Tina Turner classic, *Proud Mary.*

As soon as Rebecca stepped inside, Derrick spotted her. He, Ginger, and Mitch were seated at one of the booths directly across from the entrance. "Mitch, what's the name of the woman you're supposed to be meeting?" Derrick asked dryly.

"Rebecca Miller," Mitch replied.

"I thought you might say that. She just walked in."

Mitch turned his head toward the door and saw a petite, brown-haired woman standing just inside the entrance. "You know her?" Mitch asked.

"She's the crazy vet I was just telling you about."

Mitch threw his head back and laughed. "She sounds like fun." Then he stood and moved toward the woman. As soon as he reached her, he recognized her as the woman Derrick had knocked down in the gym the previous Saturday.

"Hi, Rebecca," he said. "It's nice to see you again."

Rebecca recognized him immediately, but she didn't remember exchanging names with him. "How do you know my name?" she asked suspiciously.

Mitch smiled down at her and said, "I'm your date."

"You're Mitch Holt?" she asked.

Mitch nodded.

"Did you know who I was when you called me?"

"No," he replied. "I didn't know you were the same person Derrick knocked down until just now. Small world, huh?" Not waiting for an answer, he held out his arm and said, "Shall we?"

Rebecca nodded numbly and slipped her hand around his offered arm. She wasn't sure how she felt about this turn of events. On one hand, she was extremely relieved that Mitch Holt wasn't the short, fat, bald man with bad teeth she'd been picturing in her mind all day. On the other hand, she was confused as to why such a good-looking man would want to go out on a blind date in the first place.

As soon as they reached the booth, her eyes locked with Derrick's. He gave her a quick smile and shrugged as if to say, "I'm as surprised as you are."

"Rebecca, this is Ginger Rollins, and you already know Derrick," Mitch said in introduction.

"Hello," said Ginger in a silky voice as she offered her hand.

"Hi," Rebecca returned, reaching out to shake the woman's outstretched hand. Ginger was stunningly beautiful. Her blonde hair flowed in soft waves to her shoulders. Her high cheek bones and thick full lips reminded Rebecca of a super-model. Rebecca felt instantly out of place among this group of gorgeous people.

Derrick nodded in acknowledgement of the introduction and said, "It's nice to see you again, Dr. Miller."

"Please, call me Rebecca. How's your puppy? Have you named her yet?" she asked as she slid into the booth to sit beside Ginger.

"Trouble," Derrick answered. "It's only been five days, and so far she's managed to chew up a pair of loafers, two pairs of socks, and one pillow."

Rebecca laughed. Derrick was struck again by how pretty she looked when she smiled. The image of her smiling up at him from the floor of the vet clinic flashed through his mind. He suddenly pictured her lying on her back in bed smiling up at him. A flash of desire ripped through him.

Ginger saw the look of male interest on Derrick's face and felt a spurt of jealousy. She'd wanted a date with Derrick Peterson ever since she'd met him two years ago when she had been dating Mitch. Now that she'd finally gotten her chance with him, she wasn't going to let this little mouse of a woman steal his attention away from her. She chuckled softly and said, "Isn't it funny? Derrick was just telling us about how you two met at your veterinary clinic. He said he thought you were crazy."

Derrick gave Ginger a sharp look. Rebecca blushed a little and said, "Well, actually, his visit to my clinic was the third time we'd met."

Mitch casually laid an arm across her shoulders and said, "You mean you've met sometime other than when he mowed you down at the community center?"

Derrick's jaw slackened, and his eyes widened in shock. "That was you?" he asked incredulously.

Seeing the comical expression on Derrick's face lessened some of her discomfort. She smiled and said, "Yes."

"When was the second time?" Derrick asked.

"In the elevator at the hospital, a few hours after you knocked me down," Rebecca replied.

A light dawned in Derrick's eyes. "You were the one with the therapy dog. Why didn't you say something?"

Just then, the waitress stepped up to the table and asked, "What can I get you folks to drink?"

Rebecca was relieved that she didn't have to answer Derrick's question. She didn't want to admit that she'd was too disappointed by the fact that he hadn't recognized her to say anything. As soon as they'd finished ordering drinks, Ginger cleared her throat and said, "How about I entertain you boys with a song?" She was confident it would get their attention focused back onto her.

Mitch grinned and said eagerly, "Sounds great." Then he turned to Rebecca and explained, "Ginger's got an amazing voice."

Rebecca returned his smile and then turned her head to watch Ginger walk gracefully toward the stage, which was currently empty. She stopped and whispered something to the sound man. Then she stepped onto the stage. The room grew silent as she grabbed the microphone.

The first bars of *Crazy* by Patsy Cline filled the silent room. Ginger started swaying slowly to the music. *There's not a man in here who isn't staring at her,* Rebecca thought. *Check that, there's not a person in here who isn't staring at her. Not that I blame them, she's beautiful.*

The entire bar listened with mesmerized awe as she sang. Mitch was right. She had a great voice. The room erupted into applause as Ginger finished the song. Rebecca didn't miss the smug look Ginger aimed at her as she returned to their booth. *What was that about?* she wondered. *Surely, she isn't jealous of me?*

As the evening progressed, Rebecca was amazed at how much fun she was having. As Mitch regaled them with stories of his life on the police force, she relaxed and forgot about the earlier awkwardness of the evening. He had a bigger than life personality. She was surprised with how quickly she'd become comfortable with him. She felt as if they'd known each other for a long time. She didn't usually feel such an easy camaraderie with someone she had just met.

However, throughout the night, her eyes kept being drawn to Derrick. He leaned casually back against the booth. He wore a white dress shirt opened at the collar. Rebecca found the contrast between the shirt and his deeply tanned skin incredibly sexy. Once, he'd caught her staring and their eyes had locked. Ginger caught the look and diverted Derrick's attention by asking him to get her another drink. Embarrassed by the fact that he'd noticed her staring, Rebecca avoided looking directly at him for the rest of the night.

"Do you sing, Rebecca?" Mitch asked late in the evening.

Rebecca shook her head in denial. She loved to sing, but alone in the shower, not on a stage in front of a room full of people.

"Come on, how about we try a duet?" Mitch suggested, standing up and tugging on her hand.

The next thing Rebecca knew, Mitch was leading her to the stage. He stopped by the sound man and whispered his song selection so quietly that Rebecca didn't hear what he said. A moment later, they were standing on the stage waiting for the song to begin. Rebecca laughed as the first strains of *Born to be Wild* erupted from the speakers. Rebecca sang the first few words timidly, but Mitch's enthusiasm soon melted her reserves. She relaxed and threw herself into the fun of the moment.

Derrick found himself captivated by Rebecca's transformation. She had been quietly reserved throughout much of the evening. Up on the stage, she came alive with a vibrancy that lit up the room.

Ginger saw that Derrick's attention was completely focused on Rebecca. She leaned into him and rubbed her breasts against his arm. He didn't even glance her way. She sat back in the booth with a pout.

A few moments later, Mitch and Rebecca rejoined them. "You were great, Rebecca," Mitch enthused as soon as they were seated. "Wasn't she, Derrick?"

Derrick's eyes shone with intensity as they met Rebecca's. "Yes, she was," he answered sincerely.

Rebecca laughed self-consciously and said, "It was fun, Mitch. Thanks for dragging me up there. I would never have done it otherwise."

"My pleasure," he answered, looping his arm around Rebecca and drawing her to him for a quick kiss.

Derrick cleared his throat and said, "I hate to break up the party, but it's getting late, and I'm on duty at the ER tomorrow."

"What? No one-on-one?" Mitch asked, turning to look at Derrick.

"Sorry, Dr. Patel asked me to cover for him," Derrick replied.

Rebecca had been surprised by Mitch's sudden show of affection. She was also a little surprised by her complete lack of response to it. It had felt like a kiss from her brother. She liked Mitch very much, but there wasn't any physical attraction there.

She checked her watch and was surprised at how late it was. "I really should be going, too," she said. "Tomorrow's our last practice before the season starts."

"Rebecca coaches a girls' basketball team," Mitch explained.

"You coach basketball?" Ginger asked in surprise.

Rebecca wasn't sure if it was her size or the fact that she was a woman that she found baffling. "Yes," she replied. "And we're really pretty good."

"How about I give you a hand tomorrow?" Mitch suggested. "Since Derrick's backing out of our weekly game, I've got the morning free."

"Sure, I can always use extra help in practice," Rebecca answered.

Derrick was disconcerted by the flash of jealousy that shot through him at the idea of Rebecca spending more time with Mitch. He slid out of the booth and offered his hand to Ginger. Mitch followed suit. They separated at the door. Derrick was sullen as he walked with Ginger to his car. He opened her door and then strode around to the driver's side. As he slid behind the wheel, Ginger pressed herself into his side. He turned toward her, and she claimed his mouth in a passionate kiss. Derrick returned the kiss. A long moment later, Ginger pulled back slightly and whispered throatily, "My place or yours?"

Derrick surprised himself by answering, "Neither. Like I said, I have to be at the hospital in the morning." Any other night, he would have taken Ginger up on her offer. *Why was tonight different?* he wondered. Then the image of Rebecca throwing her head back and laughing as she and Mitch finished their duet to a thunderous applause flashed through his mind.

When he pulled into Ginger's drive, she leaned over and ran her hand slowly up his thigh. "Are you sure you don't want to come in?"

Derrick hesitated. It had been a while since the last time he'd had sex. *What's stopping me?* he wondered. *She's beautiful, and I'm sure she's great in bed.* He shook his head and answered, "Some other time."

She pouted and said, "Your loss. We would have been great together." Then she slid out of his car and walked up the steps to her front door.

Derrick watched her walk away. Her hips swayed provocatively as she moved. *You're an idiot,* he told himself as he put the car in reverse and backed out of the drive.

~

Rebecca groaned as the ringing of her doorbell dragged her out of a deep sleep. She opened one eye and saw that the clock on her nightstand read 6:00. *Who in the world's here this early on a Saturday?* she thought grumpily. She swung her feet over the side of the bed and stumbled out of the bedroom. The doorbell sounded again.

"Coming!" she called. She opened the door and found her mother standing on her porch.

"Mom, what are you doing here so early? Is everything okay?"

"That's what I want to know," Barbara answered accusingly. "I left you several messages last night. When you never called me back, I thought I'd better come over here and make sure you're okay."

Rebecca had placed her phone on silent before she'd left for her date. She'd been so tired when she'd gotten home that she'd dropped her purse on the kitchen table without bothering to pull out the phone and check for messages.

"I'm sorry I worried you, Mom. Come in," she said stepping back from the doorway.

Barbara walked into the living room and then turned to face her daughter. With hands on her plump hips, she demanded, "So, where were you last night?"

"I went out," Rebecca replied.

"With a man or with friends?" she asked.

Rebecca flashed her mom an annoyed look and answered, "With a man. As a matter of fact, there were two men."

Barbara's demeanor changed instantly. She stepped toward Rebecca and wrapped her in a hug. "Oh, that's great, honey. Tell me all about it," she encouraged. Then she stepped back and shook her finger at Rebecca, adding, "But I'm still furious at you for worrying me like that. You could have let me know you were going out."

Rebecca smiled and said, "I'm sorry I worried you. Sit down and I'll tell you all about it."

Barbara perched on the edge of the sofa and eagerly waited for Rebecca to begin the story. When she finished, Barbara said, "I'm confused. Was Mitch or Derrick your date?"

"Mitch was my date. Although, I think Derrick's mom is the one you gave my number to. Didn't you say he was an ER doctor?"

"That's what she told me. So, do you think you and Mitch will see each other again?"

"He mentioned that he might help me practice with the girls this morning."

Barbara eyed her daughter speculatively. *This was interesting. Mitch had been her date and was the one she was going to see again, but her eyes lit up every time she said Derrick's name. Rebecca hadn't mentioned a man in months and now there were two? Very interesting indeed.*

"Have you had breakfast?" Rebecca asked, interrupting Barbara's thoughts.

"No, I rushed right over as soon as I woke up," she answered.

"Let me go shower and then we can go get something to eat," Rebecca suggested.

Barbara smiled. "Sounds like a plan."

CHAPTER 6

"All right, girls," Rebecca addressed her team. "This is the last practice. Our first game is next Saturday morning at 10:30. Let's give it all we've got today."

The players' faces reflected their excitement as they nodded their heads in agreement.

"Go ahead and get started with the lay-up drill," Rebecca instructed.

The girls formed two lines at the top of the key and began the drill. Rebecca watched closely. She still had a few girls who would jump off the wrong foot and some who shot left-handed lay-ups with the right hand. She was so focused on her team that she didn't see Mitch jogging across the gym toward them.

He stood right behind her when he spoke. "Morning," he greeted.

Rebecca let out a startled yelp and spun around, her hand going to her throat.

Mitch gave a lopsided grin. "I didn't mean to scare ya," he said apologetically. His eyes twinkled in amusement.

Rebecca returned his smile and said, "I didn't hear you. To be honest, I didn't really expect you to show up."

Mitch gave her a wounded look. "I said I'd be here, didn't I?" Actually, he was a little surprised he'd come, too. When he'd walked her to her car the night before, she'd come up onto her toes and kissed him on the cheek. He'd read the message loud and clear. She wasn't going to go to bed with him. At first, he'd been disappointed. He wasn't accustomed to a date ending without mutually satisfying sex. The women he dated were usually more than willing to enjoy a night with no strings attached. However, he'd realized that Rebecca wasn't the casual sex type. She wasn't interested in a one-night stand, and he wasn't interested in a serious relationship. He enjoyed women too much to settle down with just one. So, why had he come to practice this morning? He liked her. She was witty, intelligent, and easy to talk to. He'd decided that he wanted to give friendship a try. He'd never had a non-sexual relationship with a woman, besides that, other than Derrick, he didn't have that many real friends.

"Yes," replied Rebecca. "I'm sorry I doubted you."

Mitch grinned and moved to loop an arm around her shoulders. They had their backs to the team. Mitch leaned over and whispered mischievously, "We have an audience. Should we give them a show?"

Before Rebecca could respond, Mitch pulled her into an embrace. His eyes danced merrily as his mouth descended on hers. He gave her a long, thorough kiss. Rebecca went rigid with shock. Mitch ended the kiss with a loud smack. A thunderous applause erupted behind them. He kept one arm around Rebecca's shoulders and turned them to face the girls. Her face burned with embarrassment. She elbowed Mitch in the ribs. He threw his head back and laughed.

The girls had moved to stand a few feet from them. Their eyes sparkled with glee as they continued to clap.

"You should probably introduce me now," he whispered.

She glared at him. He grinned. Rebecca felt some of her irritation fade. *He's just a giant kid*, she thought.

Then she cleared her throat and said, "Um, girls, I'd like you to meet Mitch Holt. He's here to give us a hand in practice today."

Her friend, Marilyn, was sitting with a few of the other parents on the bleachers to their right. She caught Rebecca's eye and gave her the 'you've got some explaining to do' look. Rebecca shrugged her shoulders helplessly.

"Hello, girls," Mitch greeted in a friendly tone.

"Hi," they said in unison. Several of the girls giggled nervously.

Then Kristen asked, "Aren't you the guy who knocked Rebecca down last week?"

Mitch chuckled. "No, that would have been my friend, Derrick. He's a lot clumsier than I am. I would never knock a beautiful woman to the ground."

The girls grinned at his humor.

"Rebecca tells me that this is your last practice before your first game. So, I guess we'd better get started. What drills would you like to work on, Coach?" He turned his gaze on Rebecca. His eyes continued to dance merrily.

Rebecca firmed her jaw and determinedly pushed past her embarrassment. "We need to work on screens and cuts to the basket." She moved to stand at the top of the key. "Kristen, you come guard me. Mitch, you set the screen and let's show them the different scenarios that can develop off a solidly set pick."

Mitch nodded and moved to stand on the right wing. Rebecca and Mitch demonstrated how the player at the top of the key could use the screen to get open for their own shot. They also showed the girls how the screener could cut hard to the basket after setting the pick and be open for an easy lay-up.

It took the girls a few minutes to get over the embarrassment of having a man participating in practice, but once they did, they had one of their best practices. After several minutes of drills, Rebecca gave them a break to get some water.

"I'm impressed," Mitch said as they watched the girls jog over to the water fountain. "They're much more advanced than I expected ten-year-old girls to be. You're a great coach."

Rebecca smiled at the compliment. "I've always loved the game. I kind of got roped into coaching them a few years ago, but I'm really glad I did. It's been a lot of fun."

The girls returned and Rebecca asked, "How about a little scrimmage? Mitch gives us a tenth player, so we can play five-on-five."

"Yes!" the team shouted in unison. Rebecca divided the teams. Rebecca's team took the ball first. Kristen was playing point guard, and Rebecca set up as the shooting guard. She was standing behind the three-point line on the left side of the court when she received a pass from Kristen.

Rebecca gave Mitch a challenging look. He grinned. He was at least a foot taller than her and probably out-weighed her by 60 pounds. He knew he could stop any sort of move she made toward the basket, so he sagged off her defensively.

Rebecca returned his grin. Then she quickly rose up and shot. The ball arched high into the air. Mitch turned and watched in stunned surprise as it fell through the hoop, barely causing the net to move.

"Nice shot," he complimented.

"Thanks," Rebecca returned, feeling a little smug.

The next time she got the ball, Mitch stepped in to guard her closely. She executed a perfect ball fake that got Mitch into the air in an attempt to block her shot. Then she drove right past him, pulled up, and drilled a jump shot. She laughed at the stunned expression on his face.

The scrimmage continued for several more minutes. Rebecca had had her fun with Mitch. She spent the rest of practice making sure the girls got most of the touches. Just before she called an end to the scrimmage, Mitch challenged, "Try me again."

Rebecca couldn't resist. She took a few slow dribbles to her left. Mitch guarded her closely. As soon as she got to the left elbow, she spun quickly around and shot an over-the-shoulder hook shot with her right hand. As she came down, her left foot landed awkwardly on Mitch's. Her ankle buckled, and she fell to the ground.

Rebecca felt a pop as a pain shot through the ankle and up her leg. She looked up and saw nine worried faces staring back at her. She felt tears burn at the backs of her eyes, but she willed them not to fall. She didn't want to cry in front of everyone. Her ankle throbbed painfully. She gave them a weak smile.

Mitch knelt beside her and asked worriedly, "How bad is it?"

"Bad," she gritted out. "I felt a pop. Did I make the basket?"

Mitch admired her grit. He grinned and scooped her into his arms. He stood and said, "Of course you did. I don't think you ever miss." Then he continued, "Looks like practice is over, girls."

Marilyn ran up to them. "That looked painful from the bleachers, Rebecca. Are you okay?"

"I'm taking her to the emergency room to have it checked out," Mitch answered.

"I don't need to go to the ER," Rebecca insisted. "Marilyn can drive me home. I'll put it on ice. I'll be fine."

Marilyn glanced at Rebecca's ankle. It had already started to swell. "Go ahead and take her to the ER," she told Mitch. "She hates admitting that she's not Wonder Woman."

Mitch nodded and said, "Could you grab her things and follow me out to my car?"

"Yes, of course," Marilyn answered.

~

"Somebody get me some damned bandaging materials," Derrick barked angrily. A young, redheaded nurse standing a few feet away glared at him and then hurried off to gather the supplies. He'd been snapping at them all morning.

"What's up with Dr. Peterson?" she whispered to an older nurse as she quickly grabbed some sponges, gauze, and tape out of the supply cart.

"I don't know. I've never seen him like this before. My guess, woman problems. In my experience, about the only thing that can cause a man to be that surly is a woman," the older woman answered.

The nurse hurried back to Derrick. He barely glanced at her as he took the supplies and began bandaging the laceration he had just finished stitching. His mind turned to the source of his bad mood, Mitch and Rebecca. He'd lain awake most of the night wondering if they had spent the night together. Knowing his friend the way he did, he was sure he had been willing. He didn't understand why the idea bothered him so much, but damn it, it did. He kept picturing the way Mitch had kept his arm draped across Rebecca's shoulders all night and the way she had laughed at his stories. The picture made his stomach clench. Derrick let out a growl of frustration.

His patient winced. Derrick glanced up quickly and saw the man's face pinched in pain. He looked back down and realized he'd wrapped the bandage too tightly. He gave himself a mental shake. "I'm sorry," he apologized.

The man gave him a weak smile. "No problem, Doc. I can see that something's got you worried."

Derrick nodded and turned toward the nurse. "Claire, why don't you finish this up?"

"Sure," she replied, dropping onto the chair he had just vacated.

A moment later, the emergency doors slid open. Derrick glanced up and saw Mitch striding in carrying Rebecca in his arms.

"What the hell!" he exploded. A few of the nurses jumped at his sudden outburst. All heads turned to look toward the door.

Mitch paused mid-stride. Rebecca's eyes widened in surprise at the furious look on Derrick's face.

Mitch's eyes narrowed questioningly on Derrick. *What's got him so worked up?*

"Rebecca's hurt her ankle. Where should I put her?"

Derrick pointed to an empty bed across the room. Mitch walked to the bed and gently placed Rebecca on it.

What kind of kinky sex games were they playing? Derrick thought as he strode angrily toward the bed.

Dreading the answer, he asked, "What happened?"

"I went up for a hook shot and landed on Mitch's foot," Rebecca answered.

Derrick stared at her blankly. "What?" he asked in confusion.

"She's one hell of a basketball player," Mitch said. "She'd already schooled me a couple of times."

"You were playing basketball?"

In spite of the throbbing pain in her ankle, Rebecca bit back a laugh. She found the dazed look on Derrick's face hilarious. Derrick met her eyes and saw that she was struggling not to laugh at him.

He sighed and said with exaggerated patience, "Okay, so let me get this straight, you were playing basketball, and you twisted your ankle?"

"That's what we said," Mitch answered, eyeing his friend like he'd just gone daft. "Remember last night? Rebecca told us about the team she coaches, and I volunteered to help her out today."

Mitch could see the light come on in Derrick's brain. "Oh, yeah, now I remember," Derrick muttered. He reached out and grabbed Rebecca's leg just above her sock.

She sucked in her breath as Derrick's hand made contact with her skin.

His eyes flew to her face. "I'm sorry," he apologized.

Rebecca's cheeks burned. Her reaction had been out of shock for the sudden tingling sensation his touch had caused to shoot up her leg, not from pain, but she wasn't going to admit that to him. "It's okay," she replied with a weak smile.

Derrick dropped his eyes back to her injured ankle. He removed her shoe and sock. The ankle was badly swollen and already beginning to bruise. "I need to get an x-ray to make sure that it isn't broken, but it looks like you've at least torn some ligaments in there."

He met her gaze. She nodded in understanding. He admired her toughness. He could tell that she was in pain, but she was hiding it well. Most women he knew would be crying their eyes out right now.

There were no signs of broken bones on the x-ray, so Derrick fitted Rebecca with an ankle brace. "You'll need to ice it twice a day until that swelling goes down. Try to keep it elevated as much as possible. You'll also need to take an anti-inflammatory."

"Thanks, Derrick," she said.

"No problem. I hope it feels better soon," he replied. He felt a flash of jealousy slice through him as Mitch bent and lifted her into his arms.

"I can walk, Mitch," she laughingly protested.

"What? And miss the chance to carry you again? Not on your life."

Derrick's eyes narrowed. He turned on his heel and left to check on a patient who had just come in. Mitch caught the look. *He likes her,* he thought. *That explains his weird behavior earlier.* Mitch smiled. *Rebecca might be just what Derrick needs.* He'd have to see what he could do to encourage him to act on his attraction to Rebecca. Knowing Derrick, he would ignore the attraction.

"Will you take me back to the community center so that I can pick up my car?" Rebecca asked.

"I could take you home and then get Derrick to help me get your car after he gets off work," Mitch suggested.

"No, I need it. I only have about an hour before I'll be bringing my dog, Captain, back to the hospital for his weekly visit." Rebecca had told him about Captain's visits to the children's wing on their date the night before.

"Are you sure you're feeling up to it?"

"I promised one of the kids that Captain would be back to visit him today. It would take more than a sore ankle to keep me away," Rebecca answered firmly.

Mitch grinned. "You're something. You know that?"

Embarrassed by the compliment, Rebecca blushed. "Thanks," she muttered awkwardly.

~

An hour later, Rebecca limped back into the hospital. Her ankle throbbed painfully. As the elevator doors closed, she sagged back against the wall.

"What happened to your foot?" Allison asked as soon as she saw Rebecca.

"Accident in basketball practice this morning," Rebecca replied. "Is Robby still here?"

"Yes, he's been talking about Captain all morning."

Allison led the way to Robby's room. A bright smile lit his face as soon as they entered.

"Guess what, Captain?" he asked as Captain moved to place his paws on the edge of Robby's bed.

"They found a donor for me. I'm having surgery tomorrow. I'm kinda scared, but happy, too."

Mrs. Adams moved toward Rebecca. "That's wonderful news," Rebecca whispered.

Robby's mother nodded, tears shining in her eyes. "We'd almost given up hope."

Several minutes later, Captain and Rebecca said good-bye to Robby. "Good luck tomorrow, Robby," Rebecca said as they left.

"Thank you and thanks for bringing Captain to see me again."

"You're very welcome."

"Is there anyone else you'd like for us to visit today?" Rebecca asked Allison as they stepped out into the hallway.

"Yes, a little girl named Emma. She was hit by a car while riding her bike a few days ago. She's got a broken arm and leg. She hasn't spoken since they brought her in. Maybe Captain will be just the thing she needs."

Rebecca nodded. "Lead the way."

Allison knocked softly on Emma's door and then pushed inside. Emma's mom and dad sat on either side of her watching cartoons.

"Mr. and Mrs. Ellington, Rebecca and Captain are here to visit with Emma. Is now a good time?"

"Yes," replied Mr. Ellington. "Come in."

Rebecca led Captain into the room. A little girl who looked to be about six years old sat in the hospital bed. She had curly black hair and large blue eyes. Her right arm and leg were both covered in casts. The right side of her face was severely bruised.

"Hi, Emma," Rebecca greeted. "This is Captain. Would you like for him to come say hello?"

Emma nodded.

Rebecca released Captain, and he trotted over to Emma's bed. He placed his paws on the bed and dropped his head onto them. Emma reached out and touched the top of his head.

"Why don't you say hi?" her mother suggested.

Emma glanced at her mother and then back at Captain. Everyone in the room held their breath.

Emma didn't say anything, she just kept softly petting Captain's head.

"Would you like Captain to show you some tricks?" Rebecca asked.

Emma nodded.

"Captain," Rebecca said, pulling a tennis ball out of the bag she had slung over her shoulder. "Let's show Emma how you can balance your ball."

Captain dropped his paws off the bed and padded over to Rebecca. He sat down in front of her, and Rebecca placed the tennis ball on the bridge of his nose.

"Okay, up," she commanded.

Captain slowly rose up on his hind legs, carefully balancing the ball. Rebecca made a twirling motion with her arm. Captain turned in a circle.

"Okay, flip it," Rebecca commanded.

Captain quickly flipped his nose upward causing the ball to fly high into the air. Then he jumped up and caught the ball.

Emma gave a squeal of excitement and began clapping her hands.

"Would you like to play catch with him?" Rebecca asked, happy to see the girl was enjoying Captain's show.

Emma nodded her head enthusiastically.

"Captain, give Emma the ball," Rebecca commanded.

Captain trotted to the bed and dropped the ball near Emma's hand. He backed up a few steps and waited patiently for Emma to throw it. She picked it up and giggled at its wetness. Then she tossed it to Captain. He easily caught it and took it back to her. She threw the ball several more times.

"He knows several tricks. He can sit, roll over, beg, and shake. Why don't you give him a command?" Rebecca suggested.

Emma's eyes widened. She looked from her mom, to her dad, and then back to Captain. The silence lengthened. Then, finally, she said softly, "Roll over." Captain quickly dropped to the floor and executed a perfect roll.

Mrs. Ellington burst into tears and reached to pull her daughter close. Mr. Ellington placed his hand on his wife's shoulder as she embraced their daughter. Rebecca felt the wetness of her own tears as she witnessed their happiness.

Finally, Emma said, "Can I pet Captain now, Mommy?"

Mrs. Ellington chuckled and released her daughter. "Of course you can, honey."

Rebecca and Captain stayed for another half an hour. As they left the room, Mr. Ellington followed them out. "I don't know how to thank you for today," he said earnestly.

"Knowing that we helped is thanks enough, Mr. Ellington."

A few minutes later, Rebecca and Captain stepped off the elevator on the first floor just as Derrick was leaving the ER. He drew up in surprise when he saw her.

"What are you doing here?" he asked gruffly.

"What does it look like?" she answered, pointing to Captain.

"I meant, why aren't you resting that ankle like I told you to?"

"I had to do this first. I'm on my way home now. I plan to ice it and elevate it just like the doctor ordered."

Derrick immediately regretted snapping at her, but he couldn't think of anything to say to make up for it. After a brief pause, she said, "Well, if you'll excuse me."

He nodded and moved out of her way. *Why do I act like such an idiot every time I'm around that woman?*

CHAPTER 7

Rebecca let out a big sigh of relief when she finally arrived home at 4:30 Saturday afternoon. There was a persistent pounding in her ankle. Pain radiated through her foot and up her calf. She couldn't wait to sit down, take off her shoes, and get her foot elevated. She let Captain into the back yard and then hobbled into the kitchen. She pulled a plastic yellow bucket out from under the sink and filled it with ice water. Then she left it in the sink. On the way to let Captain back into the house, she retrieved a towel from the bathroom.

Captain padded along beside her as she made her way back into the kitchen. She grabbed the bucket of ice water out of the sink and walked over to the small oak dining table that was pushed up against the wall of the kitchen. She placed the bucket on the floor and sat down on one of the wooden chairs. She groaned loudly as she pulled off her shoe, and then the ankle brace. She rolled down her sock and shook her head in dismay when she got her first good look at her ankle. It was swollen to three times its normal size. A large, black bruise ran from the bottom of her calf, across the ankle, and down the top of her foot.

She lifted her leg and paused with her foot poised over the bucket. "Here goes nothing," she muttered as she plunged her foot into the icy water. She sucked in a quick breath. "Crap, that hurts," she whispered between clenched teeth. Captain gave a sympathetic whimper and moved to sit beside her. Rebecca reached out and placed her hand on top of his head, grateful for his moral support.

Derrick had told her that she needed to soak the ankle for ten minutes. She wasn't sure she could stand it that long. It felt as if a thousand stick pins were being jabbed into her foot and ankle at once. She bit her lower lip and glanced at the clock on the microwave. Each minute that passed seemed like an eternity. She kept hoping her foot would go numb, but it never did. At the tenth minute, Rebecca jerked her foot out of the bucket and breathed a huge sigh of relief. She grabbed the bath towel and wrapped it around her dripping foot. She took a couple of deep, steadying breaths as the pain began to ease.

"Let's go sit on the sofa, Captain," Rebecca suggested. Captain stood and followed her while she hobbled into the living room. She stacked two pillows on the coffee table that stood in front of the sofa and then propped her foot on the pillows. She leaned back and sighed. Captain leaped onto the sofa, lay down, and dropped his head onto her lap.

Rebecca had just switched on the television when her cell phone rang. She picked it up and saw that it was her mother calling.

"Hi, Mom."

"Are you home?" Barbara asked.

"Yes." Rebecca answered.

"Good. We're on our way. We've got dinner."

"Who's 'we'?" Rebecca asked apprehensively.

"Marilyn called June and me and told us what happened. We're bringing you dinner."

"You're all three coming now?" Rebecca asked in disbelief.

"As a matter of fact, we're pulling into your driveway even as we speak."

Rebecca groaned in annoyance and said, "Okay, then I'm hanging up, so I can open the door."

Just then, Captain lifted his head off her lap and started thumping his tail against the sofa cushions. He jumped down and trotted to the front door. Rebecca stood up and limped after him. She pulled the door open as Barbara,

June, and Marilyn stepped onto her porch. June and Marilyn each held a bag of Chinese takeout.

Barbara hurried forward and wrapped Rebecca in a hug. She returned her hug and glared at June and Marilyn over Barbara's shoulder. They grinned sheepishly back at her.

Barbara pulled back and asked, "How's the ankle? It's not broken, is it?"

"No, it's just a bad sprain."

Barbara sighed dramatically and said, "That's a relief."

"Why don't you all come inside, so we can get to the real reason you're here?"

June laughed and said, "You mean we're that obvious?"

Rebecca rolled her eyes. Marilyn and June chuckled and pushed their way into her house.

"Let's eat. I'm starving," Marilyn said as she walked into the living room. June followed her. They placed their bags on the coffee table, sat down on the sofa, and started pulling out the food.

"I'll get the plates and silverware. Rebecca, you go sit down and get off that ankle," Barbara commanded.

Rebecca gave a resigned sigh and limped over to resume her spot at the end of the sofa. She sat back and propped her foot back onto the pillows. Then she reluctantly waited for the other three ladies to open fire with their questions.

June glanced at Rebecca's ankle as soon as she propped it on the pillows. "Wow, you really did a number on it, didn't you?"

Marilyn glanced up from what she was doing and looked toward Rebecca. Then she let out a low whistle and said, "I can't believe it already looks so bruised. Are they sure it isn't broken?"

"Dr. Peterson said that I probably tore some ligaments in there. I'm supposed to put it in an ice bath for ten minutes twice a day. I had just finished with the first one before you girls got here. It hurt like hell."

Barbara returned with the plates and silverware. They spent the next few minutes divvying up the food. As soon as their plates were filled, Barbara said, "On the way here, I caught June and Marilyn up on your date with Mitch last night. From the way you acted this morning, I didn't think you were interested in him. I thought you seemed more interested in his friend, Derrick. Then Marilyn tells us that Mitch kissed you in front of the girls at practice. Was I wrong, is Mitch the one you're interested in?"

Was that just this morning? Rebecca thought. It felt like days not hours since she'd had that conversation with her mother. "I'm not interested in Mitch. The kiss this morning was just for show. He thought it was funny to embarrass me in front of the girls." Rebecca felt a smug satisfaction that she'd been able to answer the question without mentioning her attraction to Derrick.

"This is all very confusing," June said. "Your date was with Mitch, and Mitch is the one who came to practice this morning, but Derrick is the one you're interested in?"

Rebecca sighed, realizing that she hadn't avoided the subject of Derrick after all. "Yes, not that it matters. You should have seen the woman he was with last night. She was gorgeous. If she's any indication of his type, then I don't stand a chance."

"I wish you would stop selling yourself short like that," Barbara chided. "You don't know how wonderful you are. Any man would be lucky to have you."

"I'm confused, too. What's wrong with Mitch?" Marilyn asked. "He's gorgeous. I almost swooned when he picked you up and carried you across the gym."

"Nothing's wrong with him. I like him a lot. He's smart, handsome, and charming. I'm just not attracted to him. He's too immature for my taste. Besides, he doesn't strike me as the relationship type. I think he likes playing the field too much to settle down with anyone."

"Well, I for one was hoping to hear a much juicier story after what I saw this morning," Marilyn said with disappointment.

Rebecca shrugged. "Sorry, that's all there is to it. Mitch and I are just destined to be friends and Derrick isn't interested in me. End of story."

"We'll see," Barbara said. "I have a feeling the story is just beginning."

~

Monday morning at Animal Friends was extremely busy. Rebecca had been moving from room to room all morning. She pulled a chart out of the bin on the back of the door of exam room two. Rebecca smiled when she read it. The patient was an eight-year-old Shih Tzu named Maggie. She'd seen the dog a few times over the years for vaccines. She belonged to Mrs. Denton, a very sweet elderly woman.

"Good morning, Mrs. Denton," Rebecca greeted as she entered the room.

"Good morning," Mrs. Denton replied.

Maggie ran over and jumped up on Rebecca's legs. She chuckled softly and said, "Good morning to you, too, Maggie." She bent and lifted Maggie into her arms.

The hair on Maggie's head was pulled away from her face and held on top of her head with a pink bow. Her left eye was crusted closed. The right eye had a large amount of mucous floating across its surface.

"You poor thing," Rebecca cooed. "Let's get those eyes fixed up." She looked up and said to Mrs. Denton, "It's pretty common for this breed to have issues with tear production. When the eyes get dried out, they get crusty like this. I'm going to clean her eyes up and then test her tear production."

"Okay, whatever she needs," Mrs. Denton replied.

Rebecca spent the next few minutes using gauze soaked with warm water to loosen the crust gluing Maggie's left eye closed. Once her eyes were cleaned, Rebecca tested her tear production.

"Yep," she said, "Maggie's not producing enough tears. She's going to need to be on daily eye ointment."

Mrs. Denton nodded in understanding. Rebecca lifted Maggie into her arms and bent to place her on the floor at Mrs. Denton's feet. Out of the corner of her eye, she saw something pink flutter to the ground. *What was that?* she thought curiously as she glanced up. Her eyes widened in shock as heat rushed into her cheeks. Mrs. Denton was standing just a few inches away with her pink polyester pants around her ankles. She was pointing to a spot on her inner thigh. Rebecca quickly lowered her eyes. *What the hell?* she thought, completely caught off guard.

"Will you look at my spider bite?" Mrs. Denton asked. "My doctor's already looked at it, but I trust you more than him."

Rebecca kept her eyes down and said, "I'm sorry. I'm not allowed to treat people. It's against the law."

"I won't tell anyone," Mrs. Denton said.

Rebecca shook her head and said, "I'm sorry. I can't. Please put your pants back on, Mrs. Denton."

She sighed in relief when she heard the sound of rustling cloth. She quickly stood and muttered something about getting Maggie's medication and then hurried out of the room.

Jimmy saw her rush out with cheeks glowing. "What happened in there?" he asked curiously.

"I bent down to put Maggie on the floor and the next thing I knew Mrs. Denton had dropped her pants," Rebecca said softly.

Jimmy let out a bark of laughter. "Seriously?" he asked.

Rebecca nodded. She chuckled softly. "It's the first time that's ever happened to me."

"Why did she do it?"

"She wanted me to look at a spider bite on her leg."

Jimmy shook his head and chuckled, "We sure get some strange people in here, don't we?"

A few hours later, Rebecca finally had a break between clients. She took the chance to sit down on one of the waiting room chairs and elevate her ankle.

"How're you holding up?" June asked.

"Fine," Rebecca answered. "It hurts, but not too badly."

Just then, a loud crash of thunder shook the windows of the clinic. June went over to open the blinds that covered the front window. The sky had grown very dark. A strong wind blew debris and leaves across the clinic's parking lot. "Looks like a pretty bad storm," June commented.

A moment later, tiny hail stones started bouncing off the pavement. Lightning flashed across the sky followed immediately by a loud crash of thunder.

"Oh man," Jimmy said as he joined them in the waiting room. "I hope my car doesn't get all dented up."

June and Rebecca both laughed at his comment. Jimmy drove an old Honda Civic whose paint was so faded it was hard to tell what the original color had been. It was missing the rear bumper. Jimmy had to enter the car through the passenger side because the driver's door handle had broken off several weeks previously.

"That would be a shame," Rebecca retorted sarcastically.

A moment later, the clinic phone rang. "Animal Friends Veterinary Clinic," June answered. "How long has she been in labor?" she asked. There was a long pause as she listened to the person on the other end of the line. "Yes, it sounds like she's gonna need a c-section. How fast can you get here?" After hearing the answer, she said, "Okay, we'll see you in 20 minutes."

She hung up the phone and said, "That was Phillip Jones. He's bringing in a Chihuahua. She's been in labor for several hours with no puppies."

"Okay, Jimmy, go ahead and put some towels in the dryer to get them warmed up," Rebecca instructed as she went to prepare the surgery room.

25 minutes later, Phillip Jones arrived. The storm continued to rage outside. He rushed inside carrying a small dog crate.

"Bring her on back," Rebecca said as he came through the door. She led him to the treatment area behind the exam rooms. He placed the crate on the table. Rebecca opened the crate door and pulled out a small, black Chihuahua.

"What's her name?" she asked.

"Tinkerbell," he answered.

"How long has she been pushing?" she asked.

"A couple of hours."

Rebecca gave her a quick exam. "Feels like she's got a really large puppy in there," she said. "She definitely needs the c-section."

"Okay," Mr. Jones answered.

A few minutes later, Rebecca and Jimmy had Tinkerbell on the surgery table. Rebecca could hear the phone ringing as she made the incision to open up the abdomen. As she pulled one of the uterine horns out, June stuck her head into the surgery room.

"We've got two more coming," June said.

"C-sections?" Rebecca asked.

"Yep," June answered. "That storm's really nasty out there. It must be scaring all the pregnant dogs into labor."

Rebecca nodded in agreement as she opened the uterus and brought out the puppy. She quickly clamped the umbilical cord and handed the puppy to Jimmy. He took it into the treatment room and began rubbing it with a warm towel. Rebecca smiled when she heard the puppy's first cry. It only took her a few minutes to close the incisions in the uterus and abdomen.

She heard the bell over the front door announce the arrival of her next patient. She left Jimmy to watch

Tinkerbell wake up and went to begin the exam of the new arrival. She took a minute to glance outside. Heavy rain continued to fall. Water rushed through the gutters on either side of the street that ran in front of the clinic.

Her next C-section was Lulu, an English Bulldog. Rebecca removed ten puppies out of her. As soon as she finished with Lulu, she moved on to Muffy, a Toy Poodle. She had three puppies.

By the time Rebecca finished with Muffy, it was well after closing.

"What a day!" said Jimmy when they were finally closing down for the night. "I don't know about you, but I'm beat. You ladies drive carefully. Doesn't look like the storm's let up much."

"Thanks for all your help today, Jimmy," Rebecca said. "This was definitely a strange one."

"No problem. See ya in the morning," he said as he hurried through the door and ran to his car.

"I'm exhausted. I can't imagine how tired you must be," said June.

Rebecca nodded and said, "I'm running on fumes. I'm going to go home and soak in a long, hot bath. Then I'm going to prop up this ankle. Now that all the excitement's over, it's really starting to throb."

June nodded in understanding. She grabbed her purse and headed toward the door. Rebecca walked with her.

"See you in the morning." June said.

"Be careful, June. Jimmy's right, it's really nasty out there."

June dashed to her car while Rebecca paused to lock the door. June was just turning onto 1st Street when Rebecca jumped into her car. Rebecca and June lived only a few blocks from each other, so they traveled in the same direction from the clinic. Rebecca turned onto 1st Street and could see June stopped at the stoplight at the corner of 1st and Liberty a few blocks ahead of her. The light turned green and June moved into the intersection. Rebecca gasped in horror as a pickup blew right through the cross traffic's red light and slammed into the driver's side of June's car.

"June!" she screamed. She punched the gas and sped toward the accident. Her tires screeched as she pulled to a stop and jumped out of the car. Rebecca could see the driver of the pickup standing beside his truck. He looked dazed, but otherwise uninjured. The adrenaline that surged through Rebecca caused her to forget all about her ankle as she ran toward June. The driver's door was caved in, and the window was shattered. June was slumped over the steering wheel. Her face was covered with blood. Rebecca ran around to the passenger door and jerked it open.

"June, are you okay?" she asked as she slid into the car. There was no response. Rebecca reached out and felt for a pulse. She breathed a sigh of relief when she felt a slow, steady beat. June groaned.

"It's going to be okay, June. I'm here," Rebecca said. She could hear the sirens of rescue vehicles drawing closer. "Help is coming. Just hang in there."

A few moments later, a police car and an ambulance arrived on the scene. Rebecca slipped out of the car to give the EMTs access to June. Rain beat down on her as she stood nervously beside the car. It took several minutes for them to get June out. They loaded her onto a gurney and quickly wheeled her to the ambulance. Rebecca jogged along beside them. June remained unconscious.

"How badly is she hurt?" Rebecca asked.

"We're taking her to St. Luke's. They'll be able to answer your questions," one of the EMTs answered.

As soon as they loaded June into the back of the ambulance, Rebecca jumped into her car and followed it to St. Luke's.

CHAPTER 8

Derrick moved out from behind the curtain surrounding one of the ER beds. He'd just finished treating a man for severe burns. The man had been electrocuted when lightning struck his house causing a current to leap out of the wall socket he'd been standing near. The man had been lucky that the shock had only resulted in burns.

Derrick reached out to rub the back of his neck. Then he took a couple of deep breaths and rolled his shoulders to relieve some tension. Over the last several hours, the ER had been overrun with emergencies caused by the storm that was raging outside. Derrick had been steadily moving from patient to patient. In addition to the electrocution, he'd treated several car accident victims as well as a woman who'd been badly cut when a tree limb crashed through her living room window. He was starting to feel the effects of fatigue.

"Who's next?" he asked Gloria, the nurse who was triaging the patients.

"That's all for now. Dr. Jones is with the last patient."

Just then, the nurse's station radio beeped followed by the sound of Joe, one of the ambulance drivers, alerting them that they were on their way with another car accident victim. Joe informed Gloria that the woman was unconscious and had multiple injuries. They would arrive at the hospital in ten minutes.

Derrick sighed at the news. "Gives me just enough time to grab a cup of coffee."

He went to the employee break room and poured himself a cup. He regretted that he didn't have time to get some coffee from the cafeteria. He had to settle for the nurses' weak coffee. *At least, it's hot*, he thought as he carried the cup to a table and chairs that stood in the center of the room. He groaned loudly as he sank into the nearest chair.

After downing the coffee, he re-entered the ER. He saw the ambulance pull up at the entrance. He stood with Gloria as Joe and his partner, Rhonda, removed the gurney from the back of the ambulance. A few moments later, they were wheeling it inside.

Joe started rattling of the patient's vitals as they pushed the gurney into the ER. Gloria and Derrick fell into step beside it as Joe and Rhonda wheeled it over to one of the empty beds and carefully transferred the patient onto it. They had already started the woman on IVs. As soon as they had her transferred, Derrick stepped in and began his examination.

The woman's nose was obviously broken. She had a long laceration across her left cheek as well as several smaller cuts on her hands. Pieces of broken glass covered her hair.

Derrick's head jerked up at the sound of a familiar female voice saying urgently, "I'm here to see June Montgomery."

Rebecca Miller stood at the nurse's station craning her neck trying to see into the ER. Derrick looked back at the woman on the bed. *This is Rebecca's receptionist*, he thought as he took in the gray hair and plump features of the woman he had met at the Animal Friends Veterinary Clinic. He returned his focus to June and continued his examination.

~

Rebecca ground her teeth in frustration. Her heart pounded in fear for her friend. It had been 45 minutes since she had arrived at the ER and no one had been able to tell her anything about June. She'd been instructed to have a seat in the waiting room and that the doctor would be out to see her when he was finished. Rebecca wondered if Derrick was on duty tonight. She hoped that he was. It comforted her to think that June was in his hands. She had no way of knowing whether or not he was a good doctor, but she felt confident that he was.

Rebecca's nerves were stretched to the breaking point. She alternated between pacing the small room and sitting stiffly in the room's uncomfortable plastic chairs. She'd just sat down when Derrick stepped into the waiting room. Rebecca leaped off the chair and hurried toward him.

Derrick could see fear shining in her eyes as she stopped in front of him. She looked like she'd been put through hell. Her damp hair hung limply to her shoulders. Her face was pale and pinched with worry. He suddenly had an overwhelming urge to hug her. He gripped his hands into fists to keep from reaching for her.

"She's going to be okay," he said.

Rebecca visibly sagged with relief. The fear in her eyes was quickly replaced with the moisture of unshed tears.

"How badly is she hurt?" Rebecca asked anxiously.

"Her left collar bone and wrist are broken, so is her nose. I had to stitch several lacerations, including a pretty long one across her left cheek. She's also got a concussion. I'm going to keep her here tonight for observation. She'll be out of commission for several weeks, but she'll be fine."

Rebecca could no longer hold back the tears as relief poured through her. She unconsciously reached out and placed her hand on Derrick's arm. "I saw it happen," she said softly. "She was right in front of me, and I saw the pickup run the light and slam into her car. I thought he'd killed her."

This time Derrick couldn't resist the urge. He opened his arms, and she stepped into his embrace. He felt a flood of protectiveness surge through him. She seemed so small and fragile as he held her to him. It was such a contrast to the tough, brave woman he'd previously encountered. He was surprised at how good it felt to hold her against him.

Rebecca took a deep breath and felt some of the tension flow out of her. Her head was pressed against Derrick's chest. She could hear the strong, steady beat of his heart. It soothed her worn and frayed nerves. She felt herself relaxing for the first time in hours.

A few moments later, an older couple walked into the waiting room. They eyed Derrick and Rebecca curiously. Derrick dropped his arms to his sides. He was irritated that they had been interrupted.

Rebecca stepped back and swiped at her eyes. She felt embarrassed by her moment of weakness. "Is she awake? When can I see her?"

"Yes and now," Derrick answered. "She woke up right before I came to see you. I told her you were out here. They'll be moving her into a room soon. You can sit with her while they get her room ready."

Rebecca nodded and followed him into the ER. They received curious stares from the nursing staff as they walked across the room. It was usually their responsibility to bring the patients' visitors back to the see them. They had never seen Dr. Peterson do it personally. He usually waited until the friends and family members were with the patient before he talked with them.

Derrick and Rebecca paused outside of the third closed curtain on the right side of the room. Derrick drew it back slightly and stuck his head inside. "Rebecca's here," he said.

Rebecca was relieved to hear how strong June's voice sounded when she answered, "Well, let her in. She must be scared to death."

Derrick pulled the curtain aside, so that Rebecca could enter. "I'll leave you two alone," he said as she moved to step past him.

Rebecca gave him a grateful look and hurried toward June. She drew in a quick breath when she got her first look at June's face.

"Do I look that bad?" June asked.

She had a large bandage over the left side of her face. A splint covered her nose. Dark purple bruises were already appearing beneath both eyes. Her left arm was in a sling. A cast covered her left wrist.

Rebecca grinned and said, "You look like you've been hit by a truck."

June chuckled and then groaned. "Don't make me laugh. I feel like I've been hit by a truck, and it hurts to move." Then she asked, "How did you know I was here?"

"I was coming up to the intersection when you were hit. I followed the ambulance to the hospital."

"That must have been terrible for you."

Rebecca reached for June's hand. "It was horrible. I couldn't believe what I was seeing. I'm so glad that you're going to be okay."

June squeezed Rebecca's hand. "You look like you're about to drop from exhaustion. Why don't you go on home? I'll be fine. You've had one hell of a day. It must be really late."

"I'll wait until you're settled in your room. Then I'll go," Rebecca answered.

"Do you have your phone with you?" June asked.

"Yes. It's right here," Rebecca answered, reaching into her purse to withdraw the phone.

"May I use it to call Walter and let him know what happened? We've been talking every night after I get home from work. He'll be worried sick that I haven't called, especially with this storm."

Rebecca was surprised and pleased to hear that June and Walter's relationship was going so well. She handed June the phone and said, "Do you want me to step out while you call?"

"No, you can stay," June answered.

Walter answered on the first ring. "Hello." June could hear the anxiety in his voice.

"It's me," June answered. "I've been in an accident. I'm at the hospital, but I'm going to be okay. They want to keep me overnight. I knew you'd be worried."

"You're damned right, I've been worried," Walter answered gruffly. "I'm on my way."

"You don't have to come down here, Walter."

"Yes, I do. It'll take me about ten minutes to get there. I'll see you soon."

June handed the phone back to Rebecca. "He's on his way."

"I'm glad," replied Rebecca, relieved that June would have company.

A few minutes later, June was moved into a room on the second floor. As soon as they got her settled, June commanded, "Go home, Rebecca. Walter will be here any minute. Besides, I don't think I'll be awake much longer. The meds they gave me are really kicking in. My eyelids feel very heavy."

Rebecca knew that June was right. She was so exhausted she was having a hard time focusing, and she would need to open the clinic in just another few hours.

"Okay. Call me tomorrow to let me know when you're being discharged."

"Walter will make sure I get home," June replied. "But I'll call you as soon as I'm home."

Rebecca nodded and headed toward the door. She turned back to say something to June. Her friend was already asleep. Rebecca smiled and gently closed the door behind her. She walked down the corridor to the elevator. The doors slid open. Walter Stockton hurried out and bumped into her.

"Oh, Dr. Miller, I'm so sorry," he apologized.

"It's okay, Walter."

"How is she?" he asked anxiously.

"She's sleeping. She's got a few broken bones and a pretty major cut on her face, but otherwise, she's fine. I'm glad you're here with her. You know what room she's in?"

"Yes, they told me downstairs. You be careful on your way home. You look beat."

"I will," she replied as she stepped into the elevator and pushed the button for the lobby.

Rebecca leaned heavily against the elevator wall. She glanced at her watch and saw that it was past 11:00. She groaned. It would be after midnight by the time she was settled in her bed. That only left about five hours for sleep. Her whole body ached with fatigue. Her ankle throbbed painfully.

When the elevator doors opened, she moaned and pushed herself away from the wall. She limped across the foyer toward the hospital's entrance. Just as she passed by the ER, Derrick walked out.

She looks about ready to drop, he thought as he took in Rebecca's exhausted appearance.

He stepped up to her and grabbed her elbow. "I'm driving you home," he said gruffly.

Rebecca looked at him in surprise. "I have to be at work in a few hours. I need my car. I can drive myself."

"You're in no shape to drive. You can barely keep your eyes open. Tell me what time you need to leave for work, and I'll pick you up. We'll worry about getting your car tomorrow."

Rebecca was too tired to argue as he steered her toward his car. He stopped beside a sleek, black Mercedes. *Nice car,* she thought as he opened the passenger door for her. She folded herself into the seat, leaned back to rest her head against the soft leather seat, and closed her eyes.

Derrick jogged around the car and slid behind the wheel. "Where to?" he asked.

"322 Maple Street," she mumbled without opening her eyes.

Derrick pulled out of the hospital parking lot and turned toward the address Rebecca had given him. He glanced over at her and smiled. She had already fallen asleep. It took 15 minutes to reach her home.

The sound of Derrick shutting off the car's engine roused Rebecca. She sat up. She had not realized that she had dozed off. "Am I home already?" she asked in surprise.

Derrick let out a soft chuckle. "Yes. You were out before we'd even left the hospital's parking lot."

Rebecca gave him a rueful smile. "I guess it's a good thing you were driving."

Derrick flashed her a quick grin and then got out of the car. Rebecca opened her door. Before she could react, he leaned in and scooped her into his arms. "I don't need to be carried like a child," she protested. "What is it with you and Mitch insisting on carrying me all the time?"

Derrick smiled down at her. "What can I say? I was jealous and wanted my turn."

"Yeah, right," Rebecca said doubtfully.

Derrick didn't say anything else as he carried her toward the front door. He was honest enough with himself to admit that even though he'd been teasing her, there was some truth to what he had said. He had been jealous of the times Mitch had held her in his arms.

He set her on her feet when they reached her porch. Rebecca pulled her keys out of her purse and opened the door. As they stepped inside, she flipped on the lights in the living room.

Derrick let out a whistle. "Love the green shag."

Rebecca laughed. "It goes well with the orange countertops. Actually, I've been meaning to call a contractor, but I haven't gotten around to it, yet."

"Where's your dog?" he asked. He'd expected to be greeted at the door.

"I called my neighbor from the hospital and asked him to let Captain into the back yard for me. I often get tied up at the clinic. Jim's really great about letting him out when I can't get home at a reasonable time."

"What time should I be here to get you in the morning?"

"I need to leave around 6:30," Rebecca replied. "Are you sure you don't mind? I could call my mother and ask her to come get me."

"I don't mind." Derrick replied firmly. "I'll see you at 6:30."

Impulsively, Rebecca leaned up on her tiptoes and brushed her lips against his cheek. "Thank you, Derrick. Not only for bringing me home, but also for taking such good care of June. I really do appreciate it."

Derrick nodded. "I'm glad June is going to be okay." They stood looking at each other for a long moment. Then he turned on his heel and walked out the door.

After he left, Rebecca went to let Captain into the house. Thankfully, the rain had stopped by the time she'd called Jim, so Captain had not had to be out in the storm. She knelt down and wrapped her arms around his neck. "I'm sorry I'm so late. It's been an awful day." Captain leaned into her embrace. A few seconds later, she stood up and said tiredly, "Let's go to bed." Captain padded along beside her as she half walked, half stumbled into her bedroom. She was barely conscious of getting into her pajamas and collapsing onto the bed.

CHAPTER 9

The sound of the doorbell brought Rebecca to the edge of consciousness. She opened her eyes to slits as she tried to clear the fog of sleep from her brain. The doorbell rang again. This time Rebecca was brought fully awake. She jerked up and looked at the clock. It read 6:30. "Crap!" she yelled as she threw back the covers and swung her legs over the edge of the bed. She slipped her feet into a pair of slippers and moved to grab a robe that was slung across the back of a chair that sat in the corner of her bedroom. She pushed her arms into the robe's sleeves and tied the sash as she hurried down the hall toward the front door.

The doorbell sounded once more. "I'm coming!" she yelled.

A moment later, she jerked the door open. "I'm sorry," she apologized quickly. "I forgot to set the alarm. Just give me ten minutes, and I'll be ready to go."

Derrick chuckled softly as he stepped into the house. Rebecca's hair stuck out in a riotous mess. She wore an oversized, purple terry cloth bathrobe. The sleeves hung well past the ends of her fingers. Beneath the robe, yellow plaid pajama pants extended down to her ankles. The outfit was rounded out with fuzzy pink slippers.

She glared at him, her cheeks flaming. "Sure, I wasn't embarrassed enough, I needed you to laugh at me," she said sarcastically.

He sobered and said, "You look adorable." Derrick was surprised to realize that he meant it.

Rebecca rolled her eyes and turned to hurry back down the hall toward her bedroom. "Would you please let

Captain out while I get ready?" she called over her shoulder.

"Sure," he replied. "Lead the way," he said to Captain. He followed the dog down the same hallway that Rebecca had just disappeared into. As he passed by her bedroom, he saw that the door was slightly ajar. He glanced inside just as she pulled her pajama top over her head. He stopped short. He sucked in his breath as a shaft of desire shot through him.

Rebecca stood with her back to him. His eyes traced the graceful line of her spine down to a narrow waist that flared out slightly at her hips. Creamy-white skin covered the smooth muscles of her back. Derrick's fingers itched with the sudden need to reach out and run his hands over it.

The sound of Derrick's quickly inhaled breath caused Rebecca to glance over her shoulder. By the time she got her head around, Derrick had already moved away. *Must be hearing things,* Rebecca thought with a shrug and hurriedly finished dressing.

Less than 10 minutes later, she came out of her room.

"I found Captain's food. I thought Trouble ate fast. I think Captain had his bowl licked clean in three seconds flat."

Rebecca smiled. "Thanks for feeding him. I guess that means I'm ready to go." She walked toward the door and paused long enough to give Captain a brisk ear rub. "See you later, buddy."

"So, why so early?" Derrick asked as they drove toward Animal Friends.

"I only have to go in this early if I have patients who stayed overnight. I use a 24-hour emergency clinic in town to handle all emergencies that occur after business hours, but the patients who come in during the day and need to stay overnight still need to be fed, have bandages changed, get their meds, things like that. I had two patients stay last night. I feel bad that I didn't get a chance to check on them before I went to bed. Thankfully, they aren't there for anything life threatening, so it wasn't that big of a deal."

"How often do you have patients who stay?"

"Three to four nights a week."

"So, you go in at 6:30 in the morning, get done around 6:30 at night, and then go back to check on them again before bed?"

Rebecca nodded.

Derrick shook his head. "I thought I worked long hours."

Rebecca shrugged. "I don't mind. I love what I do."

"How are you going to manage without your receptionist?" Derrick asked.

"I'm not really sure. It's almost impossible to find good help and finding someone who's willing to work on a temporary basis might be hopeless. I've got a stack of applications from people who periodically stop by looking for a job. I guess I'll go through those and see if anyone is interested. In the meantime, it's going to be crazy."

They had reached the clinic and were pulling into the parking lot. Derrick glanced over at her and offered, "I'm free today. How about I stay and give you a hand?"

"Ordinarily, I'd politely decline the offer, but I really can't afford to turn you down," Rebecca replied. "So, thank you." She got out of the car and went to open the clinic.

What in the world did I just do? Derrick wondered as he followed Rebecca inside. *I don't know anything about working in a veterinary clinic. I've barely figured out how to care for my own dog.*

"That's Jasper," Rebecca said, pointing to a Miniature Schnauzer. Jasper wagged his short stubby tail enthusiastically at the sound of his name. "He's here because he's diabetic, and his owner needed to go out of town. I don't usually provide boarding services here, but since Jasper needs regular insulin shots, I made an exception for him. Could you please take him for a walk outside, so he can do his business?"

"Sounds easy enough," Derrick answered.

Rebecca smiled and handed him a leash. "Probably the easiest thing you'll do all day. Jasper is a sweetheart."

While Derrick took Jasper outside, Rebecca checked on her other patient, Socks, a black cat with four white feet. Socks was suffering from hepatic lipidosis, a liver disease caused by starvation. He'd gotten out and had been gone for two weeks. His owner wasn't sure where he'd been, but the cat had lost a large amount of weight. He was an indoor cat who didn't know how to find food for himself. Rebecca had him on IV fluids and was force feeding him. As soon as he started eating again on his own, he would be ready to go home.

A few minutes later, Derrick returned with Jasper. Just as he was putting him back into his cage, Jimmy arrived.

"Hi, Doc," he greeted. "Where's June? She's always here before me." He gave Derrick a curious look as he straightened away from Jasper's cage.

"She was in a car accident on the way home last night."

"No way, is she gonna be okay?"

"Yes, but she's got a few broken bones and will need to be out for several weeks. You wouldn't happen to know anyone who'd be willing to fill in for her, would you? Dr. Peterson volunteered to give us a hand today, but we're gonna need someone willing to work here until June gets back."

"As a matter of fact, my sister's looking for a job. Would you like for me to call her?"

Rebecca flashed him a relieved smile. "That would be great."

Just then, the bell over the front door jingled. "Show time," said Rebecca. As she headed to greet the new arrival, she called over her shoulder, "Derrick, come with me, and I'll show you how to get the patients checked in."

He followed her to the waiting room. A petite middle-aged woman with short black hair stood in the center of the room holding a small crate. Rebecca stepped behind the receptionist's desk and asked. "Who do we have here?"

"Tanner," the woman replied. "He's here to be neutered."

Rebecca showed Derrick how to find the appropriate paperwork. "I'll take Tanner into the first exam room. Just put whoever comes next into the other room. It looks like I have four surgery patients this morning. If anyone calls for an appointment, just get all the information you can and look for an empty spot to put them into. If you have any questions, ask Jimmy for help."

"Got it," replied Derrick as he took a seat in the chair behind the counter.

Rebecca smiled and led Tanner's owner into the exam room. As soon as she left Derrick, the next patient arrived. It was a hyperactive yellow lab mix that was there to be spayed. By the time Derrick had it situated in exam room two, the next patient had arrived. Then the phone started ringing. Before Derrick knew it, he had two patients in the waiting room and three people waiting on the line to make appointments. He answered the calls as quickly as he could. He had no idea what information to get from the clients, so he just got the basics of the owner's name, animal's name, and the complaint. Then he stuck them in the next available time slot. He was feeling pretty good about himself by the time he took care of all the phone calls and had all the surgery patients checked in. He got up and headed to the back of the clinic to check on Rebecca.

He found her in the surgery room. She was standing beside a stainless steel operating table. Derrick recognized the dog on the table as the hyper yellow lab he'd checked in to be spayed. Rebecca was holding the dog's uterus in her hands. He was surprised at how quickly she had gotten the surgery started. She had been checking in the last patient while he finished up the last phone call.

She glanced up and asked, "How's it going out there?"

"Well, the waiting room is empty, and I just finished up the last phone call," Derrick said proudly.

She smiled. "Sounds like it's going well, then."

She turned her gaze back to the dog on the table and continued the surgery. Derrick watched in fascination. He was amazed at how quickly and efficiently she worked. Within minutes, she had the surgery completed and was closing the incision.

"I think you would destroy some of the enormous egos of the hospital's surgical staff if they watched you work."

She gave him a puzzled look. "What do you mean?"

"You're an amazing surgeon. You just removed a major organ and what did that take you, ten minutes?"

Rebecca blushed. She didn't really know how to respond. She'd never been good at receiving compliments. She was relieved when the phone rang.

"Duty calls," Derrick said as he hurried back to the receptionist's desk.

"So, is that guy your boyfriend, or what?" Jimmy asked as he came in to help Rebecca move the dog off the surgery table.

"No, he's just a friend," Rebecca replied.

"The dude likes you, Doc. He wouldn't be here if he didn't."

Rebecca shook her head in denial. "He's just a really nice guy, that's all. I've seen the kind of women he dates. Believe me when I say, he's not interested in me."

Jimmy shrugged and grinned. "Whatever you say, Doc."

A few hours later, Rebecca had finished her surgeries and was seeing patients. So far, the day had gone amazingly well considering the circumstances. She was in the first exam room giving a Labradoodle her first set of shots, when she heard raised voices coming from the waiting room. A moment later, Jimmy stuck his head into the room. "You'd better get out here," he said.

Rebecca excused herself and hurried toward the waiting room.

"I need to see Doctor Miller this instance! Can't you see this is an emergency?!" a female voice yelled.

"Ma'am, please calm down. I don't think there's anything she can do for you," Derrick said in a tone of voice that indicated he was on the verge of losing his patience.

As Rebecca rounded the corner, she saw Derrick standing rigidly behind the receptionist's desk, his hands were clasped into fists. He looked as if he were about ready to jump across the desk and strangle the large, Hispanic woman who stood across from him. A cardboard box rested on the counter between them. Rebecca bit back a laugh. Marcia Cruz had a habit of picking up turtles she found in the road. Sometimes they were past the point of saving when she brought them in. Rebecca guessed this must be one of those times.

"Hello, Marcia, do you have another turtle?" Rebecca asked as she walked into the room. Out of the corner of her eye, she saw Derrick give her a surprised look.

"Yes, Doctor and this man would not let me see you," replied Marcia.

"Thank you for bringing it in, Marcia. I'll take it back and see what I can do."

Marcia nodded. Then she gave Derrick a withering look as she turned on her heel and marched out of the clinic.

"The damn thing's flat as a pancake," Derrick grumbled.

Rebecca glanced into the box. Sure enough, the turtle inside was well beyond her help. She grinned at Derrick's disgruntled expression.

"Marcia's been bringing us smashed turtles since I opened this place. Occasionally, she'll bring in one that isn't quite so smashed. We all have our quirks I guess."

"Quirks? She's certifiable."

Rebecca shrugged. "Maybe so, but she's harmless."

"Marcia gone?" Jimmy asked stepping out from his hiding place around the corner.

"Thanks for your help," Derrick said dryly.

Jimmy grinned. "I thought you could use a little initiation into the life of Animal Friends Veterinary Clinic."

Derrick's eyes narrowed threateningly. Rebecca saw the look and said, "I'm finished with the client in exam room one. Why don't you get her checked out while I get rid of the turtle?"

Derrick gave a quick nod as Rebecca grabbed the box containing the deceased turtle and headed toward the back of the clinic. Jimmy chuckled softly as he followed her.

A few minutes later, she returned to the front and asked, "So, who else do we have today?" as she moved around the receptionist's desk to look at the schedule.

Derrick looked down at the top of her bent head. She was standing very close to him. Her hair smelled faintly of strawberries. He felt the tension caused by the crazy client leave his body. He was once again surprised by how her nearness affected him. She glanced up, and he saw moisture shimmering in her eyes.

Concerned by her sudden shift in emotion, he asked, "What is it?"

"Tucker's coming in today. Mark must have finally decided to euthanize him. He's a great dog. He's had cancer for about a year. It's been a real struggle for Mark to make the decision to let him go. It's always so hard to witness someone saying good-bye to their beloved pet."

Derrick met her gaze. He was completely confused by her. Rebecca Miller was the most complex woman he'd ever met in his life. In his experience, he'd found women to be shallow, silly, and selfish. Rebecca was none of those things. She was smart, brave, hardworking, and compassionate.

The jingle of the bell over the door broke into his thoughts. They both turned to see a short, bald man carrying a medium-sized crate step into the waiting room.

"Hello, Mr. Jackson. Did Tom get into another fight?" Rebecca asked.

"Yes. He's got a big abscess on his head this time."

Tom was a large yellow tomcat who was allowed to roam the streets. He was continuously getting into fights. Rebecca had advised Mr. Jackson on several occasions to get Tom neutered, but he refused. He said that he felt like it was better to allow Tom his fun, even if it meant he would have a shorter life. Rebecca found his attitude very frustrating. She loved her job because of the animals. Sometimes dealing with the humans that came with the animals pushed her patience to the limits.

"I'll take him back," she said, reaching for Tom's cage.

Jimmy came out of the ICU as Rebecca came into the treatment area. "Is that Tom again?" he asked.

"Yes. Poor cat. It really aggravates me that Mr. Jackson won't let me neuter him. I seriously don't understand the attachment men have to their animals' testicles. They act like having their animal neutered is somehow a reflection on their own manhood."

Jimmy shrugged. "It's a guy thing, Doc."

"Yeah, well, it's stupid," Rebecca answered.

An hour later, Mark Reeves arrived. Jimmy prepared the exam room by placing a warm blanket on the stainless steel table. Tucker was too weak to walk, so Mark carried him into the room.

"I'm so sorry, Mark," Rebecca said. "I know how hard this is for you."

Mark nodded. "It's for the best. He's too weak to eat. I should have made the decision a few weeks ago, but I just wasn't ready to say good-bye."

Rebecca reached out and gently ran her hands across Tucker's head and neck. "The only thing he'll feel is the prick of the needle. Once the medicine is injected, he'll go to sleep and his heart will stop."

Mark nodded in understanding.

"Are you ready?" she asked.

"Yes," Mark whispered.

Rebecca injected the solution into Tucker's vein and watched as he took his last shuttering breath. She listened to his heart and announced softly, "He's gone."

Large tears streamed down Mark's face as he whispered, "Good-bye, Tucker. You were a great dog."

Rebecca felt the warm wetness of her own tears as she witnessed the man's painful good-bye. She turned and quietly left the room to allow Mark a few minutes to gather himself.

Derrick was standing in the treatment area. "You okay?" he asked.

Rebecca nodded. "It was for the best. It's never easy, but I'm glad that I have the option of ending their pain and suffering."

After Mark left, it was time to close up for the day. "Jimmy, did you get a chance to talk with your sister about filling in for June?"

"Yeah, she was pretty excited. She'll be here tomorrow."

Rebecca smiled with relief. "Great. I didn't look forward to going through the stack of applications tonight trying to find someone."

"I'll see you tomorrow then," said Jimmy as he prepared to leave.

"See ya," Rebecca replied.

She walked into the waiting area where Derrick was busy printing out the paperwork for the next day's appointments.

"How about I buy you dinner as a small thank you for today?" she asked as she walked up to him.

"Sounds great. I'm starved. I have a new respect for June after today and for you, too. I thought the ER was a hectic place, but this is non-stop. Is it like this every day?"

She smiled and said, "Actually, this was a pretty slow day."

Derrick gave her a disbelieving look. "Really?"

"Yep. There are some days when I see about twice as many patients as I did today."

Derrick shook his head in amazement. "Now I'm really impressed."

Rebecca laughed and said teasingly, "Good, you should be."

CHAPTER 10

Later that evening, Rebecca called June. When Derrick took her to pick up her car from the hospital, she'd found out June was discharged earlier that morning. "How are you feeling?" Rebecca asked as soon as June answered her phone.

"Sleepy. All I've done all day is sleep, and I'm still tired. They've definitely got me on some strong drugs."

Rebecca was relieved to hear the humor in June's voice. "Good. Your body needs to heal. Is Walter with you?"

"Yes, he's been such a sweetheart. I tried to send him home, but he refused to leave. He's determined to play nursemaid."

Rebecca chuckled. "I'm sure you're loving every minute of it."

June laughed and asked, "How did things go at the clinic today?"

"You won't believe it. Derrick Peterson filled in for you."

"What, as in Dr. Peterson? Okay, you've got to start at the beginning and tell me everything."

"By the time I left the hospital last night, I was barely functioning. He insisted on driving me home. Then this morning he took me to work and stayed to help."

"You mean he stayed the night with you last night?" June asked in surprise.

"No, he dropped me off last night and picked me up this morning," Rebecca clarified.

"Sounds like you have a sweetheart of your own," June commented.

"No, we're just friends, I think. I'm not really sure what we are. I mean, I barely know him. To be honest, I was shocked when he offered to help, but I'm really thankful that he did. It made for a much easier day."

"I'll tell you why he helped, he likes you, Rebecca."

"Like I told Jimmy this morning, I'm not his type. The women he dates are tall with big breasts and flawless features."

"Tell yourself that if you want, but a man doesn't give up a day off to work as a receptionist in a veterinary clinic for a woman he isn't interested in."

Rebecca thought about June's comment for a moment. Jimmy said almost the same thing to her earlier. *Were they right? Was Derrick interested in her?* She shook her head. No, he'd only helped because she'd needed it. Their conversation at dinner had been relaxed and light-hearted. There hadn't been anything flirtatious about it. They were developing a friendship and nothing more. Not that she wouldn't have liked for there to be something more between them. He was smart, considerate, and gorgeous.

"By the way, have you found someone who will fill in for me until I get back? I'm assuming Dr. Peterson was just a one-time thing."

Rebecca chuckled. "Yeah, even if he didn't have another job, I don't think he'd be back. He seemed very relieved when the day was finally over. Jimmy's sister is starting tomorrow. Have you ever met her?"

"No. I think he mentioned once that she was a couple of years older than him, but that's all I know." June yawned loudly into the phone. "Sorry," she apologized sleepily.

"I better let you get back to sleep. I'll try to stop by and visit you tomorrow."

"Okay, we can talk more about Derrick Peterson then. Don't sell yourself short, Rebecca. There is no reason why he couldn't be interested in you. You would be a great catch for any man."

"You sound like my mother," Rebecca sighed.

"Well, Barbara is a smart woman."

"Take care, June. I'll see you tomorrow." Rebecca disconnected and leaned back. She was sitting on her sofa with her ankle elevated. Captain was curled up next to her.

"What do you think, Captain? Do you think Derrick is interested in me? I think I'd just be fooling myself, if I thought that he was. He's too perfect for me."

~

The next morning, Jimmy introduced Rebecca to his sister, Kara. Rebecca fought not to stare. *What was Jimmy thinking?* she wondered. *She's going to scare off all the clients.* Kara had multiple facial piercings. Her dyed black hair jutted out from her head in long pointed spikes. She had a spider web tattoo covering the left side of her neck.

"Hi, Kara, it's nice to meet you," Rebecca greeted politely.

"Yeah," Kara replied with a shrug.

Jimmy saw the disapproval on Rebecca's face at the rude response from his sister. "Um, come on Kara, let me show you how to handle things up front," he said, grabbing his sister's arm and pulling her toward the receptionist's area.

Rebecca shook her head and sighed. *I don't have any choice but to give her a chance. I shouldn't judge her by her looks. I almost didn't hire Jimmy, and that has worked out just fine.*

A few hours later, Rebecca walked into the waiting room and stopped short. Her eyes widened in shock. Kara was leaning back in the chair behind the receptionist's counter with her booted feet propped up on the desk talking on her cell phone. Three people stood in the waiting room waiting for her to acknowledge them. The light on the phone console was blinking, indicating that she had a call on hold.

"Kara…"

Kara held up her hand to silence her. Rebecca's mouth closed with a snap. She couldn't believe the girl's audacity. Her eyes narrowed angrily.

"I've got to go," Kara said to the person on the other end of the phone. "Yeah, my new boss is giving me the evil eye." She rolled her eyes dramatically.

Rebecca felt her temperature rise. As soon as Kara ended the call, she asked through clenched teeth, "Who's next?"

"That guy," Kara said, pointing to a man sitting in one of the waiting room chairs holding the leash of a large pit bull.

Rebecca took a deep, calming breath and asked, "Do you have his file?"

Kara grabbed the paperwork and shoved it toward her. Rebecca saw that the light on the phone had stopped blinking, indicating that whoever it was had given up. Her irritation returned.

"Please keep your personal calls to a minimum," she said evenly. "And put the next client in exam room two." She moved around the counter and called the man with the pit bull into the exam room.

Later that afternoon, Rebecca stepped out of an exam room to find Kara in a full lip lock with a man wearing a white tank top and baggy blue jeans that sagged to the middle of his backside revealing red boxer shorts. Both of his arms were covered in tattoos. His hair was dyed a bright yellow. Rebecca's mouth dropped open in stunned amazement. The woman whose kitten Rebecca had just vaccinated sucked in a shocked breath as she followed Rebecca out of the room.

"Kara!" Rebecca exploded.

The couple slowly drew apart and turned to look at her.

"What?" Kara asked sullenly.

Rebecca felt heat flush her cheeks. She took a deep breath trying to calm her rising anger. "Please check out Mrs. Snider. Then we need to talk." She turned her angry gaze on the man who stood with his arm draped across Kara's shoulders. "You," Rebecca said, pointing a finger at him. "Leave, now."

He looked questioningly at Kara. "You better go. I'll call ya later," she said.

He shrugged and sauntered out of the clinic. Rebecca turned on her heel and strode angrily away from the waiting room. She knew she was on the verge of losing her temper completely.

Jimmy stood at the treatment counter peering into a microscope. He was searching for any parasite eggs in the stool sample Mrs. Snider had brought in with her kitten. He looked up at the sound of Rebecca's approach. He knew immediately that she was furious.

"What did Kara do?" he asked warily.

"She was playing kissy face with a man in the waiting room. Mrs. Snider saw it," Rebecca said through clenched teeth.

"That must have been Dalton, her new boyfriend. I'm sorry, Doc. Please don't fire her. She really needs the work. She's got a little boy at home. Let me talk to her," Jimmy pleaded.

Rebecca met Jimmy's beseeching gaze. She didn't want to have to fire his sister, especially knowing she had a child. "All right, talk to her, but I really can't allow that kind of behavior."

A relieved smile lit Jimmy's face. "Thanks, Doc. I'll make sure she understands."

They heard the jingle of the bell over the door. Jimmy went to talk to his sister. He pulled her into the first exam room.

"I stuck my neck out for you, Sis. You need to straighten up, or you're gonna get fired. Trevor needs diapers, baby food, and clothes. I can't afford to keep buying his supplies. He's your son. You need to start taking responsibility."

"I don't need a lecture from you, Jimmy. I'm the older one here, remember?" Kara said irritably.

"Sometimes it's hard to remember. Please don't blow this, Kara."

They locked gazes for a long moment. Finally, she sighed dramatically and said, "Okay, Jimmy. I'll behave."

Jimmy gave her a quick hug. "Thanks, Sis. You need to apologize to Dr. Miller."

They walked out of the room and found Rebecca in the ICU checking on the morning's surgery patients. She turned to face them as they approached her. Jimmy nudged Kara forward. She threw him an irritated glance. "I'm sorry for my behavior earlier, Dr. Miller."

"Okay, Kara. I really do appreciate you being here to fill in for June, but I can't tolerate having my clients offended like that."

"I understand. It won't happen again."

Rebecca nodded in acknowledgement. Kara returned to the receptionist's area.

"Thanks, Doc," said Jimmy gratefully.

Rebecca smiled. "You're welcome, Jimmy. I just hope she means it."

The rest of the day passed without any issues. Rebecca was relieved when it was finally time to close up for the day. The weather had warmed considerably. Since June only lived a few blocks from her, she decided to go home to get Captain and walk to June's.

An hour later, she rang June's doorbell. Walter opened the door. He flashed her a smile and said, "Hi, Dr. Miller, June will be so glad to see you. She's dying to drill you with more questions about Dr. Peterson."

Rebecca groaned. She'd forgotten about that. Walter's smile widened. He stepped back from the door to allow her inside.

"Rebecca, is that you?" June called from the living room.

"Yes," Rebecca replied as she moved into the foyer. She followed Walter to the living room. June was sitting in a large brown leather recliner. The bandage covering the laceration on her face had been removed revealing a row of neat stitches. Both of her eyes had deep purple bruises under them. She still had a splint across the bridge of her nose. Rebecca was relieved to see that her color was good, and her eyes sparkled with humor.

"You look good," Rebecca said as she moved to grasp June's outstretched hand.

"No, I don't. I look like Frankenstein's monster."

Rebecca chuckled and said, "Well, yeah, there is that." She squeezed June's hand and then moved to sit on the sofa that was at a right angle to June. Captain placed his paws on the arm of the recliner and nudged June gently. She laughed and reached out to rub his head affectionately.

"I could hardly wait for you to get here. I want you to tell me everything that happened between you and Dr. Peterson yesterday."

Rebecca shrugged. "I've already told you everything."

"Well, tell me again."

Rebecca started at the hospital the night of June's accident and recounted everything that had happened since then. When she finished, June nodded in satisfaction and said, "Yep, the man's crazy about you."

Rebecca shook her head. "I really don't think so, June. We haven't even been out on a real date."

"Walter, you're a man, what do you think?" June asked.

"I agree with June," Walter answered.

"See there," June said smugly. "I bet you'll hear from him again real soon. So, how did things go with Jimmy's sister?"

Rebecca shook her head ruefully. "She's quite a character, to put it mildly. I'm not sure if she's going to work out. I had to get on to her twice. First, for talking on her cell phone while there were people in the waiting room. Then later, Mrs. Snider and I walked out of an exam room to find her and her boyfriend all over each other in the waiting room. I was so embarrassed."

June laughed. "I imagine you were."

"Jimmy begged me not to fire her. Apparently, she has a little boy and Jimmy's been helping to take care of him."

"I'm surprised he's never said anything," June commented.

"Yeah, I have a new respect for him. He's a good kid."

June nodded in agreement.

~

Saturday morning, Derrick met Mitch for their weekly game of one-on-one. He'd been in a foul mood all week, and he wasn't sure why. Work had gone well. Things were relatively slow in the ER. He hoped the physical exertion of a basketball game would help ease the tension he'd been feeling.

He and Mitch had been playing for about half an hour when Mitch panted, "Time Out. I need to catch my breath."

He and Derrick were both drenched in sweat. They moved to sit on the bleachers. Mitch took a long swallow of water and asked, "What's going on with you today? You're running me ragged."

Derrick shrugged. "I needed a workout."

Mitch gave him a quizzical look. "Want to talk about it?" he asked.

"Nothing to talk about."

Just then, Derrick saw Rebecca walk into the gym. His whole body tensed. Mitch noticed the change in Derrick's demeanor and followed his gaze. A wide smile stretched across his face. "I forgot all about Rebecca's basketball game today. Let's go get cleaned up. Then we can stay to watch them play," Mitch suggested.

Derrick was confused by his reaction to seeing Rebecca. His mood had improved significantly in the space of a few seconds. *What's going on?* he wondered. *Why does just the sight of her make me feel better?*

Just then, Rebecca turned to look at them. Mitch waved and started jogging toward her. Derrick felt a shaft of jealousy knife through him when Rebecca smiled widely and waved back at Mitch. He still wasn't sure what was going on between the two of them. He suddenly felt an overwhelming urge to bury his fist in Mitch's face. He shook his head in frustration and moved to join them.

As he walked up, he heard Mitch ask, "What time does the game start, Rebecca?"

She checked her watch and said, "It starts in 30 minutes. The girls will be arriving soon."

"Great, that gives us enough time to get cleaned up," Mitch answered. "We thought we'd be your cheerleaders."

Rebecca smiled. "The girls will like that. I'm sure the other team will be completely jealous that my girls have two hunky guys cheering them on."

Mitch wiggled his eyebrows at her and said, "So, you think I'm hunky, do you?"

Rebecca laughed and said, "You're gorgeous, and you know it."

Derrick scowled. Mitch saw his look and grinned. "Come on, let's hit the showers."

Twenty minutes later, Mitch and Derrick joined Marilyn and the other parents on the bleachers behind Rebecca's team's bench.

"Hi, Mitch," Marilyn greeted warmly. Her eyes moved admiringly over Derrick.

"Hi, Marilyn. This is Derrick." He jerked his thumb toward Derrick.

"It's nice to meet you, Marilyn," Derrick said politely.

"It's nice to meet you, too," Marilyn returned. "Rebecca told me about you helping out at the clinic the other day. That was really sweet of you."

Mitch glanced at Derrick in surprise. "You worked at Rebecca's vet clinic?" he asked incredulously.

Derrick nodded. "She didn't tell you?"

"No, I haven't talked to her since practice last Saturday," Mitch replied.

Maybe they aren't sleeping together, Derrick thought, his mood lightening.

The game began a few minutes later. Derrick found himself cheering loudly right along with the girls' parents each time one of Rebecca's players scored. He admired how well they played. It was obvious that Rebecca was a good coach. They easily won the game.

As soon as the game ended, Mitch jumped down off the bleachers and went to give the girls a round of high fives. Not for the first time in their friendship, Derrick envied Mitch's easy way with people. He would have felt like an idiot acting like that, but Mitch looked completely at ease. The girls flushed and giggled at his attention.

Derrick walked up behind Rebecca and said, "Congratulations, Coach."

She whirled around to face him. Her face was slightly flushed, and her eyes danced with excitement. Derrick was struck by how pretty she looked. "They played great, didn't they?" she asked proudly.

He grinned and replied, "They're obviously well coached."

Mitch walked up and wrapped Rebecca in a bear hug. "How about Derrick and I buy you a congratulatory lunch?" he asked.

Rebecca laughed softly. "Sounds great, but it's gotta be somewhere fast. I'm supposed to have Captain at the hospital by 1:00."

"Burgers it is," replied Mitch as he released Rebecca.

After Rebecca said good-bye to her players and made sure they all had rides home, she, Derrick, and Mitch settled on a restaurant near Rebecca's house. Derrick and Mitch met Rebecca there 15 minutes later.

Derrick barely got a word in edgewise as Mitch dominated the conversation during lunch. He began to think that maybe he was wrong about Mitch and Rebecca's relationship, maybe there was something going on between them. He grew more withdrawn as the meal progressed.

Thirty minutes later, they watched as Rebecca backed out of the restaurant's parking lot. As soon as she left, Derrick turned to Mitch and asked bluntly, "Are you two sleeping together?"

"What?!" Mitch asked in surprise.

"You heard me," Derrick growled.

Mitch laughed. "Is that why you looked like you wanted to punch me in the face in there? No, we're just friends."

Mitch saw the tension leave his friend's face. He grinned. "So, when are you going to ask her out?" he asked.

Derrick scowled and said, "She isn't my type."

"I think she's exactly your type. You just haven't figured that out, yet," Mitch replied.

Derrick turned on his heel and walked stiffly to his car. He jerked open the door and slid behind the wheel. Mitch followed after him. He started to say something more, but decided it was better to let his friend chew on that for a little while.

CHAPTER 11

The next week passed quickly for Rebecca. She did not have any more trouble from Kara. She had actually settled in and done a pretty good job. As Rebecca headed to the community center for her team's second game, she wondered if she was going to see Derrick. She hadn't heard from him since the previous Saturday. If she was honest with herself, she'd have to admit that she had been disappointed when he hadn't called her. In spite of the protests she'd given June, a small part of her had hoped that June had been right, and Derrick would call. However, the week had rolled by without a word from him.

I wonder if he'll be here today, she thought as she walked into the gym, her heartbeat quickened at the thought. She stopped at the edge of the gym floor that consisted of three full-sized basketball courts and looked around for Mitch and Derrick. She felt a flash of disappointment when she didn't see them. Marilyn waved at her from across the gym. Rebecca smiled and returned her wave. Marilyn's daughter, Emma, and a few of the other members of the team were already warming up on the far court. Rebecca jogged over to join them.

"No sign of the gorgeous duo," Marilyn commented as soon as Rebecca joined her.

"They never promised to come to all the games," Rebecca replied with a shrug.

"You can't fool me. I know you were hoping they'd be here. I saw you looking around for them when you came in. So, what exactly is your relationship with those two anyway?"

"We're friends. They're both really great guys."

"Hey, Coach, can you watch my shot and tell me what I'm doing wrong?" Emma interrupted.

Rebecca was relieved to have an excuse to end the conversation. "Sure. Let me watch you shoot one."

Emma put up a jump shot from the right wing.

"You need to pull your elbow in and flick your wrist a little harder to get a better arch and backspin," Rebecca advised. "Toss me the ball and I'll show you what I mean."

Emma threw her the ball. Rebecca shot. It sailed high into the air and fell through the net with a *swoosh.*

"Nice shot, Coach."

"Thanks. Let me see you try it again," she instructed.

Emma put up another shot. This time she made it.

"Good," Rebecca praised. "That was much better."

A few minutes later, they tipped off. This game was a lot closer than the previous week. Rebecca's team won by three.

"Great game," Rebecca praised her team. "I'm proud of how tough you played. Next week will be our biggest challenge. We play the Shockers. They beat us pretty badly last year. They have several really tall girls on their team. I want you all to work on your box-outs and rebounding. It's going to be a key part to us getting a win."

"Okay, Coach," the girls replied.

Rebecca smiled and said, "See you all next week."

Marilyn stepped off the bleachers to join her. "Are you taking Captain to the hospital today?" she asked.

"Yes. Last week, we met a little girl who has leukemia. Her mother told me that meeting Captain was the first time she'd laughed in weeks. We're going to visit her again today."

"Since Derrick and Mitch aren't here to take you to lunch, why don't you join Emma and me?" Marilyn suggested. "We aren't as fascinating as those two, but it would still be fun."

"Sure, I'd like that," replied Rebecca.

~

First thing Monday morning, Rebecca glanced at the schedule to get an idea of what to expect for the day. She saw that Derrick had an appointment to bring Trouble in for her second set of vaccines. Rebecca smiled. *I guess he never found anyone else to take her.*

Early in the afternoon, Rebecca stepped into an exam room to see a chocolate Labrador Retriever with an ear infection. As soon as she entered the room, she noted that the owner wore a hunter green polo shirt with blue stitching that read, "Brian McAllister, Contractor." The man looked to be around 30. He had dark-brown hair and blue eyes. He was short and had a muscular build. He flashed her a friendly smile that revealed dimples in both cheeks. *What a great smile*, Rebecca thought.

"Hello, Mr. McAllister. I'm Dr. Miller," she greeted.

"Nice to meet you and please, call me Brian."

"So, Digger's got an ear infection, huh?" Rebecca asked as she bent to greet the lab. His whole body wagged enthusiastically when she reached to pet his head. She laughed and said, "Well, aren't you a friendly one?"

Brian chuckled. "He thinks everyone's his friend. It's his left ear. It's been bothering him for a few days."

Rebecca spent the next few minutes examining Digger. When she finished, she illustrated how to properly clean and medicate the ear. Then she said, "I noticed that your shirt says you're a contractor. Do you do remodeling? I've got an old house from the 70s that needs to be brought into the 21st century."

He flashed her another dimpled smile. "Sure, we pretty much do everything from new construction to minor repair jobs."

Rebecca returned his smile. "Great. Would you be willing to come take a look and give me an estimate?"

"How does Friday night sound? I could check out the house and then take you to dinner."

Her eyes widened in surprise. She hadn't expected that. *Why not?* she thought. *He seems like a nice guy. He's definitely cute. Maybe a date's just the thing I need to get my mind off Derrick Peterson.*

"Sounds good," she replied.

He grinned. "What time should I be there?"

"I usually finish up here around 5:30. How would 6:30 work for you?"

"Perfect."

Just then, they heard someone in the waiting room give a terrified scream.

~

Derrick found himself smiling as he headed toward Animal Friends for Trouble's vaccine appointment. He was looking forward to seeing Rebecca. He still couldn't define what it was that he felt for her, but he couldn't deny that he enjoyed being around her.

"Come on, Trouble," he said affectionately as he opened the door to let out the dog. She'd grown to about twice the size she'd been when she had followed Derrick home. He had to admit he'd grown very fond of her. It was nice to come home from a day at work and have someone there to greet you, even if that someone had four legs instead of two. In fact, it was even better. When he'd had a tough day, Trouble didn't mind that all Derrick wanted to do was kick off his shoes, drink a beer, and watch sports. She just wanted to be near him while he did it. She didn't nag or demand anything from him. She really was the perfect companion.

Derrick pulled open the front door to the clinic and stopped cold. A woman with spiked black hair stood on the receptionist's counter screaming hysterically. An elderly woman stood on a waiting room chair clutching a small carrier to her chest. She gazed around the room with wide frightened eyes. Jimmy was running around the room chasing a long furry creature.

"Close the door!" Jimmy yelled at him.

Derrick hadn't realized he was standing halfway through the front door. He quickly stepped inside and closed it.

Just then, exam room one's door flew open and Rebecca stepped out. "What's going on?" she asked just as a large chocolate lab burst out of the room behind her, knocking her against the door frame in its haste. The dog was barking loudly. Trouble decided to join in the fun. She began barking wildly and pulled hard against the leash that Derrick was holding. The room was in complete chaos. The woman standing on the receptionist's desk continued to emit an ear-piercing scream.

Derrick glanced toward Rebecca and saw a small trickle of blood above her right eye. A man stepped up behind her and grabbed her shoulders supportively. He whispered something in her ear. She nodded her head. Then he stepped past her and dove toward the chocolate lab.

Derrick reeled Trouble in closer to him and knelt to wrap his arms around her. The furry creature flew past him followed closely by Jimmy. As the creature passed, Derrick recognized that it was a ferret. He would swear that it looked like it was enjoying the commotion it was causing. Jimmy was right behind it. It took a sharp turn to the left. Jimmy lost his footing and fell hard to the ground. The ferret darted past Rebecca and into the exam room. Rebecca quickly pulled the door closed.

Derrick stood and moved toward her. "Never a dull moment, huh?" he asked in an amused tone.

She grinned at him. "Not in this place," she replied. She reached to touch the cut above her eye.

"Just a small cut. Do you have a first-aid kit?" Derrick asked.

Rebecca nodded.

"Lead the way and I'll patch you up."

"Sorry, Rebecca," Jimmy said as he got to his feet. "Jinx jumped out of his cage and took off before I could catch him."

Rebecca chuckled. "I should have warned you. He's a sneaky little thing. He's done that to me before. He thinks it's a fun game."

She turned toward the woman who stood on the chair. "I'm sorry, Mrs. Douglas. Jinx is harmless."

"What is it?" the woman asked shakily.

"Jinx is a ferret. They're known for being mischievous little things."

"Some help you were, Kara," Jimmy said grumpily. "You can get off the counter now."

The spiky haired girl stuck out her tongue at Jimmy and then hopped down off the counter.

"Are you sure you're okay?" Brian McAllister asked as he joined Derrick and Rebecca. "I'm sorry Digger knocked into you like that."

Rebecca smiled. "It's okay, Brian. He was just caught up in the excitement. I'll be fine. Kara can get you checked out."

"I need your address for Friday," Brian commented.

"Oh yeah, um, can you give me a minute? Dr. Peterson's going to get me bandaged up."

"Sure," Brian replied. "I'm in no hurry."

He glanced speculatively toward Derrick and received a dark scowl. *Wonder what's going on between those two*, he thought as he turned toward the receptionist's counter.

Derrick followed Rebecca to the treatment area. She moved to the counter that held all the diagnostic equipment. She reached overhead to open a cabinet. Derrick spotted the first-aid kit and reached over her to retrieve it.

Rebecca inhaled his scent. *Wow, he smells good*, she thought. She turned slowly around to face him. He stood a few inches in front of her. His intense hazel eyes bore into hers. She felt her pulse leap at his nearness. She glanced nervously downward and noticed for the first time how well dressed he was. He wore a starched royal blue dress shirt that was open at the collar and charcoal gray slacks.

Derrick saw the color creep into Rebecca's cheeks and felt a smug satisfaction that his nearness was affecting her. "Look up, so I can get a look at that cut," he instructed softly.

Rebecca raised her eyes to look into his face. Her pulse pounded in her ears. She clenched her fists at her sides, resisting the urge to reach out and touch him. She felt completely flustered. She desperately wanted to step back from him, but she was pushed up against the counter.

He reached out and dabbed at the cut over her eye. She winced and pulled back slightly. Tears sprang into her eyes.

"This is going to sting a little," he said mildly.

She pursed her lips and said dryly, "Well, thanks for warning me after the fact."

He grinned. "So, you have a date with that guy Friday?"

"Yes, as a matter of fact, I do," Rebecca replied.

His eyes narrowed on her face. His glance fell to her lips. For a brief moment, Rebecca thought he was going to kiss her. Her lips parted slightly in anticipation. The gold flecks in Derrick's eyes seemed to glow with intensity. Then he suddenly reached up to place a small band aid over her cut. He stepped back abruptly and muttered, "You'd better go get him that address."

Rebecca hesitated. Then she slid past him and hurried into the waiting room. Brian smiled warmly at her when she joined him. She grabbed a pen and paper from the receptionist's desk and quickly jotted down her address and phone number.

He reached for the paper and said, "Great, I'll see you Friday around 6:30."

"See you Friday," she replied.

Jimmy walked up to stand beside Derrick just as Rebecca handed Brian the paper. He quickly glanced at Derrick. The man looked like he wanted to smash something. Jimmy smiled. *Yep,* he thought. *He definitely likes her. Wonder how long it's gonna take him to realize it.*

As soon as Brian left, Jimmy said, "So, who's the guy, Doc?" He slid a glance toward Derrick. The man's scowl grew even darker. Jimmy grinned.

"Oh, he's a contractor. He's going to work on remodeling my house."

"On a Friday night?" Kara asked.

"Well, he's going to come give me an estimate, and then we're going to have dinner." Rebecca's ears burned with embarrassment at being the center of all this attention.

"Good for you," Kara commented. "That guy's really cute."

"Um, Mrs. Douglas, why don't you come on into exam room one and let me take a look at Bubbles," Rebecca said, grateful for an excuse to leave the room.

Derrick's eyes followed Rebecca as she disappeared inside the exam room.

"You gonna let her go out with that guy?" Jimmy asked.

Derrick jerked in surprise. He hadn't realized that Jimmy was still standing beside him. "It's not any of my business," he replied gruffly.

Jimmy gave a bark of laughter. "Man, when are you gonna admit ya like her?"

Derrick glowered at him. Jimmy threw up his hands and said, "Hey, don't get mad at me. I'm not the one who's about to steal your girl." Jimmy grinned and turned to walk back to the treatment area.

A few minutes later, Rebecca called Derrick and Trouble into the room. He remained silent as Rebecca examined Trouble and gave her the vaccines. *It isn't any of my business if Rebecca wants to date that guy. So, why is it bothering me so much?* he wondered testily.

"Did you and Mitch get called into work yesterday?" Rebecca asked as she injected Trouble with the vaccines.

"Not that I expected you to come to the game. I just didn't see you at the gym." She wanted to kick herself as soon as the question came out.

"Mitch got called in to investigate a series of break-ins. Apparently, there have been three places that carry prescription drugs robbed in the last two weeks. The third one happened early Saturday morning."

"I heard something on the news about one of the break-ins a few days ago. It was a pharmacy over on 3rd Street, I think."

Derrick nodded. "Some of those drugs are worth a lot on the streets."

"Do you know if they have any idea who's behind the robberies?"

"Mitch said it's two guys. They wear ski masks and loose-fitting clothes. So, they really don't have much to go on."

"I hope they catch them soon," Rebecca replied. There was a long pause. Then she continued, "Trouble looks great. She needs to come back for her last set of shots in about three weeks. She should be spayed then, too."

Derrick nodded and moved toward the door. "I'll make another appointment. Enjoy your date Friday night."

Rebecca felt her cheeks flush again. "I will. Thanks."

CHAPTER 12

On Wednesday night, Rebecca was lounging on the sofa watching a corny sci-fi movie when her cell phone rang. "Hi, Mom," she answered.

"Hi, honey. I was calling to see if you would like to catch a movie with me Friday night? We haven't hung out in a while. I thought it would be fun."

"I can't," Rebecca replied.

"Does that mean that you have another date with Mitch?" Barbara asked.

"No. I have a contractor coming by to give me an estimate on remodeling the house. Then we're going to dinner."

"Come on, Rebecca. You know I'm not going to let you get away with that kind of vague answer. So, spill it. Who? What? When? Where?"

Rebecca rolled her eyes toward the ceiling. She should have known she wouldn't be able to sneak this one past her mother. She sighed and said, "His name is Brian McAllister. He brought his dog into the clinic on Monday. His shirt said he was a contractor. So, I asked him if he would be willing to come over and give me an estimate. He suggested that he come on Friday night, and then we could have dinner afterward."

"Is he cute?" Barbara asked.

"Yes. He's got a really nice smile," Rebecca answered.

"Hah!" Barbara said excitedly. "This is wonderful. You haven't gone out in over a year. I'd about given up on grandchildren, and suddenly, there are three men in your life. My odds of becoming a grandma are increasing by the minute."

"Mom, get hold of yourself, it's only dinner," Rebecca replied dryly.

"You never know, Rebecca. Most marriages started with 'only dinner'."

"You're one of a kind, Mom."

Barbara chuckled. "So, how's June?"

"She's doing great. I stopped by to see her last night on my way home. They took her stitches out on Monday. It'll be a few more weeks before they remove the cast off her wrist."

"Is that man, Walter, still staying with her?" Barbara asked.

"Yes, he's pretty much moved in. I think they're getting serious. I haven't seen her this happy since her husband passed away."

"Good for her. I think I'll try to visit her this week."

"I'm sure she'd like that."

"Well, I guess I had better let you go. Call me and let me know how it goes with Brian."

"I will. Love you, Mom."

"I love you, too. I only want you to be happy."

~

Rebecca's doorbell rang at 6:25 Friday night. "Well, he's punctual. That's good," Rebecca said to Captain as she went to answer the door.

Brian stood on her porch wearing a light-blue dress shirt and khakis. He flashed her a friendly smile.

"Hi, Brian," she greeted. "Come on in." She stepped back to give him room to enter.

When he stepped inside, he gave a low whistle. "I can see why you're ready to remodel," he chuckled. "Let me guess, the bathtub is lime green."

Rebecca laughed. "Yep and the sink is salmon. There's also lovely flowered wallpaper."

Brian grinned. "Why don't you take me through and point out everything you'd like updated? Then we can discuss options, and I can give you some suggestions over dinner."

"Sounds good," Rebecca replied.

They spent the next 30 minutes walking through the house. After they finished, they walked out and climbed into his silver Ford F-150. The truck sat so high off the ground that Rebecca had to hop up into the seat.

"Is Italian okay?" Brian asked.

"Sure, I love Italian food."

"Great. There's a really nice place just a few miles from here. The owner is a friend of mine."

They sat in companionable silence on the short drive to the restaurant. When they arrived, Brian jumped out and hurried around to assist Rebecca out of the truck. He grinned up at her as she braced a hand on his shoulder and hopped down. He lightly pressed his hand to the small of her back and guided her into the restaurant.

The interior was dimly lit. The tables were covered with white linen tablecloths. A votive candle and a vase containing a single red rose rested in the middle of each table. Rebecca was glad she had settled on the black slacks and silk blouse instead of the jeans and polo shirt she'd almost worn.

They were seated at a table toward the back of the restaurant. A short time later, a gentleman wearing a black tuxedo approached them. He stopped at their table and rested a hand on Brian's shoulder. "Brian, it's good to see you. Who is the lovely lady?"

"Gregory Milano meet Rebecca Miller. This is Gregory's restaurant."

"It's nice to meet you, Rebecca. Please let me know if there is anything I can do for you."

"Thank you. It's nice to meet you, too. You have a beautiful place."

Gregory nodded his head in acceptance of the compliment. "We are very proud of it. I'll leave you to enjoy your dinner."

They watched as Gregory walked away. "I helped build this place a few years ago. Gregory and I hit it off, and we've been friends ever since."

Just then, the waitress arrived to take their order. After she left, Brian said, "Before we get to business, I want to get to know more about you. Have you always lived in Spring Valley?"

"Yes, except for my college years, I spent those in Oklahoma. What about you?"

"No, I grew up in Connecticut. I moved here after my divorce three years ago."

They spent the next several minutes making small talk and getting to know more about each other's backgrounds. Rebecca found out that he had three brothers who had all gotten advanced degrees. Brian was the only one who had decided to skip college and learn a trade. He'd started out working as a roofer and worked his way up to foreman for a contracting company in Connecticut. After his divorce, he decided to move to Spring Valley and start his own business. Rebecca admired his ambition. She understood how much hard work and determination it took to start a business from scratch.

The waitress arrived with their food. Rebecca had ordered the eggplant parmesan. "It smells great," she commented.

"Wait until you taste it," Brian replied.

Rebecca took her first bite and gave a little moan. "Wow, this is absolutely delicious."

Brian grinned. "I'm glad you like it."

After they finished the meal, Brian said, "Okay, so let's talk about what we can do with your house."

Rebecca nodded eagerly. Brian drew some brochures out of the briefcase he'd brought with him. He made several suggestions for ways to modernize and improve the kitchen, living room, and master bath. Rebecca was impressed with how well he seemed to understand what she was looking for. The ideas were both creative and practical. After she'd made several selections, Brian said, "I'll go over everything on Monday and draw up an estimate."

Rebecca glanced at her watch. Her eyes widened in surprise at how late it was. "I really should be getting home. I have a basketball game tomorrow morning."

Brian grinned. "You play basketball?"

Rebecca shook her head. "No, I coach a team of ten-year-old girls at the community center."

"Then I guess we'd better get you home," said Brian as he pushed back from the table.

When they arrived at Rebecca's house, Brian walked her to her door. He leaned in and pressed a gentle kiss to her lips. "I had a really nice time, Rebecca."

"Me, too," she replied truthfully.

"I'll call you Monday with that estimate."

Rebecca nodded and turned to unlock her door. Brian stepped off the porch and returned to his pickup. As Rebecca swung her front door open, she glanced back and waved good-bye. Brian returned the gesture as he climbed into his truck.

Later that night, as she lay awake in bed, Rebecca thought, *Well, Mom's right. This is an interesting turn of events. Brian doesn't make my pulse pound in my ears and my palms get all sweaty from just being in the same room with him like Derrick does, but I really did have a nice time tonight. Besides, Derrick hasn't given any indication that he's interested in me. I'd be smart if I just forgot all about Derrick Peterson.*

~

Rebecca watched as her team went through their warm-ups. *Looking good,* she thought proudly. Then she turned and surveyed their competition. *This is going to be tough. They look good, too.* The other coach saw her watching and waved. Rebecca smiled and returned the wave.

A moment later, she saw Derrick and Mitch exit the hallway that led to the showers. *They must have finished their game and went to shower before I got here,* Rebecca thought. She'd looked for them when she had first arrived and had been disappointed not to see them. They made their way across the court toward her. Rebecca admired Derrick's athletic grace as he jogged across the gym. She felt her heart rate quicken. *Why do I let him affect me so much?* she thought, frustrated by her body's automatic response.

"Hi, girls," Mitch called out to the team. "Good luck, today."

"Thanks," they replied in unison.

They stopped beside Rebecca. Derrick gave her a hard stare and then said, "How did your date go last night?"

"Date, what date?" Marilyn asked from her spot on the bleachers behind them.

Mitch's eyes widened in surprise. He glanced from Derrick to Rebecca and back again. Derrick's stance was combative. He stood with his feet spread wide and his arms crossed over his chest. Mitch smiled. *A little competition, huh? This is getting interesting.*

Just then, the referee blew his whistle indicating it was time to start the game. *Saved by the whistle,* Rebecca thought with relief. "Game time," she said, giving Derrick and Mitch a smug smile. She turned her back on them as her players trotted over to her.

Derrick growled in frustration and moved to sit beside Marilyn on the bleachers. "Rebecca had a date last night?" she asked Derrick.

He gave a curt nod.

"But I thought you..." her voice trailed off as Derrick's eyes narrowed on her face. "Um, who was it with?" she asked instead of finishing what she had been about to say, which was that she thought Derrick was the one who had a thing for Rebecca.

"Some guy who came into her clinic on Monday. Apparently, he's a contractor and is going to fix up her house."

The game was underway. Rebecca's team had the ball. Emma drove to the basket and made a lay-up to give them the lead. "Way to go, Emma!" Marilyn yelled at her daughter. Then she turned back to Derrick. "We'll get Rebecca to spill the beans after the game."

A few minutes later, Derrick's cell phone rang. He cursed under his breath when he saw that it was the hospital.

"Dr. Peterson," he answered curtly. He listened to the person on the other end. Finally, he said, "All right. I'm on my way." He turned to Mitch and said, "Apartment fire. Apparently, there are several victims."

Mitch nodded in understanding. "Call me later. I'm free tonight, if you'd like to grab a beer."

"Sounds good," replied Derrick.

After he left, Marilyn asked, "So, what's with that guy? He obviously likes Rebecca. He looked madder than a red hornet at the idea of Rebecca going out with someone else."

Mitch laughed. "In his experience, women are shallow and not worth investing in emotionally. His mother had several affairs before she finally ran off with a truck driver when Derrick was 11. After that, he built a wall around his heart. He doesn't know how to take a woman like Rebecca. She's everything his mother wasn't. She's smart, hardworking, dedicated, and compassionate. Every time he's around her the wall crumbles a little, and it scares the hell out of him."

"Well, he'd be lucky to have Rebecca. She's one of the best people I know."

"I agree. I think her date last night might be the wake-up call he needs."

They grew silent as they watched the rest of the game. It was back and forth. Both teams played hard. In the end, Rebecca's team lost by two.

After the game, Mitch moved off the bleachers to join the team. "That was a great game, girls. You were playing a good team. You almost pulled it out."

"Thanks, Mitch. It was really nice of you to come watch us," Kristin replied. The other girls nodded in agreement.

"It was my pleasure," Mitch replied. "I'm sorry I missed last week."

As the girls moved to join their parents, Mitch said, "All right, Rebecca, Marilyn and I are taking you to lunch, so you can tell us about this date you had last night."

Rebecca scowled in annoyance and said, "My love life isn't any of your business, Mitch."

He gave her an offended look. "Sure it is. You're like a sister to me. I've got to protect you from men with bad intentions."

"Come on, Rebecca, you know you're going to tell me everything. Mitch might as well get to hear it, too," said Marilyn.

Rebecca threw up her hands in surrender. "All right. There really isn't that much to tell."

Mitch grinned and looped an arm around her shoulders. "Great, that's settled. Where would you like to go?"

"It doesn't matter. I'm not going to the hospital today. So, I have plenty of time."

Mitch glanced at Emma. "What about you? Do you have any suggestions?"

"How about Chinese?" she suggested.

"Is that okay with you, Marilyn?" Mitch asked.

She nodded. He looked at Rebecca questioningly. "Fine with me, too," she said.

A few minutes later, they arrived at the Hidden Dragon. As soon as they had filled their plates from the buffet and settled into their seats, Marilyn said, "Okay, spill it."

Rebecca shrugged nonchalantly. "His name is Brian McAllister. He's a general contractor. He came over last night to give me an estimate on fixing up my house. Then we went to dinner. That's all there is to it."

"What does he look like?" Emma asked eagerly.

Rebecca shrugged. "I don't know. He's average height. Has brown hair. He's got really cute dimples."

"Dimples are good," Emma replied, grinning widely.

"Yes, they are," Rebecca agreed.

"Did you have a good time? Are you going to see him again?" Marilyn asked.

"Yes and I don't know. He's going to call me on Monday with an estimate for work on the house. We didn't make any plans for another date."

Mitch had remained thoughtfully silent while Rebecca answered the questions. *Looks like Derrick better throw his hat in the ring soon, or he might be out of the game.*

~

"How did things go at the hospital?" Mitch asked Derrick later that night as they sat at a table in Jack's Place, their favorite bar.

"One of the victims was an eight-year-old kid. He suffered severe burns over half his body. He's in ICU. I'm not sure if he'll make it. If he does, he's going to need several skin grafts."

Mitch shook his head. "That's too bad."

"There were five people in his family. They all had injuries, but his were the worst."

"How did the fire start?"

"The mother fell asleep while smoking a cigarette," Derrick said in disgust. "The woman's got four kids in the house, and she does something that stupid."

They sat in silence for a few minutes. Finally, Mitch said, "So, Rebecca's dating someone, huh?"

Derrick stiffened. After a long pause, he asked, "Did she say they were going out again?"

"Well, he's supposed to call her on Monday. From what Rebecca said, it sounded like last night's date went pretty well." Mitch paused, trying to judge Derrick's reaction. He grinned in satisfaction when Derrick's eyes narrowed and the muscles in his jaw tightened. "She seems to really like the guy," he added for good measure.

Derrick grunted and glowered down at his beer. "I think the guy's a weasel," he finally muttered.

Mitch's grinned widened. "What makes you think that?"

"He's just too smooth. I bet he asks all the single women he bids jobs for out on a date. I think he's just trying to get Rebecca to agree to a higher price for the renovation job."

"Rebecca's an attractive, smart, and capable woman. Maybe he just likes her."

"Maybe," Derrick grumbled. "But I don't trust him."

"You know what I think?" Mitch asked. "I think you're jealous."

Derrick glared at Mitch. If he didn't know his friend as well as he did, Mitch would have been intimidated by that look. Instead, he just grinned back at him. Finally, Derrick dropped his gaze to stare into his beer. Then he picked it up, drank it down in one long swallow, and called for another one.

Yep, he's got it bad, Mitch smirked. *It's about time he met a woman who could break down his defenses.*

CHAPTER 13

Derrick wasn't drunk when he arrived home later that night, but he was close. He felt extremely aggravated by the fact that he still felt lousy. *It's been too long since I took a woman to bed,* he thought. He decided that if alcohol wasn't enough to get the little veterinarian out of his head, then sex with a beautiful woman was what he needed. He picked up the phone book and thumbed through until he came to the name he was looking for, Ginger Rollins. He picked up his cell phone and punched in her number.

"Hello," she answered in a sleepy voice.

Derrick glanced at his watch. It was after 1:00 in the morning. He felt a little embarrassed that he hadn't checked the time before he'd called.

"Hi. It's Derrick Peterson. I'm sorry to call so late. I didn't realize the time."

"Oh, Derrick, you're welcome to call me anytime," Ginger said in a silky-smooth voice.

A warning bell went off in his head telling him that this was a bad idea. He stubbornly pushed the feeling aside and said, "Um, well, I called to see if you'd like to have dinner with me Monday night."

She sighed into the phone. "I'd love to. I get off work at 5:30."

"Okay, I'll pick you up at 6:30," replied Derrick.

"I look forward to it," Ginger replied breathlessly.

~

Late Monday afternoon, Rebecca walked out of one of the exam rooms to find Brian sitting in the waiting room. He flashed her one of his dimpled smiles. She returned his smile and then turned her head to look at the elderly man who had followed her out of the room. He was carrying a tiny, apricot Poodle in his arms.

"Please bring Melvin back to see me in about 10 days, so that I can remove his stitches," she instructed.

The man nodded and moved to the receptionist's counter to pay his bill. As soon as he stepped away from Rebecca, Brian stood and walked toward her.

"This is a nice surprise. I thought you were just going to call with the estimate," Rebecca greeted.

"I have the estimate in the car. I thought I might be able to convince you to let me take you to dinner to discuss it," Brian responded with a grin.

Rebecca felt a little flustered at being caught off guard. She didn't have a good excuse to say no, and she wasn't sure she wanted one. She enjoyed their date on Friday, so why not go out with him again?

"That was my last patient, but I do have several things I need to do to shut down for the night. I could be ready to go in about half an hour, if you want to wait."

Brian grinned. "I'd be happy to wait for you. Is there anything I can do to help?"

"No, I just need to give a few meds and then finalize the day's paperwork. You can make yourself comfortable."

Rebecca hurried toward the ICU to check on her overnight patients and give them their afternoon meds.

"You going out with that guy again?" Jimmy asked, sounding less than happy about the idea.

Rebecca looked at him curiously. "Yes. Why should that bother you?"

Jimmy shrugged. "I don't know. There's just something I don't trust about that guy. He's too smooth. I like Dr. Peterson better."

"Well, Dr. Peterson isn't the one who asked me to dinner," Rebecca replied.

"I'm sorry, Doc, forget I said anything. Have a good time. I'll see you tomorrow."

Rebecca thought about Jimmy's remark after he left. Brian had been a perfect gentleman on their last date. She wondered what it was about him that bothered Jimmy. She pushed the thought from her mind as she went back up front to help Kara close out the register.

Fifteen minutes later, she was ready to go. "Let's take my truck. I'll bring you back to get your car after we finish with dinner," Brian suggested.

"Sounds good," replied Rebecca.

They chose a steak house a few blocks from the clinic. "How did the rest of your weekend go?" Brian asked after they were seated.

"It went well. My team lost Saturday. That was kind of a bummer, but otherwise, it was a good weekend."

They continued to make small talk until their food arrived. After they finished eating, Brian pulled out the estimate for the renovations.

"I've broken it up by section, so you can see how much the floors and each room would cost individually. Then I have the total. You can choose to do any or all of it."

Rebecca looked over the estimate. She knew from her experience building the vet clinic a few years ago that Brian's pricing was reasonable.

"This looks doable," Rebecca said after she finished looking over the proposal. "How soon could you start?"

"I've got several crews. I could have the guys out to start the master bath next week."

Rebecca's eyes widened with surprise. "Wow, I didn't expect you to be able to make it so soon. That sounds great."

Brian grinned. "Good. Would you be able to let them in, say around 8:00 Monday morning?"

"Sure, that will give me time to get the surgery patients checked in. Then I can run home to let your crew in and start the surgeries after I get back."

They spent the next hour in pleasant conversation. They covered everything from their favorite movies to their worst dates. Rebecca laughed out loud when Brian recounted the time he'd picked up a woman at a bar only to discover later that she was actually a man.

"That did not happen," Rebecca said laughingly, shaking her head in disbelief.

"I swear it's true," Brian said earnestly.

A moment later, Derrick walked into the restaurant. Ginger, the bombshell, was hanging on his arm. She wore a skin-tight red dress that stopped mid-thigh, emphasizing her long, well-shaped legs. Derrick wore a dark tailored suit that fit his tall, muscular body perfectly. They made a beautiful couple. Rebecca felt a wave of jealousy wash through her. *Like he would ever be interested in me, when he can have someone who looks like that,* she thought with self-derision.

Brian followed her gaze. He gave a low whistle. "Wow. They look like they belong on the big screen. Do you know them?"

"That's Dr. Peterson. You met him in the clinic a few days ago," Rebecca replied in a slightly strained voice.

"Oh, yeah, I remember him. His girlfriend is a knockout."

~

Ginger felt Derrick's muscles tense beneath her hands. Her eyes flew to his face. He clenched his jaw tightly. His narrow-eyed gaze was focused on a table behind her. She turned to see what had brought about this sudden change in mood. A moment ago, he had been relaxed and smiling, now he looked like he wanted to break something. Then she saw Rebecca Miller sitting with a nice-looking man at a table across the restaurant. *Her again,* Ginger thought angrily.

Derrick met Rebecca's eyes and gave a slight nod. Rebecca dropped her gaze to stare at the table. *So, she's really dating that guy,* he thought in disgust. *I'd bet my house he's up to something. It's too bad she can't see it.*

The waitress arrived and led Derrick and Ginger to their table. He intentionally sat with his back to Rebecca's table. He'd come out on this date to clear her from his mind. He'd be damned if he was going to let her ruin it. *Get a grip, Peterson,* he thought, giving himself a mental shake.

"Derrick," Ginger's voice interrupted his thoughts.

"Huh?" he asked distractedly.

"The waitress just asked you what you'd like to drink," Ginger replied.

Derrick glanced up in surprise. He turned his head slightly to see a petite, blonde waitress looking at him expectantly. "I'll have an iced tea," he said, smiling apologetically at the waitress. He'd regretted the hangover he'd had after his night out with Mitch. He'd decided to stay away from alcohol for a while.

Ginger cocked an eyebrow in surprise at his order. "The same for me, please," she said.

After the waitress left, Ginger reached for Derrick's hand. "I'm really glad you called," she said silkily.

Derrick focused on her face. "Yeah, me, too," he replied. He was determined to drive thoughts of Rebecca Miller out of his mind.

~

Rebecca's eyes tracked Derrick as he followed the waitress across the restaurant to his table. She found herself admiring the way his suit jacket emphasized his broad shoulders. She scowled and shook her head in agitation. She'd been having such a good time. Why did he have to show up and why did he have to be with Ginger?

"Ready to go?" Brian asked, interrupting her thoughts.

Rebecca jerked in surprise. She'd forgotten he was there. She blushed and said, "Um, yeah, sure."

Brian placed a hand at the small of her back as they exited the restaurant. After they were settled in his truck, he asked, "So, what is it with you and Dr. Peterson? Is he an ex-boyfriend?"

"No, we're just friends. Not even friends, more like acquaintances."

"Hmm," Brian said. "It sure looked like there was something going on between you."

Rebecca didn't respond. What was there to say? She couldn't tell Brian that she had a major thing for Dr. Peterson, but other than the day he'd helped out at the vet clinic, all their interactions had been filled with a weird tension. She didn't understand what was going on between them. How could she explain it to someone else?

As they pulled into the Animal Friends parking lot, Brian asked, "So, how about a do-over? Are you free Friday?"

"Sure, I'd like that," responded Rebecca. She felt bad at the way dinner had ended. She shouldn't have let the sight of Derrick and Ginger affect her so strongly.

Brian grinned. "Great. I'll pick you up at 6:30." He leaned across the truck and placed a light kiss on her cheek.

Rebecca nodded and reached for the door handle. "See ya then," she said as she hopped out of the truck.

~

Derrick found his mind wandering through most of his dinner with Ginger. She talked incessantly about everything from her favorite TV reality shows to the latest fashions. Derrick found her conversation mind-numbingly boring. He strongly resisted the urge to continually glance at his watch. When the waitress arrived to ask if they wanted dessert, he answered a curt, "No. Just bring the check."

Ginger's eyes widened at his brusque tone. Then they took on a warm glow. She interpreted his eagerness to leave as eagerness to get to the point in the evening where he took her to bed. She smiled seductively. "In a hurry, are we?" she asked in a low, silky tone.

Derrick didn't answer. He'd invited Ginger out on this date with every intention of taking her to bed. However, as he gazed across the table at her, he felt mildly repulsed by her brazenness.

As soon as the waitress returned with their receipt, Derrick stood and reached for Ginger's arm. She tried to slide closer to him, but he firmly held her away as they moved out of the restaurant. When they were settled in his car, she slid her hand over his thigh and lightly brushed his crotch.

He pushed her hand away and flashed her an irritated look. She flounced back against her seat and crossed her arms over her chest.

"I don't get you," she said angrily. "It's that little bitch, isn't it? As soon as you spotted her, you changed."

"Watch your mouth, Ginger," Derrick warned.

"You have the hots for her, don't you? I can't imagine what you think she's got that I don't."

"Class for one," Derrick grumbled as he threw his car into reverse. Then he instantly felt bad. This wasn't Ginger's fault, and she was right; it was the sight of Rebecca that had changed the way Derrick felt. He slammed his hand into the steering wheel and cursed under his breath. *That damned woman is driving me nuts,* he thought angrily. *I just need to stay as far away from her as possible, then things can get back to normal.*

Ginger pouted silently on the drive back to her house. As soon as Derrick pulled his car to a stop in her driveway, she threw open the door and jumped out. She leaned back down and said, "Don't call me again." Then she slammed the door closed and marched angrily away.

~

The next few weeks passed quickly for Rebecca. She went out on a few more dates with Brian. He had remained a perfect gentleman, but she could sense that he was ready to take their relationship to a more physical level. Rebecca was grateful that he hadn't pushed things, but she knew that she couldn't hold off taking that step for too much longer. She wasn't sure why she was so reluctant.

The work on her house was progressing well. The master bath was completed last week. She loved it. She'd soaked in her Jacuzzi tub almost every night since they put it in. She couldn't believe how much it helped to relieve tension after a long day at the clinic.

She pulled into the Animal Friends parking lot after returning from letting the crew that would be working on the kitchen into her house. She was excited to see if it turned out as well as her bathroom. As she stepped out of the car, she spotted Kara and her boyfriend, Dalton, having a heated discussion in his car. This was Kara's last week. June was due to return on Monday. Although, she'd grown accustomed to Kara, Rebecca had to admit that she was looking forward to getting June back. She felt bad about Kara losing her job, but she'd been told from the beginning that it was only temporary.

Just then, Dalton lifted his arm and slapped Kara hard across her face, splitting her upper lip. Rebecca saw red. She didn't think. She just reacted. She rushed up to Dalton's car and jerked open his door. He swung his head around in surprise. She pulled her fist back and slammed it into his face with all of her strength. Pain shot through her hand as it made contact with his face. She winced and clutched her hand against her chest.

"You bitch!" he roared, jumping out of his car. He pressed a hand against his injured left eye. "You're going to pay for that."

Rebecca took a step backwards. Dalton advanced toward her.

"Leave her alone, Dalton," Kara pleaded. She stood on the other side of the car.

"Shut up," Dalton commanded. "You know I've got to teach her a lesson about butting into other peoples' business."

He reached out and painfully grasped Rebecca's wrist.

"Let her go," an angry voice spoke from directly behind Rebecca.

Rebecca saw Dalton's eyes widen and the color leave his face as he glanced past her shoulder toward whoever had spoken. He shoved back on her arm and released her wrist. Rebecca stumbled backwards. She slammed up against a warm, solid body. A strong arm encircled her waist, steadying her. She craned her neck to see her rescuer. Derrick looked down at her. Rebecca felt her heart jump. She hadn't seen him since that night at the restaurant two weeks ago.

His jaw was clenched so tightly that a muscle twitched on the left side. The gold flakes in his eyes glittered with anger. Now she knew why Dalton had looked so scared, Derrick looked deadly.

"Did he hurt you?" he asked, running his eyes quickly over her face.

She shook her head. "No."

Just then, Dalton made a move toward his car. "Don't move," Derrick commanded. Dalton drew up short. He glared angrily at Rebecca. Derrick reached into his pocket and pulled out his cell phone. He flipped it open and pressed three. He had Mitch on speed-dial.

"What's up?" Mitch asked when he answered.

"I need you to come down to Animal Friends, pronto. Some punk-ass kid just assaulted Rebecca," Derrick bit out.

"What?!" Mitch exclaimed.

"You heard me, now get your butt down here," Derrick answered.

"I'm on my way. Is Rebecca okay?"

"Yes."

"I'll be there in ten minutes."

Derrick ended the call. "Get inside the clinic," he commanded Dalton.

"Was that the cops? I ain't waitin' around for no cops to show up," Dalton responded.

Derrick released Rebecca and stepped toward Dalton. "Get inside the clinic, now," he said threateningly.

Dalton shrugged and sauntered inside the clinic. "She's the one that punched me anyways. She's the one they should arrest. I ain't done nothin'."

"You hit Kara," Rebecca sputtered, seething in anger. "Or have you forgotten that little fact?"

Derrick turned toward her. "Why don't you take Kara inside and see about that cut on her lip? Mitch said he'd be here in ten minutes."

Rebecca nodded and moved to where Kara still stood by Dalton's car.

"Are you all right, Kara?" she asked with concern.

"You shouldn't have interfered, Doc," Kara said in reply. "Dalton's got a mean streak."

"Has he hit you before?" Rebecca asked.

Kara hunched her shoulders defensively and nodded.

Rebecca sighed. "Kara, you don't have to put up with anyone hitting you."

"He treats me good most of the time," Kara answered weakly.

Rebecca felt anger burn in her belly. Anger at Dalton for thinking he could go around hitting women and anger at Kara for making such poor choices in her life. She led Kara inside and back to the treatment area. Jimmy came out of the ICU, just as they arrived.

"What happened to your lip, Kara?" he asked with concern.

"Dalton hit her," Rebecca answered angrily.

"What? I thought you told me you were through with that guy."

Kara shrugged helplessly. "I know, but he said he was sorry and that he was going to change."

"What happened to your hand, Doc?" Jimmy asked.

Rebecca glanced down and saw that her knuckles were puffy and bruised. "I must have popped a blood vessel when I punched him," she said, making a fist. She winced slightly at the movement.

"You punched him?" Jimmy asked incredulously.

Rebecca quickly explained what had happened while she gently wiped the blood away from Kara's split lip. As soon as she finished, Jimmy turned on his heel and strode angrily into the waiting room. Dalton slouched in one of the chairs with his arm slung nonchalantly across the back of the one next to it.

"You come near my sister again, and I'll beat the shit out of you," Jimmy growled, pointing an angry finger at him.

Dalton smirked and said, "I'd like to see you try, you little bitch."

"Hold it, Jimmy," Derrick said, when he stepped threateningly toward Dalton. "The cops are on their way. They'll take care of him."

Jimmy stopped. He glowered down at Dalton. Then he grinned. "Doc sure gave you one hell of a shiner. How you gonna explain that to your friends?"

Just then, the front door opened and Mitch stepped inside. Right behind him was a middle-aged man leading a Jack Russell Terrier. Rebecca hurried into the waiting room when she'd heard the bell jingle.

"Jimmy, why don't you go ahead and take Mr. Robinson and Jack into exam room one," Rebecca suggested. "I'll be there in just a minute."

Turning toward Mitch, she said, "Thank you for coming."

"Is this the guy who hit you?" he asked, eyeing the tattooed young man slouching in the chair.

"She hit me, man. See?" Dalton said, pointing to his swollen eye.

"Only after he hit Kara," replied Rebecca.

"Who's Kara?" Mitch asked.

"She's Jimmy's sister. She's been filling in for June as my receptionist. She's in the back. She refused to come out to talk with you. She says she doesn't want to press charges against Dalton."

"Then I can go now, can't I?" Dalton smirked.

"Not so fast," Mitch replied. "What about you, Rebecca? Did he strike you?"

"No, he just grabbed my wrist after I punched him. Then Derrick showed up."

"Well, then, I guess you're free to go, Dalton." Mitch said.

"What?!" Derrick exploded. "That's it? He just gets to walk out of here?"

"As much as I'd like to take him down to the station, if Kara doesn't want to press charges, then there's really nothing else I can do," replied Mitch.

Derrick growled in frustration as Dalton leisurely stood, stretched, and sauntered out of the clinic. As the door banged shut behind him, Derrick said, "I wish I'd smashed my fist into his face."

"I did," replied Rebecca grinning. "And it felt pretty damn good."

Mitch threw his head back and laughed. "That's my girl, tough as nails."

"What you did was stupid," Derrick bit out angrily. "What would you have done if I hadn't shown up?"

Rebecca shrugged. "I don't know. I didn't really think about that. When I saw him hit Kara, I kind of lost my head." She grinned and added, "But I'm glad you did show up. Why are you here, anyway? I haven't seen you for weeks."

Derrick suddenly remembered that he'd left Trouble in the car. "Trouble is supposed to be spayed today. I left her in the car. Excuse me." He hurried out the door to retrieve the dog.

"You really are lucky that Derrick showed up. That guy could have seriously hurt you," Mitch said.

"I know," Rebecca replied. "I just got so mad when I saw him hit Kara."

Derrick returned just as Mitch asked, "So, you still seeing that contractor?"

"Yes," replied Rebecca, meeting Derrick's eyes as he stepped through the door. Derrick's gaze narrowed in annoyance.

"I don't know what you see in him," Derrick grumbled.

"He's sweet and we enjoy each other's company," Rebecca replied. "Not that it's any of your business. Now, if you'll excuse me, I need to check Jack in for his surgery. Then I'll take a look at Trouble."

After she left, Mitch said, "So, you're still not ready to admit that you like her, huh?"

"It wouldn't matter if I did. Apparently, she's got a boyfriend."

"I don't think she's too serious about him, yet, but you'd better make your move soon."

Just then, Rebecca and Mr. Robinson stepped out of the exam room. "You can pick Jack up any time after 1:00." The man nodded in understanding and left the clinic.

"Okay, Derrick, bring Trouble in."

"I'll see you Saturday, Rebecca," Mitch said. "I don't want to miss the last game of the season. I'm sorry I missed the last two. This string of robberies is taking up all of my time. Every time I think we're getting close to nailing the guys, they slip away."

Rebecca shook her head. "I hope you catch them soon. The girls will be happy to see you at the game. You've become like a mascot for them."

Derrick led Trouble into the room. Rebecca crouched down next to her. "She's grown. She looks good."

As Rebecca reached out to rub Trouble on the head, Derrick saw her swollen knuckles. He cursed. She jerked her head up in surprise. "What?" she asked.

"Your hand," Derrick bit out angrily.

Rebecca shrugged. "It looks worse than it feels." She finished examining Trouble and stood up. "Okay, just like I told Mr. Robinson, you can pick her up any time after 1:00."

Derrick nodded. He opened his mouth to say more, then clamped it closed again. He wasn't sure what he wanted to say. When he'd seen that guy grab her arm, he'd wanted to kill him. He'd never experienced that kind of rage before. He still hadn't processed what it meant. He was starting to think that maybe Mitch was right, perhaps he did have feelings for Rebecca. He needed time to sort it out in his own mind before he said anything to Rebecca, especially since she was seeing someone else. Maybe he was too late. "I'll see you at 1:00," he said. Then he turned and left the clinic.

CHAPTER 14

Saturday morning, Mitch and Derrick met to play their weekly game of one-on-one.

"What's with you?" Mitch asked after easily driving past Derrick for a lay-up to end the game. He was pretty sure he already knew the answer, Rebecca Miller.

Derrick grabbed the ball as it came through the net and asked, "What do you think of that guy Rebecca's dating?"

Mitch shrugged and started walking toward the bleachers to grab his water bottle. Derrick walked with him. "I don't know anything about him, but I'm sure that if Rebecca likes him, then he must be a pretty good guy."

"There's something about him that I don't trust," Derrick commented.

"Are you sure you're not letting your own feelings for her cloud your judgment?" Mitch asked.

Derrick paused before answering. Then he sighed and answered simply, "No."

Mitch smiled. "So, you're finally ready to admit you like her, huh?"

Derrick frowned. "Yeah, I like her. I just don't know what to do about it," he grudgingly admitted.

"You could try telling her how you feel," Mitch suggested.

Derrick shook his head. "No, I can't do that while she's seeing someone else. It wouldn't be right. I'm not going to step in on another man's territory."

Mitch knew there was no use arguing with him. Derrick lived by a very strict ethical code. It was one of the things Mitch admired most about him. Unless Derrick had proof that the guy was going to hurt Rebecca, he wouldn't try to steal her from him.

Mitch reached out and clasped Derrick on the shoulder. "I guess you're just going to have to wait and see if your instincts about the man are right. In the meantime, it won't hurt to be her friend. How about staying to watch her game with me?"

Derrick nodded in agreement. They grabbed their gear and headed to the locker room.

A few minutes later, they returned to the gym. Derrick spotted Rebecca on the far side. She was shooting three-pointers. He stopped to watch her for a moment, admiring the fluidity of her movements.

"We've been spotted," Mitch said, lifting his arm to wave at Rebecca's friend Marilyn.

Derrick saw Marilyn say something to Rebecca. She stopped and turned to look their way. He lifted his arm in salute and started jogging across the floor toward her.

~

Rebecca felt her heartbeat quicken just like it did every time she laid eyes on Derrick Peterson. *Man, he's gorgeous,* she thought. Within a few moments, Mitch and Derrick reached her.

"Hi, girls," Mitch greeted the team who was warming up behind her. "Good luck today. Who are you playing?"

"It's a re-match with the Shockers," Emma answered.

"Isn't that the only game you've lost this season?" Mitch asked.

"Yep," Emma replied. "They're a really tough team."

"We'll be sure to do our part cheering you on from the bench," Mitch said, giving the girls his most dazzling smile.

They blushed and giggled, then returned to their warm-ups.

"I'm glad you're here," Rebecca said. "It means a lot to me and the girls."

Derrick met her eyes and smiled warmly. "Every team needs a good cheering section," he said.

Rebecca's eyes widened a little in surprise. Derrick usually seemed so tense and aloof. However, today, he appeared relaxed and friendly. She felt flustered by this new Derrick.

"Um, yeah, the louder the better," she finally agreed.

"How's your hand?" he asked.

Rebecca glanced down at her knuckles. "Fine. The swelling's gone, just a little bruised now."

"I'm glad. Well, we'd better join Marilyn. Good luck," he said, flashing her another smile before moving away to sit with Marilyn. She turned a questioning gaze on Mitch. He just grinned and shrugged, then followed Derrick to the bleachers.

A few minutes later, the game got underway. "So, where's Rebecca's new boyfriend?" Mitch asked Marilyn.

"I don't know. He's never come to one of her games," she replied.

"Don't you think that's a little odd?" asked Derrick.

"Now that you mention it, it does seem a little strange," Marilyn agreed.

"Have you ever met the guy?" Mitch asked.

"No. He and Rebecca have been out several times, but I've never met him."

"Too bad. I was hoping you could tell me what you think of him," replied Derrick.

"Well, Rebecca seems to think he's really nice. They apparently have a good time together. I think it's starting to get pretty serious."

Derrick frowned and turned his gaze to watch Rebecca. She continually yelled out instructions to her team. She was completely focused on the game. Derrick felt an odd sense of pride watching her work the sidelines. *Is there anything the woman can't do?* he wondered.

The Shockers gave Rebecca's team another tough game. Marilyn's daughter, Emma, scored a lay-up in the last second to pull out the victory.

"Way to go, Emma!" Marilyn yelled. Mitch and Derrick both added whistles and thunderous applause. Emma beamed as the other members of her team rushed to give her a group hug.

After extricating herself from the hug, Rebecca turned toward them. A radiant smile lit her face. Derrick felt his guts tighten. *I can't believe it took me so long to see how beautiful she is,* he thought.

He was brought out of his momentary trance when Mitch's booming voice yelled, "Great game!", only inches from his ear.

"Thanks!" Rebecca called as she moved toward the bleachers to join them. "We're all going out for a post-season pizza party. You two are welcome to join us."

"I'd love to, but I need to get back to work on that robbery investigation. I'm supposed to meet someone this afternoon who may have some information about the case," Mitch said.

"Too bad. What about you?" she asked Derrick.

He shook his head. "Sorry, a restaurant full of overly exuberant girls is way out of my comfort zone."

Rebecca smiled. "Under normal circumstances, I agree completely." After a brief pause, she added, "I guess I'll be seeing you around then."

Derrick suddenly realized that he didn't have any reason to see her again now that Trouble was up to date on her shots and the basketball season was over. His only chance of seeing her would be accidental meetings. He felt a heaviness move into his heart.

"Yeah, good luck to you," Derrick answered.

"Hey," Mitch put in, "You sound like this is good-bye. I don't know about Derrick, but you can't get rid of me that easily."

Rebecca chuckled, "I didn't mean to sound like I wanted to get rid of you. It's just that now that the season's over, I don't know when we'll be seeing each other again."

"Well, we'll find the time. You're welcome to join us for our Saturday morning ball game anytime," Mitch replied.

"I'd like that," Rebecca said.

Derrick and Mitch congratulated the girls on a great win. After they were gone, Marilyn commented, "Those are two incredible guys."

"Yes, they are," Rebecca agreed, feeling a little pang in her heart at the thought that she might not see them again.

Later, as they sat at a booth with a red and white checkered vinyl tablecloth enjoying victory pizza, Marilyn asked, "So, why didn't Brian come to the game today?"

"He usually works on Saturday mornings. He's got to organize the work of all his crews, so he knows where to send them on Monday. Why?"

"Mitch and Derrick asked me, and we all thought it was strange that he didn't come to support you at your last game."

"Oh," Rebecca replied. She hadn't thought of it like that, but it was strange that two men who were only friends came to watch the game and the man she was dating didn't. "I'm sure he would have liked to be here," she said in Brian's defense.

"If you say so," Marilyn replied. "So, how serious is it getting between you two, anyway? Have you slept with him yet?"

Rebecca felt heat rush into her cheeks. "Marilyn," she admonished. "The girls might hear you or even worse the girls' parents." She glanced furtively toward the two long tables the girls and the group of parents surrounded.

"Are you kidding? I don't think they can even hear each other it's so loud in here. So, have you?"

Rebecca shook her head. "I've been seriously thinking about it, though. Brian has been really sweet. He hasn't pushed it, but I don't know how much longer he'll be understanding about it."

"What are you waiting for?" Marilyn asked.

Rebecca shrugged. "I don't know. I guess I was waiting to feel swept away by the moment."

"So, basically, you were waiting to see if he could make you feel like Derrick does every time you're near him," Marilyn said knowingly.

Rebecca started to protest, but stopped herself. There was no use. Marilyn knew her better than anyone. She was right. That is what she had been waiting for.

She sighed. "I'm sure you're right, but that isn't really fair to Brian, is it?"

Marilyn shook her head. "The thing you need to ask yourself is whether you're going to hold out for the fairytale ending or settle for pretty good."

~

Rebecca and Captain had just returned from their weekly visit to the hospital when her cell phone rang. "June, is everything okay? You're still planning on being back Monday, aren't you?"

"Everything's fine. I just had some news that couldn't wait until Monday," June replied.

"What?" Rebecca asked curiously.

"Walter asked me to marry him."

"Wow! That's fantastic. I'm assuming you said, 'yes'."

June chuckled. "I certainly did. He's been so wonderful these last weeks. I love him dearly. I didn't think it would be possible for me to find love again after losing Cal."

"Oh, June, I'm so happy for you. Have you set a date?"

"We'd like to have a June wedding. It just seems appropriate."

"So soon?" Rebecca asked in surprise. "It's already mid-May."

"Yeah, so we've got some major planning to do. Of course, I want you to be my maid of honor."

"I'd love that. Thank you," replied Rebecca.

"We don't want anything fancy. We're too old for that. We just want a few friends and family. Do you think Barbara and Marilyn would be willing to help with the planning?"

"Of course. My mom's great at that kind of thing. You'll make her year if you ask her to help."

June chuckled. "I guess I'll call her next. Are you busy tomorrow afternoon? Maybe we could all get together and come up with a game plan."

"That sounds great. I'll call Marilyn. What time do you want us?"

"How about 2:00?"

"Okay, see you tomorrow at 2:00. Congratulations again, June. I'm really very happy for you."

"Thanks, Rebecca, see you tomorrow."

When Rebecca hung up the phone, she called Marilyn. After giving Marilyn the news, she asked, "Can you believe June's getting married? Isn't it funny how quickly our lives can change? And just think, if June hadn't gotten into that car accident, who knows how long it would have taken her and Walter to fall in love."

"Yeah, you never know what or who might be just around the corner," Marilyn agreed. "Sorry to cut this short, but I promised Emma that I'd take her to the movies tonight. We really need to get going."

"All right. Have fun. I'll see you tomorrow."

A few minutes later, Rebecca's phone rang again. She reached for it expecting it to be her mother. She was surprised to see that it was Brian. "Hi, Brian," she greeted.

"Hi. How did the game go?" he asked.

"We won, but it was close," Rebecca answered.

"I'm sorry I missed it. Look, about tonight, I had something come up, and I'm going to have to back out," he said regretfully.

"No problem. Is everything okay?" she asked with concern. This was the first time Brian had canceled one of their dates.

"Yes, a friend of mine called a few minutes ago to say they were flying into town for a last minute business meeting and wanted to meet me for drinks. I hope that's okay."

"Sure, I understand. By the way, I have some news," Rebecca commented.

"Oh, yeah, what?" Brian asked.

"June just called to tell me she and Walter are engaged. She asked me to be her maid of honor. The crazy part is that she wants to have a June wedding. That means we only have a few weeks to pull it off. I'm supposed to meet with her, my mom, and Marilyn tomorrow, so we can put together a game plan."

"Sounds like that will keep you busy for the next few weeks. I'm guessing I'll be taking a back seat for a while," he teased.

Rebecca chuckled. "Yeah, I guess you will be. Sorry, but weddings do kind of take priority."

He laughed. "I understand completely. Let me know if there's anything I can do. I'd be happy to build an arbor or gazebo for her if she decides to do an outdoor theme."

"That's really generous of you. I'll tell her. You may regret making that offer."

"I'd be happy to do it. Take care, Rebecca. I'll call you in a couple of days."

"Okay, have fun with your friend tonight."

~

"Hi," June greeted as she swung the door open for Rebecca.

"Hi, yourself," Rebecca greeted, stepping in and wrapping June in a hug. She pulled back and looked at June's face. "You're glowing with happiness," she commented.

"I feel wonderful," June replied. "It's surreal. I keep pinching myself to make sure I'm not dreaming."

Rebecca chuckled. "Marilyn said that helping you plan your wedding sounded like the most fun she's had in years. She should be here any minute."

"Your mom shrieked so loudly that my ear rang for a good hour afterwards," June said in an amused tone.

Just then, they heard the sound of a car pulling into the drive. Rebecca turned to see her mom's blue Honda Civic. "Looks like she's right on time," she commented.

Barbara sprang out of the car and hurried toward Rebecca and June, who still stood in the open doorway. She carried a large yellow bag slung over her shoulder. "Oh, Rebecca, isn't this going to be so much fun?" She patted the bag and said, "I brought a few magazines for us to look through."

"How many magazines do you have in there?" Rebecca asked. "That bag looks like it weighs a ton."

"Well, I've been collecting bridal magazines for the last few years, so I'd be prepared for the day you called me with news of your engagement. I'm glad they're finally going to come in handy, even if it isn't your wedding I'm planning."

Rebecca rolled her eyes. June smiled and said, "Come on in, Barbara. Rebecca's right, that bag looks like it's heavy."

"It is," Barbara replied.

They moved to sit at the dining room table. Barbara reached into the bag and pulled out about 20 bridal magazines. She spread them out on the table. "Now, the first thing we should think about is whether you want an indoor or outdoor wedding," she said.

"Oh, by the way," Rebecca interjected, "Brian said that he was willing to build an arbor or gazebo if you decided you wanted to do something outdoors."

"That was really sweet of him," June responded.

A moment later, the doorbell rang. "That must be Marilyn," said June as she hurried to answer the door.

"So, how are things between you and Brian?" Barbara asked as June moved out of the room.

"Good," responded Rebecca. "We've been seeing each other pretty regularly. Nothing too serious, but things are going well."

"I guess that means Dr. Peterson is completely out of the picture," Barbara commented.

"I wouldn't say that's entirely true," said Marilyn as she walked into the room. "He came to Rebecca's basketball game yesterday."

Barbara raised her eyebrows at this bit of news. "He did, did he?"

"We're not here to discuss me," said Rebecca, wanting to change the subject. "Let's get back to the wedding."

"Right," said Barbara, letting the subject drop for now. She'd have a chance to quiz Rebecca later. "So, indoor or outdoor, June?"

"We were thinking something outdoors. Walter has a beautifully landscaped back yard. Do you think Brian was serious about his offer to build something for us?" June asked.

"Yes," replied Rebecca. "I'm sure if you tell him what it is that you want, he could have one of his crews put it together for you."

They spent the rest of the afternoon looking through the magazines that Barbara had brought with her. They put together a timeline of events that needed to be done and divided up some of the planning responsibilities. Marilyn was friends with a woman who owned a bakery, so she volunteered to call her about setting up a meeting to discuss the cake. Barbara volunteered to coordinate the meeting with the florist. Rebecca and June decided to close down the clinic early on Wednesday, so that they could go dress shopping. Rebecca also told June that she would show Brian some of the ideas from the magazines that June liked and set up a time for them to meet at Walter's to see which ideas would fit with his yard.

"Brian's got a great eye for what will work best in a given space. My house is looking fantastic. The kitchen is almost done. I can't wait to have you all over, so that you can see the finished product," Rebecca commented.

June sat back and sighed happily. "Looks like we have a plan."

"We certainly do," Barbara agreed. "I think we just might pull this off."

June smiled widely. "I think you're right."

"Well, I don't know about you ladies, but I'm starving," Marilyn commented. "How about we go have dinner? The champagne's on me."

"In that case, what are we waiting for?" June asked enthusiastically. Rebecca and Barbara laughingly agreed.

CHAPTER 15

After spending Sunday afternoon planning June's wedding, Rebecca was in a particularly romantic mood. She decided that it was time to take her relationship with Brian to the next level. He was a great guy. He was funny and thoughtful, and she definitely had feelings for him. She decided that after she closed the vet clinic on Monday, she would pay him a surprise visit. She could use the excuse of bringing over the bridal magazines to show him some of June's ideas and then let things progress from there.

Monday morning, she was whistling a happy tune as she unlocked the clinic door. It was a beautiful spring day. Birds chirped at her from nearby trees. A few fluffy white clouds floated lazily in the bright blue sky. Rebecca smiled and drew in a deep breath. The brisk morning air was filled with the sweet fragrance of flowers in bloom.

She had not had any patients stay over the weekend. So, she set about getting ready for the morning's surgery patients. A few minutes later, the bell above the front door jingled. Rebecca moved into the waiting room to see who had arrived. The sight of June sitting behind the receptionist's desk brought tears to her eyes. It felt like forever since she'd last been there.

"Now, that's a sight for sore eyes," Rebecca said as she walked up to the counter.

June smile and asked quizzically, "What is?"

"You, sitting behind the counter. I've really missed you, June. I'm so glad to have you back."

"It's good to be back. I've missed this. Everyone who comes in here is like family."

A moment later, Jimmy strolled through the back door. "June!" he said enthusiastically. "It's great to see ya. How are you feeling?"

"I feel great. I've got several more weeks of physical therapy for the wrist and shoulder, but otherwise, I'm good as new."

Derrick had done an excellent job of stitching the laceration on June's face. The wound was still in the healing phase, so it was a fairly pronounced pink line running down her left cheek. Once it healed, the scar would be barely noticeable.

"June has some news," Rebecca said, her eyes twinkling with good-humor.

"What?" Jimmy asked curiously.

"Walter Stockton and I are getting married," June said, blushing slightly.

Jimmy's mouth stretched into a wide grin. "Wow, the old guy doesn't waste any time. Maybe he could give me some pointers," Jimmy teased.

The front door opened and a young, attractive blonde walked in leading a well-groomed black and tan Cocker Spaniel. Jimmy's eyes widened in appreciation as the woman approached the counter.

"Hello," she said. "My name is Amy Brennan. This is Cocoa. She's here to be spayed."

"Hi, Amy," Rebecca greeted. "I'm Dr. Miller. Let's take Cocoa into the first exam room, so that I can give her a quick exam."

Rebecca took Cocoa's paperwork from June's outstretched hand. Amy followed her into the room. Rebecca spent a few minutes giving Cocoa a pre-surgical exam. When she finished auscultating her heart and lungs, Rebecca said, "Cocoa looks very healthy. We'll be starting her surgery in about an hour. She'll be ready to go home any time after 1:00. All of her stitches will be internal, so you won't need to bring her back to have them removed. Do you have any questions about the procedure?"

"Would it be possible for me to stay and watch?" Amy asked. "I'm in my second year at Spring Valley Community College, and I'm trying to decide what to do after I finish up my general studies classes. I was thinking about applying to get into the veterinary technician program."

Rebecca smiled. "You are more than welcome to stay. I'm pretty accustomed to being observed. In fact, I've had a few of the students in Spring Valley's vet tech program spend some of their clinical time with me."

Amy's face lit up with a bright smile. "Thank you."

"Let me introduce you to Jimmy. He was the young man you saw when you first came in. He's my tech. He can show you how we set everything up. It will take me a while to get all the patients checked in. I'll put Cocoa at the front of the line, but you're welcome to watch all of them if you'd like."

Rebecca led Amy to the treatment area. Jimmy was busy setting up the anesthesia machine and making sure they had enough surgical packs available.

"Jimmy, this is Amy. She'd like to observe surgeries today. She's thinking about applying to Spring Valley's vet tech program."

Jimmy's mouth stretched into a wide smile. "Great!" he enthused. "Let's get Cocoa settled. Then I'll be happy to show you around."

Rebecca left the two alone as she went to get the next patient checked in.

Jimmy couldn't believe his good luck. He thought Amy was just about the prettiest girl he'd ever seen. She had an oval face that was dominated by two large round blue eyes. Her hair was the color of honey and hung straight down her back almost reaching her waist. She was several inches shorter than him. She was thin, but not skinny. He liked girls to have a few curves. He didn't understand guys that were attracted to girls who looked like skeletons.

"So, you attend Spring Valley Community College?" he asked as they walked back to put Cocoa in a cage.

"Yes. I'm in my second year," Amy replied timidly.

"How do you like it?"

"It's okay, I guess."

"Did you go to Spring Valley High School? I graduated two years ago. I don't remember you."

"No," Amy answered. "I went to Travis High School. We played you guys in football every year."

Jimmy spent the next few minutes explaining how the anesthesia machine worked and pointing out the supplies they would need for the surgeries that morning. He kept trying to work up the courage to ask Amy out, but he couldn't quite come up with the right words.

A few minutes later, Rebecca joined them. "Everyone's checked in. Are you ready to get started? We just have Cocoa, a dog neuter, and two cats to spay today."

"Sure, we're all set. I've got Cocoa's meds all drawn up."

"Okay, bring her out and let's get started," Rebecca instructed.

Jimmy carried Cocoa to the treatment table. Rebecca reached out and stroked her head. Amy stood off to the side watching anxiously.

"Don't worry, Cocoa," Rebecca soothed. "It's just a little poke of a needle. You'll hardly feel a thing." She said the words for Amy as much as for Cocoa.

Jimmy hugged Cocoa against his chest. He held her right arm at the elbow to give Rebecca access to the vein that runs down the top of the lower part of the dog's front leg. Rebecca gripped the forearm firmly and inserted the needle to begin injecting the anesthetic. Before she had even finished the injection, Cocoa's body went limp. Jimmy pried open her mouth and Rebecca inserted the endotracheal tube. Then she connected the end of the tube to the anesthesia machine that would deliver Isoflurane gas to keep Cocoa asleep during the surgery.

Jimmy rolled Cocoa onto her back and began shaving her abdomen.

"Have you ever watched anything like this before?" Rebecca asked Amy.

Amy shook her head. Her eyes were nervously watching Jimmy shave Cocoa's belly.

"There usually isn't much blood, but it can still be pretty overwhelming the first time you see it. If you start to feel faint, you'll need to leave the room. I won't be able to catch you."

Amy laughed nervously. "I think I'll be fine."

Rebecca smiled. "Most people do until it happens. You wouldn't be the first person to pass out on me."

"I'm sure you'll do great," Jimmy said encouragingly. He scooped Cocoa into his arms and turned to carry her into the surgery suite.

Amy gave him a weak smile and then followed him into the room.

A few moments later, Rebecca was ready to make the incision into Cocoa's abdomen. She glanced up at Amy, who stood on the opposite side of the stainless steel surgery table. Her pupils were dilated and she was taking quick, shallow breaths. Her hands were clasped so tightly together that her knuckles were turning white.

"Relax," Rebecca said in a soothing tone. Then she returned her gaze to Cocoa and began to make the incision. She heard Amy inhale sharply as the scalpel sliced through the skin. Rebecca's eyes flew to Amy's face.

"You okay?" she asked.

Amy nodded, but didn't answer. She'd grown very pale.

"Your skin's almost white," Jimmy commented, sounding concerned. "You might want to sit down."

"I'm fine," Amy said shakily.

Rebecca finished opening Cocoa's abdomen. She inserted the spay hook that was used to fish out the ovaries and uterine horns. She pulled up the hook and saw that she'd grabbed a loop of bowel instead. She used her index finger to push the piece of intestine back into the abdomen.

She heard Amy give a slight groan. She glanced up just in time to see Amy's eyes flutter shut and her legs collapse. Jimmy dove toward her, but was unable to reach her before she hit the floor. He rushed to her side. He knelt down and lightly brushed his fingers over her cheek. Her eyes fluttered open.

"What happened?" she asked weakly.

He gave her a crooked grin. "You fainted."

Color rushed into her cheeks. "Did I really?"

"Yep."

She pushed herself into the sitting position. "This is so embarrassing. I can't believe I passed out. I've never done that before."

"Jimmy, why don't you help her into one of the exam rooms and give her a drink of water," Rebecca suggested. "I can finish this up by myself."

Jimmy nodded and reached to assist Amy to her feet. He placed an arm around her waist to steady her as she swayed against him. *Man, she smells great,* he thought as she leaned into him for support. He walked beside her as they shuffled out of the surgery room. Amy carefully kept her eyes averted away from the table.

Jimmy helped her down into the chair in exam room one and then hurried away to get her a cup of water.

"Thanks," she said as he handed it to her.

"No problem. How are you feeling?"

"Other than mortified, I feel fine. I'm still a little shaky. I guess vet tech school is out of the question."

"Maybe it wouldn't have affected you so much if it hadn't been your dog," Jimmy suggested.

"You might be right, but I still think I should look into trying something else. I'll probably stick with my first thought, which was to be an elementary school teacher."

"I bet you'd be a great teacher."

Amy gave him a small smile. "You're very sweet."

"Do you think I'm sweet enough to go out with me Friday night?" Jimmy asked. He held his breath waiting for her answer.

"Sure," she replied. "I'd like that."

Jimmy exhaled the breath he'd been holding. "Great!" he said enthusiastically. "I get off around 5:30. Could I pick you up at 6:00? That would give us enough time to grab a bite to eat and then take in a movie."

"Sounds fun," Amy said.

Jimmy reached into the pocket of his jeans and pulled out his cell phone. "If you give me your number, I can put it in my phone. I'll call you in a couple of days to get your address."

His hands were shaking from excitement as he punched in her number. He couldn't believe she'd agreed to go out with him. He'd never dated anyone like her before. She was a beautiful college student. He was a skinny goofball who'd barely made it through high school.

A moment later, Rebecca stuck her head around the door. "How are you feeling?" she asked.

"Much better. I'm sorry. I felt fine and then the next thing I knew I was on the floor."

Rebecca smiled reassuringly. "I'm glad you're okay. Like I said before, you're not the first person to pass out on me. Cocoa's doing great. She's just waking up. You're welcome to come sit with her for a while."

Amy nodded and slowly stood.

"Jimmy, we need to get started on the next patient."

"Sure thing, Doc. Who do you want next?"

"I've already given Mittens her shot. She should be about ready," Rebecca replied.

The rest of the morning passed uneventfully. Amy sat with Cocoa while Rebecca and Jimmy finished the surgeries. As soon as Cocoa was awake enough to go home, Amy left.

"What a pretty young lady," June commented after Amy had gone.

"Can you believe she agreed to go out with me Friday night?" Jimmy asked.

"Well, congratulations, Jimmy. You treat that girl right. She's a sweetheart."

"Yes, ma'am," Jimmy agreed, grinning from ear to ear.

~

Later that evening, Rebecca drove toward Brian's. After observing the way Jimmy hovered protectively around Amy all morning and seeing the happiness painted all over June's face, she was more convinced than ever that she was making the right decision. As she drew closer to his house, she felt a nervous tightness in her stomach. *There's nothing to be anxious about,* she admonished herself. *It's not like I'm a virgin. It's just sex, no big deal.*

It was almost 8:00 when she pulled into Brian's driveway. She could see a few lights on inside the house. *Looks like he's here,* she thought. She wasn't sure whether she felt relieved or disappointed.

Her heart beat an unsteady rhythm in her chest. Her palms felt slick with sweat. She put her car in park and wiped her moist hands on the legs of her jeans. She'd gone home to shower and change before driving over. It had taken her several minutes to decide what to wear. She'd finally settled on keeping it casual with a pair of blue jeans and a T-shirt.

She took a deep breath, grabbed the magazines off the passenger seat, and stepped out of the car. She felt her nervousness increase as she made her way to his front door. He lived in a two-story house that was covered with dark tan vinyl siding. The windows had decorative maroon shutters. The house sat at the end of a cul-de-sac in a quiet suburban neighborhood. Rebecca had only been here on one other occasion. They usually either went out or met at her place.

Her hand trembled slightly as she reached to ring the doorbell.

She heard voices coming from inside. *I wonder if his friend is still in town. I should have called first,* she thought, feeling a little foolish.

A moment later, the porch light came on and the door swung open. A tall, slender, red-headed woman with strikingly beautiful green eyes stared at her curiously. "Can I help you?" she asked.

Rebecca was momentarily robbed of speech. "Um, is Brian here?" she asked weakly.

"Darling!" the woman called. "There's a woman here to see you."

Darling? Rebecca thought, her confusion increasing by the second. A few seconds later, Brian joined the woman at the door.

"Rebecca," he said in surprise. "What are you doing here?"

"I, uh, see that I should have called first. I'm sorry. I didn't realize you had company," Rebecca rushed.

"I'm not company," the woman said. "I'm his wife."

Rebecca's eyes widened in surprise. *His wife?* she thought incredulously. *What is she talking about?* Her eyes flew to Brian.

"Will you excuse us for a moment, Jill?" Brian asked stepping around the woman to join Rebecca on the porch.

"Sure," the woman replied. Rebecca could have sworn she saw pity in the woman's eyes as she closed the door.

"I thought you said you divorced three years ago," Rebecca said as soon as the door clicked shut.

Brian stood with his hands shoved into the pockets of his jeans. He stared at the tops of his shoes. Rebecca squeezed the magazines to her chest defensively and waited impatiently for Brian's response.

Slowly, he raised his eyes to meet hers. "I'm sorry, Rebecca. Everything I told you was the truth, except that Jill and I never officially divorced. We've been separated for three years. Then a couple of weeks ago she called me out of the blue. We've talked almost every night since. We decided that maybe we weren't ready to give up on our marriage yet. She came to visit for the weekend to test the water. Things went well enough that she decided to stay the week. Listen, I know this isn't fair to you, but I'm glad you came tonight. I didn't know how to tell you. I really like you, but I need to see if I can save my marriage. I hope you understand. I never meant to hurt you."

Rebecca's eyes narrowed angrily on his face. "You're an ass. I can't believe you told me you were divorced. I never would have agreed to go out with you, if I'd known you were still married!" she said, her voice rising angrily on the last syllable.

"I know. That's why I said what I did. I really thought the marriage was over." He noticed the magazines she was holding. "Are those for June's wedding? I would still be happy to build something for her."

Rebecca stared at him in stunned amazement. She was at a complete loss for words. She couldn't believe this was happening. Finally, she said stiffly. "I'll let her know." Then she turned on her heel and hurried toward her car.

Rebecca angrily shoved the key into the ignition. She felt hot tears streaming down her face. *Maybe dogs aren't men, but sometimes men sure act like dogs,* she thought as she swiped at the tears. *At least I hadn't slept with the jerk yet.*

CHAPTER 16

When Rebecca got home, she grabbed a pint of chocolate-chip ice cream out of the freezer and curled up on the sofa to cuddle with Captain. "Well, boy, I guess it's back to just you and me," she said. He thumped his tail and rolled onto his back to give her better access to his belly.

Rebecca smiled slightly. "You're right, Captain, we do make a good team. Why did I mess with a good thing? We were doing great before Brian came into our lives." Although talking to Captain made her feel better, she still felt like she'd been slapped in the face. Derrick and Jimmy had both tried to tell her there was something off about Brian, but she hadn't seen this coming. He'd seemed like such a great guy. Maybe she was just a lousy judge of character.

She devoured the tub of ice cream and then decided that she needed to talk to Marilyn.

"What's up?" Marilyn asked when she answered her phone.

"Brian's married," Rebecca blurted out.

"What?!" Marilyn exploded into the phone. "How did you find out? Tell me everything."

"Well, after all the wedding talk yesterday, I got caught up in the romance. So, I decided to surprise Brian after work today. I was planning on seducing him. When I got to his house, his wife answered the door."

"The bastard!" Marilyn interjected.

Rebecca spent the next few minutes relaying the rest of the conversation she'd had with Brian.

"I can't believe he told you he was divorced. Did he tell you why they'd been separated for three years without getting divorced?"

"No, and I didn't ask. It doesn't really matter now. The part that matters is that they're back together."

"I'm sorry, Rebecca. I know you were starting to have feelings for this guy. You wouldn't have been ready to go to bed with him, if you didn't think it was going somewhere special."

"Thanks, Marilyn. You're always so supportive. I don't know what I'd do without you."

"That's what best friends are for."

~

The next morning, when June arrived at Animal Friends, Rebecca told her about what had happened.

"What a jerk," June said. "I'm just glad you found out about what was going on before it was too late. I wonder what he told his wife about you after you left."

"I'm not sure, but I got the feeling she knew exactly what was going on. I swear she looked at me like she felt a little sorry for me. I bet she's been through something like this with him before. I'm guessing that a girlfriend showing up on his front porch is not something new."

"If that's true, then why on earth would she want him back?"

Rebecca shrugged. "Maybe it's a two-way street. I don't know, and I don't care. She can have him as far as I'm concerned. I just wish I would have been able to see what kind of man he was before I let my heart get involved."

"Do you still feel up to dress shopping tomorrow? We could postpone it, if you need some time," June offered.

"Of course, I still feel up to it. I'm not going to let Brian ruin our fun. By the way, he said that he was still willing to build something to put in Walter's yard for the wedding."

"He thought I would still want him to?" June asked, sounding affronted. "Walter has two sons who are pretty handy. I'll have him ask them if they think they could do something for us. If not, then we'll just stand out in the open."

Rebecca gave June a hug. "You're a great friend, June."

June squeezed Rebecca tightly. "I'm just sorry that he hurt you."

"I'll recover. I won't pretend that it didn't hurt, but I was pretty happy with my life before Brian came into it."

~

The next day, Rebecca and June closed the clinic at 2:00. Barbara and Marilyn joined them 30 minutes later at Betsy's Bridal Shop. Rebecca had called her mother the previous night to tell her about what happened with Brian. As soon as she climbed out of her Camry, Barbara hurried over and wrapped her in a hug.

"Are you okay, sweetheart?"

"I'm fine, Mom. I'll get over it."

"You always put on such a brave front. It's okay to cry a little," Barbara said as she released her and stepped back. Rebecca rarely cried. Barbara didn't think it was healthy for Rebecca to be constantly keeping her emotions in check.

"He hurt me, but he also made me furious. I don't feel like crying, but if I see him again, I might punch him in the nose."

Marilyn laughed. "That's the spirit, Rebecca."

Rebecca smiled. "Now that that is out of the way, let's find June a gorgeous dress."

Barbara clapped her hands together. Her eyes sparkled with joy. "Oh, yes, let's," she agreed enthusiastically.

As soon as they entered the large bridal shop, a petite, older woman with short gray hair hurried toward them. Her mouth curved into a wide, friendly smile. "Welcome to Betsy's. My name is Teresa. What can I do for you ladies?"

Barbara grabbed June's arm and pulled her forward. "This lovely woman is getting married in three weeks. We're here to find her a fabulous dress."

"Three weeks?" Teresa asked incredulously.

"Yep," said Marilyn. "So, lead the way. We've got some serious shopping to do."

Teresa chuckled and said, "Okay, follow me." As she started toward the racks of gowns, she asked June, "What is your name?"

"June."

Teresa's smile widened. "Oh, I can see why you want to have the wedding so soon. Do you have any idea what you are looking for, June?"

"Something simple and elegant. I'm not a real fancy person. In addition, I want it to be in cream or maybe a pale pink, definitely not white."

"Okay, let's see what we've got," answered Teresa.

She stopped at the end of a long row of gowns. She eyed June critically for a moment, then she started moving quickly down the row. She grabbed dresses off the rack as she moved. She practically threw them at Rebecca and Marilyn, who exchanged amused glances as they snatched at the flying gowns.

Within in a few moments, Teresa had selected ten dresses for June to try on. She led the way to the dressing area. Three changing stalls lined one wall. In front of the stalls was a large, open area with a small, elevated platform taking center stage. Surrounding the platform on three sides were giant, floor-length mirrors. To the left of the platform was a seating area with two large, overstuffed leather sofas.

"You ladies can hang the gowns on that rack," Teresa instructed, pointing to a long metal rack just to the right of the three changing stalls. "Then you can have a seat while I help June try them on."

Rebecca and Marilyn obediently hung the dresses on the indicated rack and moved to join Barbara in the seating area. Teresa grabbed the first gown and she and June disappeared inside the middle stall.

"She's a whirlwind, isn't she?" Marilyn asked in an amused tone. "I'm already tired."

Rebecca grinned and nodded in agreement.

A few minutes later, June emerged. The gown she wore was a very pale shade of pink. It had a sleeveless, fitted bodice that flared out to a full-length, pleated skirt that was slightly longer in the back than in the front. A light-weight jacket covered the bodice and flowed down to the tops of her thighs. June looked beautiful.

"Wow," Barbara said, jumping to her feet. "You look fabulous."

June beamed. Her cheeks had a rosy flush, and her eyes sparkled with happiness.

"Step up on the platform and see what you think," Teresa instructed. "Remember, this is only the first dress."

"Mom's right, June. You look terrific," said Rebecca as June looked at herself in the mirrors. "What do you think?"

"It's wonderful," June breathed. "Don't laugh if I start crying." Her eyes shone brightly with the moisture of unshed tears.

Rebecca smiled. She and June were polar opposites when it came to shedding tears. June cried at the drop of a hat. "I won't. Go ahead and cry."

"Ready for the next one?" Teresa asked.

"It will be hard to beat that one," Marilyn observed.

For the next few hours, June continued to try on dresses. They were all very lovely. Teresa had picked the perfect gowns to suit June. However, in the end, she chose the first one she'd tried on.

"I just couldn't get it out of my mind. I kept comparing all the other dresses to that one and none of them quite surpassed it," June said, reaching out to lightly stroke the jacket.

"I think you made an excellent choice, June," Barbara commented.

Rebecca and Marilyn agreed. Once June had selected her gown, they spent the next hour trying to find a maid of honor dress for Rebecca. They finally settled on a simple, teal colored dress that complimented the color of June's gown.

The women were in happy spirits when they left the bridal shop. They decided to celebrate their successful shopping trip by enjoying dinner at La Mesa, their favorite Tex-Mex restaurant. It served the best margaritas in town.

~

Friday night, Rebecca and Captain were curled up on the sofa watching *Tombstone*, one of Rebecca's all-time favorite movies. The credits were just starting to roll across the screen when the doorbell sounded. Captain leaped off the sofa and padded to the door. Rebecca glanced at the clock and saw that it was 11:00. *Who in the world?* she wondered as she hurried to the door. She pulled it open to find Kara standing on the porch. Her left eye was swollen closed. Blood trickled from a small cut above it. Both of her lips were swollen and bloodied. Her T-shirt was torn, exposing her left shoulder.

"I didn't know where else to go," Kara mumbled around her swollen lips.

"What happened?" Rebecca asked in a shocked whisper.

"Dalton," Kara whispered.

"That son-of-a-bitch," Rebecca cursed. "Why does he think he has the right to do this to you? Come in, let me get you cleaned up." She stepped back from the door to allow Kara room to enter.

"Have a seat at the table," Rebecca instructed, pointing at her dining table. "I'll get my first-aid kit."

Kara shuffled stiffly into the kitchen. Rebecca watched her lumbered movements. *The bastard must have cracked her ribs, too,* she thought angrily.

Within moments, she joined Kara at the table. "That cut above your eye could use a couple of stitches and from the way you were walking, I'd say you have a few cracked ribs. I should take you to the hospital."

Kara shook her head. "Please, don't," she whispered.

Rebecca sighed. She went to the sink to moisten a wash cloth. Then she dropped down into the chair next to Kara. "Where's Jimmy?" she asked as she gently cleaned her wounds. She opened the first-aid kit and dug out some antibiotic ointment. After she applied the ointment to the wound above Kara's eye, she placed a butterfly bandage over it.

"He's out with that girl, Amy," Kara mumbled.

Rebecca suddenly remembered Kara's son. "Where's your son?" Rebecca asked.

"He's with my mom. I didn't want him to see me like this, so I came here."

Rebecca sighed with relief. "I'm going to call my friend, Mitch. He's the cop you met at the clinic the day Dalton hit you in the parking lot. I want you to tell him what happened. You can't let Dalton get away with it again, Kara."

Kara didn't respond as tears began to stream down her face. Rebecca went into the living room to grab her cell phone. Mitch answered on the third ring.

"Everything all right, Rebecca?" he asked worriedly. Her name had shown up on his caller ID.

"Yes. I'm sorry to bother you on a Friday night, Mitch."

Mitch glanced over at the naked brunette sleeping next to him. *It had been a good night, too,* he thought. "No problem, Rebecca. You know I'm here for you, anytime. What's going on?"

"Do you remember Jimmy's sister, Kara? You met her at Animal Friends that day her boyfriend hit her and then threatened me."

"Sure, I remember," Mitch said. "What about her?"

"She showed up at my house a few minutes ago. Her boyfriend's beaten her up pretty badly. Would you mind coming over here to talk with her?"

"I'm on my way. I'll be there in 15 minutes."

"Thanks, Mitch," said Rebecca as she ended the call.

Rebecca reached out and placed a hand on Kara's shoulder. "Go sit in the living room where it's more comfortable. He'll be here in a few minutes. In the meantime, I'll get you some ice."

Kara nodded and pushed herself slowly to her feet. She shuffled into the living room and took a seat on the sofa. Captain jumped up beside her and gently placed his head on her lap. Kara absently reached down and started stroking his head.

"No matter how upset I am, it always makes me feel better when he does that," Rebecca commented when she joined them a few minutes later.

Kara took the bundle of ice from Rebecca and pressed it to her swollen lips. She winced painfully as the ice made contact with her skin.

"I know you're scared, but you really need to press charges this time, Kara."

Kara didn't say anything. She just continued to slowly stroke Captain's head with one hand while she held the ice with the other. They sat in silence for the next several minutes. Rebecca felt relief pour through her when she heard Mitch's car pull into her driveway. She jumped up and hurried outside to meet him. She felt her heart constrict at the sight of him getting out of his car and striding confidently toward her. She hadn't realized how much she had missed him. As soon as he stepped up onto her porch, she wrapped him in a hug.

"It's really good to see you," she whispered into his ear.

He returned her hug. "It's good to see you, too. I wish it were under better circumstances, though," he replied.

Rebecca stepped back and said, "She's inside. I hope she's going to be willing to talk with you."

Mitch nodded and followed Rebecca into the house. The girl sitting with Captain on Rebecca's sofa looked frail and frightened. *He sure did a number on her,* Mitch thought, feeling anger burn in his belly. He hated men who felt like they needed to show how tough they were by beating up women and children.

"Hi, Kara. Can we talk?" Mitch asked as he sat in the chair next to the sofa.

Kara gave a slight shrug.

"Was it Dalton again?" Mitch asked.

Kara nodded. She kept her eyes averted, refusing to meet his gaze.

"Want to tell me what happened?" Mitch asked gently. "Or if you'd feel more comfortable, I can have one of my friends, Lacy, who's a female officer meet us at the station, and you can tell her what happened." In Mitch's experience, abused women felt more relaxed talking with other women about what happened to them. They had an understandable distrust of men.

"I'd rather tell you," Kara said softly.

"I'm glad," Mitch replied.

Rebecca felt affection swell in her heart as she watched how gently Mitch handled Kara. *He's such a great guy,* she thought. *I'm lucky to have him for a friend.*

Kara told Mitch that Dalton had beaten her because she'd picked up the wrong brand of toilet paper. She said that he had been more on edge over the last few weeks and had finally exploded. Mitch asked her if she knew what was making him so edgy and Kara replied that she didn't. She said he and his brother had been hanging out with a new set of friends, and they'd been going out a lot late at night. She said she'd tried to ask him about it that day in the Animal Friends parking lot, and that was what caused him to slap her.

"Do you know where he is now?" Mitch asked.

Kara shook her head. "He got a phone call while he was hitting me. Then he left."

"Do you have a picture of him?" Mitch asked.

"On my phone," Kara answered.

"Excellent. Send it to my phone, then I can send it out to the patrol cars. What kind of car does he drive?"

"A black Beetle with purple flames."

Mitch remembered the car from the day at Rebecca's clinic. A patrol car would be able to spot it quickly. "We should have him in custody in a matter of hours. In the meantime, do you have someplace you can stay? You shouldn't go back to your place until we pick him up."

"She can stay here until morning," Rebecca said.

"Good," replied Mitch. "Would you be willing to bring Kara down to the station in the morning, so that I can get her official statement, say around 10:00?"

"Sure," Rebecca replied.

Mitch rose to leave. "Thank you for telling me what happened, Kara."

She looked up at him through wide, frightened eyes. "Please don't let him hurt me again."

"I won't," Mitch promised.

Rebecca walked him out. "I'd like to take that guy behind a barn and beat the shit out of him," Mitch muttered angrily when they were outside.

"I'd like to help," replied Rebecca.

Mitch flashed her a quick grin. "I've missed you, Rebecca. Are you still seeing that guy, Brian?"

Rebecca shook her head. "No, as it turns out, he's married."

Mitch blew out a soft whistle. "That must have been a shock."

"About as big as you could get," replied Rebecca.

Mitch shook his head. "His loss," he said, then added, "I'll see you in the morning. We should have the bastard in custody by then."

"Thanks for coming, Mitch. I'll see you tomorrow."

They exchanged another brief hug before he returned to his car.

CHAPTER 17

The next morning, Mitch met Derrick at the community center for their weekly game.

"Rebecca called me last night," Mitch commented just as Derrick went up for a jump shot. He grinned as the shot sailed awkwardly out of Derrick's hands causing him to shoot an air ball. Mitch ran after the ball as it bounced across the gym.

Derrick stood with arms crossed waiting for Mitch to return with the ball. Mitch could see a muscle twitching in Derrick's jaw. He'd been as surly as an angry bear for the last several weeks. Mitch knew that Rebecca's involvement with Brian was the source of Derrick's foul mood. He wondered how his friend was going to take the news he was about to give him.

When Mitch was within a few feet of him, Derrick impatiently asked, "Why did Rebecca call you last night?"

"Remember that girl, Kara, who worked for Rebecca, the one whose boyfriend hit her in the parking lot?"

Derrick nodded.

"She showed up at Rebecca's last night. Her boyfriend beat her up pretty badly. Rebecca called me to come talk with her about pressing charges against him. They're meeting me at the station this morning to file the paperwork."

"How did she look?" Derrick asked, trying not to sound too eager for information about Rebecca. He'd worked hard over the last few weeks to push her from his thoughts, and he'd failed miserably. Everything seemed to remind him of her. He compared every woman he met with her. This one didn't laugh like Rebecca. That one didn't have Rebecca's understanding of sports. This one didn't love dogs like Rebecca. In addition to finding that every woman he met failed to measure up to her, he kept coming up with reasons to call or visit her vet clinic. Thankfully, he'd recognized them as the lame excuses they were before he'd actually acted on any of them.

"She looked like she'd been hit by a truck," Mitch said, intentionally misunderstanding Derrick's question.

Derrick's eyes narrowed. "I meant Rebecca," he said through clenched teeth.

Mitch grinned mischievously. Derrick's eyes glittered with irritation. Mitch knew that if he pushed his friend any further, he'd end up taking a fist to the face.

"She's not seeing Brian anymore," he replied. He was fascinated by the immediate change in Derrick's expression. The muscles in his face relaxed, making him look younger. The hard line of his mouth eased into a crooked grin. The gold flecks in his eyes glowed intensely.

"What happened?" he asked.

"Apparently, she found out that he's married. She didn't offer any more details, and I didn't pry."

Derrick's expression changed to one of concern. "How did she seem to be taking it?"

"She acted like the same-old Rebecca. She told me she wanted to help me beat the shit out of Kara's boyfriend."

Derrick grinned. "That sounds like Rebecca."

"I should hit the shower, so I can get to the station in time to meet them," Mitch commented.

Later, as Derrick drove toward home, his thoughts were consumed with images of Rebecca. He wasn't sure what to do about this new piece of information. He knew he needed to give her enough time to get over the break-up, but how much time? He'd never set out with the intention of wooing a woman before. He had no idea how to go about it. He began to hum along to the music on his radio as the last remnants of the wall he'd built around his heart fell away.

~

Rebecca and Kara arrived at the station at 10:00. She felt Kara tense beside her as she pulled open the door.

"Are you okay?" Rebecca asked.

"Yeah," Kara mumbled. "I hate police stations."

Rebecca had never been inside one before. She wondered how many times Kara had. They entered a large foyer with white tile floors and white walls. A long counter with a plate-glass window and a sign that instructed all visitors to check in stood directly in front of them. Closed doors flanked either side of the counter. They walked up to the counter and asked to see Mitch Holt.

Within a few minutes, Mitch walked through the door to the right of the counter. He smiled warmly when he spotted them.

"Good morning," he greeted. "I'm glad you're here, Kara. Let's go back to my desk and talk."

Rebecca and Kara followed Mitch through the door and down a long corridor. They turned a corner and Mitch pushed open a glass door that led to a room filled with a maze of desks. The room was buzzing with activity. Several of the desks were occupied by officers who were talking on phones, taking statements, and working on computers. Rebecca was fascinated by the sight.

Mitch led them to a relatively quiet area at the back of the room. He borrowed a chair from a nearby desk and placed it next to the one that already sat next to his.

"Have a seat," he instructed, pointing to the two chairs.

Rebecca and Kara sat facing Mitch, who took a seat behind the desk.

"We arrested Dalton last night. His Beetle wasn't too hard to find. He'd gone to his brother's house. His arraignment is scheduled for this morning. That's when the judge sets his bail. He seemed pretty confident that his brother will post it for him. I'm not sure where he's going to get the money, but if he does, then he could be out by as early as this afternoon. You can file a restraining order against him to keep him away from you until the trial."

Kara sat stiffly in the chair. Her eyes were wide with fright. Her face had gone very pale.

"What if he comes after me?" she asked in a scared whisper. "I didn't think he'd be out so soon."

"Like I said, I doubt he'll be able to come up with the bail money, but if he does, then the restraining order will give us the right to arrest him if he comes anywhere near you. If you see him, you call me. Okay?"

Kara gave an almost imperceptible nod. Rebecca reached out and placed her hand on Kara's arm.

"You and your son are welcome to stay with me, Kara," she offered.

"That's really nice of you, but we'll be okay. Jimmy lives with us. He'll make sure Dalton stays away."

"Kara," said Mitch. "I'd like to take some pictures of you to use as evidence. Would that be okay?"

Kara nodded.

They spent the next half hour taking pictures of Kara's battered face. Mitch helped Kara file the restraining order and promised to get it to the judge that afternoon. When they finished, Rebecca took Kara to her mother's.

A few hours later, Mitch received word that Dalton's brother had posted his bail. He decided he needed to look into how Dalton's brother was able to come up with that kind of cash so quickly. He lived in a shabby, one-room apartment in a rundown neighborhood.

~

Later that afternoon, Rebecca and Captain headed to the hospital. Rebecca was glad to have something to take her mind off the drama of the last several hours. She'd never been involved in anything like that before. She hoped that Dalton would stay away from Kara. There was a part of her that feared he would ignore the restraining order and go after her. She knew that Kara believed he would. Rebecca could sense how scared Kara was when she dropped her off at her apartment. Jimmy had been there. As soon as he'd seen Kara's face, he'd exploded with rage. It had taken them several minutes to convince him not to go after Dalton. Rebecca had stayed until she was sure Jimmy wasn't going to do something stupid.

Rebecca glanced over at Captain and smiled. He wore the same happy expression he always did when he knew they were on their way to visit kids at the hospital. Rebecca felt some of the tension she'd been carrying since last night ease. She reached out and rubbed his shoulder. Suddenly, she heard her mother's voice say, "Dogs aren't men, Rebecca." *No,* she thought, *they're much more loving and compassionate. They would never treat the ones they supposedly care about the way men sometimes do.*

A few minutes later, they arrived at the hospital. Rebecca and Captain both walked toward the hospital entrance with a sense of eagerness. It had been a few weeks since their last visit.

"Hi, Rebecca," Allison greeted as they stepped off the elevator. "It's good to see you guys." She bent to give Captain a brisk ear rub.

"You, too," Rebecca agreed. "Who do you have for us today?"

The first patient they visited was a six-year-old girl who'd been in a car accident. She'd broken both of her legs and had already undergone two surgeries to repair them. She was in a great deal of pain. Her face lit up with joy when Captain laid his big head on her bed. She and Captain played catch for several minutes. The girl's parents were overjoyed by their daughter's response to Captain.

The other patient they saw was Nate, a nine-year-old boy. He and his older brother had been lighting some old fireworks they'd found stored in their grandmother's garage. One of the fireworks hadn't gone off. They'd assumed it was a dud and Nate had picked it up. It went off in his hand. He'd lost the ends of two fingers. His hand and forearm were badly burned. He'd been angry and belligerent since the accident. He loved playing sports and felt like he'd never be able to play now that he was missing part of his fingers. He stubbornly refused to look at Captain. Rebecca had tried to encourage him to interact by getting Captain to perform a few tricks, but Nate kept his eyes glued to the television. They finally gave up and left the room. Nate's mother followed them out.

"I really thought this would help," she said, her voice filled with disappointment.

"These things take time," Allison said. "It's only been a few days. I'm sure he'll start to feel better once he's allowed to go home."

"Thank you for trying."

"We were happy to do it," replied Rebecca, her heart ached for the pain in the woman's voice. She couldn't imagine how it must feel to see your child hurting like that. Coming to the hospital always helped her put her own problems into perspective.

~

The sun was shining brightly as they left the hospital. Rebecca decided to take Captain to the park for a walk. They deserved a few minutes of relaxed fun in the sun. As soon as they pulled into the park, Captain began to whimper with excitement. His tail beat a happy rhythm against the car seat.

Rebecca laughed at his happiness. "I agree, boy, let's go have some fun."

Rebecca chose Forrest Park. It consisted of several hiking trails that wound through heavily wooded areas. The paths were wide and easy to traverse. Rebecca decided she needed a long walk and picked the Rabbit Hole Trail. It was a three-mile loop that followed a winding stream.

She and Captain set out at a brisk pace. They passed several other hikers. A few of them were clients. She stopped to talk to Sheila Daniels, the owner of a handsome Newfoundland named Beast.

"It's good to see him getting some exercise," Rebecca commented. "Keeping him fit will be good for his hips."

Sheila nodded. "It's good for me, too," she chuckled.

They were standing a few yards from a point where the path disappeared around a bend. A flash of blue caught Rebecca's eye and she glanced toward the movement. Her eyes widened in surprise as Derrick and Trouble jogged around the corner. He was wearing black shorts and a snug blue T-shirt that accentuated the smooth muscles of his chest and stomach. The powerful muscles in his tanned legs bunched and rippled with the force of each stride. Rebecca felt her heart rate accelerate, and her palms grow clammy.

"What a hunk," Sheila whispered.

Rebecca had forgotten Sheila's existence. Just then, Derrick noticed her and altered his path to jog toward her.

"Do you know him?" Sheila asked as Derrick approached them.

Rebecca nodded. She couldn't seem to get her brain to work well enough to speak.

A wide grin stretched across Derrick's face when he stopped beside them.

"Rebecca," he said, panting with exertion, "it's nice to see you."

"Hi, Derrick," Rebecca replied. Sheila nudged her with her elbow.

"Um, Derrick, this is Sheila Daniels. She's a client of mine."

"It's nice to meet you, Derrick," Sheila said, smiling and offering him her hand. She was a pretty woman with long, blonde hair and big, blue eyes. She had a small dimple in her left cheek when she smiled. She stood several inches taller than Rebecca. She wore a tight jogging outfit that accentuated her curves. Rebecca felt an unexpected flash of jealousy as she realized that Sheila was exactly Derrick's type.

Derrick flashed her a quick smile as he took her outstretched hand. "It's nice to meet you, too, Sheila," he said politely.

He turned his gaze back to Rebecca. "Could I walk with you? I'd like to talk."

"Sure," replied Rebecca, eyeing him curiously. *What could he want to talk about?* she wondered.

She turned her attention back to Sheila. "It was nice seeing you. Don't forget to bring Beast in for his annual vaccines."

Sheila recognized that she was being dismissed. She smiled coyly at Derrick. "My name's in the phone book. Give me a call sometime."

Derrick smiled politely, but didn't respond. Sheila shrugged and continued down the trail.

Derrick fell into step beside Rebecca as she started to walk in the opposite direction.

"How are you doing?" he asked, sounding genuinely concerned. "Mitch told me about last night."

"I'm doing fine. I'm worried about Kara though. Did Mitch tell you that the guy made bail?"

Derrick shook his head. "I'm surprised he could come up with the money. He didn't look like he'd have too much spare cash laying around."

"That's pretty much what Mitch said, too. Apparently, his brother posted it for him."

"I want you to be careful, Rebecca. You never know if that punk might try to take this out on you. I don't like the idea of you being alone, especially hiking down a relatively deserted trail."

"It's not deserted. I've been hiking for an hour, and I've passed someone every few minutes. Besides, I really don't think Dalton will come after me. He's in enough trouble already."

"I'm just suggesting that you be careful until you know the guy's behind bars."

They fell silent as they continued down the trail. Derrick was struggling to come up with a way to approach her new single status. Everything he thought of to say sounded awkward. Finally, he said, "Mitch also told me that Brian is married. I'm sorry. I know that must have come as a shock to you."

Rebecca shrugged. "It came as a big shock. I really thought we were developing a relationship."

"Do you want me to punch the guy out for you?" Derrick asked, trying to lighten the mood.

Rebecca chuckled. "That's sweet, but not necessary."

A few minutes later, Rebecca surprised herself by suddenly blurting out. "June is getting married in two weeks. How would you feel about being my date?"

Derrick couldn't believe his ears. She'd given him the opening he needed. His mouth spread into a wide, sexy grin. "I'd be happy to be your date. However, I do have one stipulation."

"What's that?" she asked.

"I want to have a real date with you before the wedding."

Rebecca's eyes widened in surprise. "Okay," she replied. "That sounds fair."

"Are you free Friday?" he asked.

Rebecca nodded.

"Good, I'll pick you up around 6:30."

By the time they finished the conversation, they had made it back around the loop. They stopped at the water fountain and allowed the dogs to drink. When they'd had their fill, Derrick bent and placed a quick kiss on Rebecca's cheek. "I'll see you Friday."

Rebecca watched him jog to his car. She was in a mild state of shock. *What in the world just happened? I just ruled out men and suddenly, I have two dates with Derrick Peterson. Could things get any stranger?*

CHAPTER 18

As soon as Rebecca got home, she called Marilyn.

"Hi, Rebecca. What's up?"

"You won't believe the weekend I've had," Rebecca replied. She spent the next several minutes describing what had happened to Kara.

"So, the guy's out on bail? Aren't you scared?" Marilyn asked.

"No, I don't think he'll try to do anything to me, but I'm worried about Jimmy and Kara. If Dalton shows up at their apartment, I'm not sure what Jimmy will do. It could get really ugly."

"Well, you never know about a guy like that, Rebecca. He might know that you live alone and try something. Just be careful and make sure you have Mitch's number on speed dial," Marilyn replied, her voice filled with concern.

"You sound like Derrick did when I ran into him this afternoon," Rebecca replied. She knew that dropping Derrick's name like that would pique her friend's curiosity. She grinned into the phone when the tone of Marilyn's voice changed from concern to excitement.

"You saw Derrick this afternoon? Where? What happened?"

Rebecca chuckled. "I took Captain for a walk in Forrest Park. He was jogging with his dog, Trouble. Mitch had already told him what happened to Kara. Derrick gave me a lecture on the dangers of being alone on the trail."

"When is that man going to admit how much he likes you?" Marilyn said in response.

"That's my other piece of news."

"Oh, do tell," Marilyn said eagerly.

"I asked him to be my date for June's wedding."

"What did he say?" Marilyn asked, her voice filled with excitement.

"He agreed to be my date for the wedding, as long as I agreed to go out with him this Friday."

Marilyn let out a squeal. "I knew it! I knew he liked you!" Rebecca could picture Marilyn doing one of her famous "happy dances" on the other end of the phone.

Rebecca chuckled. "Calm down. It's just a date. Besides, I'm not sure I'm ready to get into another relationship. I just broke up with Brian last week, remember?"

"Do you remember who you're talking to? I've been your best friend for years. I know that you've had a thing for Derrick Peterson ever since you met him. You can't tell me that you're not tingling with excitement and anticipation. I'm just glad the man finally came to his senses and asked you out."

"You're right, I am excited, but I'm trying not to get my hopes up too high. What if he just thought it was the friendly thing to do, since I had asked him to be my date for the wedding? Maybe he only wants to renew our friendship."

"Rebecca, I've seen the way that man looks at you and friendship is not what he has in mind."

Rebecca sighed. "You might be right, but I think it will be best if I don't read too much into this."

~

Monday morning, Rebecca filled in June on everything that had occurred over the weekend. When she finished, June shook her head in amazement, "My goodness, Rebecca, I can't believe all of that happened in one weekend. I hope Kara's okay. And I agree with Marilyn, Derrick Peterson is crazy about you."

Just then, Jimmy walked through the back door.

"Jimmy, how's Kara?" Rebecca asked.

He shrugged. "She's okay, I guess. She hasn't said too much. I think she's really scared Dalton will come after her."

"Does she have someone with her now?" June asked.

"Yeah, she's with my mom. They know to call the police if they see any sign of Dalton."

"I'm sorry, Jimmy. I know this must be really hard for you, too. Hopefully, it will go to trial quickly, and you can all have peace of mind," Rebecca replied.

"Thanks again, Doc, for everything you did for us this weekend. I don't know what would have happened if Kara hadn't shown up at your house."

Rebecca gave him a quick hug. "I'm just glad that she did come to me, and that she's safe. By the way, I didn't get a chance to ask how your date with Amy went."

Jimmy's mouth stretched into a wide grin, and his eyes took on a dreamy quality. "It was great. She's great. We had a great time."

"So, things went great?" June asked with a chuckle.

Jimmy blushed slightly. "Yeah, they did."

"Speaking of dates," June said, "guess who finally asked Dr. Miller out?"

"Who?" Jimmy asked, his eyes glowing with curiosity.

"Dr. Peterson," June replied.

Jimmy grinned. "Congratulations, Doc. I knew that dude liked you."

Now it was Rebecca's turn to blush. "I'm not really sure there's any need for congratulations. We're just going to dinner."

A few minutes later, Steven Milner, one of Spring Valley's animal control officers, walked through the front door. Animal control occasionally brought injured animals into Animal Friends for Rebecca to treat or sometimes, euthanize, depending on the severity of the injury. Rebecca usually donated her services and only charged them the cost for the medications she sent with the animal. She also donated space if the animal needed to be hospitalized for a few days.

"What have you got today, Steven?" she asked.

"A mutt with a terrible case of mange. He's missing most of his hair, and his skin is oozing pus. He stinks to high heaven and to top it off, he's got a pretty nasty disposition. It doesn't look like he's had an owner for a while. This one might be a euthanasia candidate."

"Okay, go ahead and bring him through the back and straight into the treatment area, so that I can take a look at him."

Steven nodded and left to retrieve the dog. A few minutes later, he re-entered through the back door. He used a rabies pole, which consisted of a long PVC pipe with a noose at the end of it, to lead the dog into the treatment area.

Rebecca's heart constricted, and she felt her eyes fill with moisture at the sight of the poor dog. His skin was thickened, bright red, and covered in bloody scabs. The skin around his eyes was swollen to the point that he was looking through slits. He barely had any hair left on him. His ribs and hip bones stuck out sharply. It was difficult to tell what breed he was. Based on his size, Rebecca guessed that he had some lab in him. He was growling a low warning.

Rebecca squatted a few feet away from the dog, so that she could get down on his level. "Hi, buddy," she said soothingly. "I'm really sorry this happened to you. I can help, if you'll let me."

The dog eyed her warily from the corner of his eye. He continued to emit a low growl. Rebecca gazed into the dog's eyes and quietly contemplated what to do. The dog looked frightened and pitiful, but not aggressive. Finally, she glanced up at Steven.

"Put him in the first exam room. I just can't euthanize him. He only looks to be about a year old. The mange can be treated, and I have a feeling that given a little love and attention, he'll be a nice dog."

"All right, Doc. I'll trust your judgment. I've known you long enough to know that you're usually right about these things."

Rebecca stood up and stepped out of the way, so that Steven could walk the dog into the exam room. She went into the ICU and filled a bowl with food. She grabbed another bowl and filled it with water.

"Open the door for me, Jimmy. I'll let you know when we're ready to come out."

Jimmy hurried to open the door. Rebecca stepped quickly inside as he pulled the door closed behind her. The dog crouched on the other side of the room. He no longer growled, but his eyes were still filled with fear. Rebecca set the bowls down on the floor a few feet in front of her. Then she sat down and leaned back against the door. She could see the dog's nose working as he took in the scent of the food.

"All you have to do is come and get it," Rebecca said softly. "I promise I won't hurt you."

Rebecca kept her eyes averted away from the dog and continued to talk to it in low tones. She saw him take a tentative step toward the bowl.

"That's it. Come on. The food's delicious."

The dog took another step forward. He paused and then took another step. Rebecca continued to talk to him. After a few more steps, he reached the bowl. He sniffed the food, then quickly snatched a piece of kibble and hurried back to the opposite side of the room.

"Pretty good, huh?" Rebecca asked. "There's plenty more."

This time the dog approached the bowl by taking slow, steady steps. Rebecca smiled when he dipped his head and started eating. After he finished the food, he took a long drink of water. Then he raised his head and looked shyly at Rebecca.

"Feel a little better?" she asked. "Do you mind if I pet you now?"

The dog stood with his head lowered and his tail tucked tightly between his legs. Rebecca scooted a little closer to him. He was still a little out of reach. She paused to give him a chance to get used to her nearness. He didn't move away, so she finished closing the gap between them. She held out her hand palm down. He stretched out his neck and sniffed it. Rebecca smiled. She knew she was making progress.

She slid a little closer to him. Then she reached out and gently placed her hand on his shoulder. She knew that if she stroked his inflamed skin, it would cause him pain, so she just softly pressed her hand against him. He pushed the top of his head into her chest. Rebecca felt a tear run down her cheek.

"It's going to be okay," she choked. "I'm going to get you all fixed up. You won't have to hurt anymore."

She stayed that way for a few more minutes. Then she stood and moved to the exam room door. The dog followed her. They stepped out into the treatment area.

"Okay, Jimmy, he's ready for his bath now."

"What do you think we should call him?" Jimmy asked.

Rebecca squatted down beside the dog. He leaned his shoulder against her. She smiled and reached out to place her hand on his head. "How about Roscoe?"

"Yeah, that suits him," Jimmy replied as he moved around the treatment area to pick the dog up. "Come on Roscoe, let's get you cleaned up a little," he said as he gently lifted the dog in his arms.

Jimmy gave the dog a medicated bath. Roscoe seemed to enjoy the warm water. After the bath, Jimmy set him up in a comfortable cage in the ICU. Rebecca went to begin checking in her surgery patients. The rest of the day passed smoothly. Rebecca made a point to spend as much time with Roscoe as she could throughout the day. She wanted him to feel safe and confident. By the end of the day, he had started wagging his tail each time she or Jimmy approached his cage. Rebecca knew that he'd start to feel much better in a few days when the medications she had him on had a chance to start working.

~

Friday night came quickly. Rebecca's palms were slick with moisture as she tried to clasp the necklace she'd chosen to wear. She still couldn't quite believe that she was actually about to go out on a date with Derrick Peterson. She kept telling herself not to read too much into it, but she couldn't help the excitement she was feeling.

The doorbell rang at exactly 6:30. She hurried toward the door with Captain right on her heels. She pulled it open and her breath caught in her throat. Derrick stood on her porch wearing a dark-blue dress shirt that was open at the collar and pressed black trousers. He held a small bouquet of red roses. He flashed her a gorgeous smile.

"Hi," he greeted.

"Hi," she said, embarrassed by the slight breathy quality to her voice.

He held out the roses and said, "These are for you."

"They're beautiful," she said, reaching for the flowers. "Come in, while I find a vase for them."

She turned from the door and headed to the kitchen. Derrick followed behind her. His eyes ran appreciatively down her back. She wore a tight fitting, black dress that fell to the tops of her knees. It was open in the back revealing smooth, pale skin. He felt his gut clench at the gentle sway of her hips as she walked away from him. He forced himself to look away as she bent to retrieve a vase from under the sink. When she stood, she caught him surveying the kitchen. Several of the cabinet doors were missing their hardware, and half the counter top was missing.

"Brian's crew showed up to finish the work the Monday after I found out about his wife. I sent them packing and told them to tell him to send me a bill for the work they'd completed. I haven't gotten around to finding another contractor."

"I think one of the nurses who works in the emergency room has a brother who's a contractor. Would you like me to have her give him your number?"

Rebecca grinned. "That would be great."

"Done," Derrick replied. "Are you ready to head out? I have 7:00 reservations at Rochelle's."

Rebecca raised her eyebrows in appreciation. Rochelle's was one of the nicest restaurants in town. She'd never eaten there before.

"How did you get a table? I heard you had to make reservations weeks in advance if you wanted to get in."

Derrick grinned. "You do, but I know the owner and gave him a call."

Rebecca returned his smile. "All right, then, let's go."

A few minutes later, they arrived at the restaurant. They were immediately taken in and shown to their seats. They were seated at a cozy table toward the back of the restaurant. Within moments, their waitress arrived to fill their water glasses and hand them their menus.

Rebecca decided on a shrimp pasta dish and Derrick chose the filet mignon. He ordered a bottle of wine. As the waitress took their menus, he met her eyes across the table.

"I realize that I don't really know that much about you other than you own a vet clinic, coach basketball, and volunteer at the hospital."

Rebecca smiled. "Well, let's see, I was born here in Spring Valley. My dad died when I was 12. My mom, Barbara, finished raising me."

Derrick was surprised to hear that she was an only child raised by a single parent just like he had been.

"Are you and your mom close?" Derrick asked.

"Yes, very," Rebecca replied. "She drives me nuts sometimes, but she's also my biggest supporter."

Derrick suddenly grinned. "I wish that I had called your number when Stella got it from your mom, instead of giving it to Mitch."

"You call your mom, Stella?" Rebecca asked.

"She's my step mom. My mom ran off with a truck driver when I was 11. My dad remarried five years later. Stella and I barely tolerated each other while I was in high school. We've developed a more civil relationship over the years and for the last few, she's made it her mission to try to find me a wife."

"I know what you mean. Since I turned 30, getting me married has become my mom's primary goal in life. She's worried about grandchildren." Rebecca felt her cheeks grow warm as soon as the words were out of her mouth. She couldn't believe she'd just broken the golden rule of dating and mentioned marriage and children on their first date.

In order to change the focus of the conversation, she asked, "When did you decide you wanted to be a doctor?"

Derrick shrugged. "I wanted to do something constructive with my life, and I wanted a career where I could make a decent living. Becoming a doctor seemed like the perfect combination."

"Why work in the ER?"

"During my residency, I got hooked on the fast-paced action. I love the adrenaline rush."

Rebecca smiled. "I can relate to that. There are days in the vet clinic when things are happening so fast I don't have time to think. It can be very exhilarating."

"What about you? When did you know you wanted to be a vet?"

"I decided I wanted to be an animal doctor as soon as I was old enough to know they existed. I've always been passionate about animals. Spending my life helping them seemed like the obvious choice."

Derrick and Rebecca continued to talk for another couple of hours. Finally, Derrick said, "I hate to bring this to an end, but I'm on duty tomorrow."

Rebecca glanced at her watch. She couldn't believe how much time had passed. She nodded and stood to leave.

When they arrived at her house, Derrick got out and walked Rebecca to her door. He reached out, brushed a strand of hair off her cheek, and tucked it behind her ear. Then he gently cupped the side of her face. His other hand grasped her waist and pulled her toward him. Rebecca was mesmerized by the intensity of his gaze as his eyes bore into hers. She had to tilt her head back to look up at him as he brought her body into contact with his.

She sucked in a quick breath when she felt the heat of his body caress her skin through her dress. His face descended slowly toward hers. His eyes were focused on her mouth. When his lips made contact, Rebecca felt a bolt of electricity scorch through her body. His lips were soft and gentle as they played across hers. Rebecca melted against him. His lips turned firm and demanding as he gave her a long, thorough kiss. Then he slowly raised his head and pulled her head into his chest. She wrapped her arms around his waist.

Derrick gave a soft chuckle. "I only meant for this to be a gentle goodnight kiss, but dammit I'm having a hard time convincing myself to let go and leave."

Rebecca felt the chuckle rumble in his chest. She also felt the steady beat of his heart against her cheek. She let out a soft sigh.

He held her for a few more seconds, then he dropped his arms and stepped away. He placed the tip of his finger under her chin and tilted her head back. She met his gaze. The gold flecks in his eyes burned with hot intensity.

"Good-bye, Rebecca. I had a great time. I'll call you in a couple of days." He bent and placed a chaste kiss on her forehead and then stepped around her and headed to his car. It took Rebecca a moment to gather her scattered senses and get her keys out to open her front door.

As soon as she got inside, she leaned back against the door and ran her fingers over her still tingling lips. *Wow,* she thought. *He's got to be the sexiest man alive.*

CHAPTER 19

The next morning, Rebecca went to Animal Friends to feed Roscoe. He'd blossomed into an animated and affectionate dog over the past week. His skin was no longer inflamed, and he was starting to regain some of his fur. He had a tuft of white fur on his chin and a white patch on his chest. It was now obvious that he was a black lab mix as Rebecca had first guessed. She would probably keep him at the clinic for another week. Then he would be ready to go to the animal shelter to be put up for adoption. Rebecca was seriously considering keeping him. He had a great personality, and she thought that Captain might enjoy having a friend.

"Good morning, Roscoe," she greeted.

He danced around in his cage wagging his tail enthusiastically. She grabbed a leash off the wall and moved to open his cage door. As soon as she released the latch, he pushed the door wide and leaped out.

"In a hurry this morning, huh?" Rebecca asked in an amused tone. "I'm sorry I didn't get back last night to let you out. I was on a date."

Woof!

"It went very well. Thanks for asking," Rebecca said as she slipped the leash around Roscoe's neck. She bent and gave him a quick hug. She was in high spirits as she walked Roscoe outside. The sky appeared bluer and the air smelled fresher than she could ever remember it. She knew she had a goofy grin on her face, and she didn't care. The children's song, *If You're Happy and You Know It* kept running through her mind. She was happy, and it felt great.

She was walking Roscoe through a grassy area that ran along the east side of the clinic when she heard the sound of a car with a loud muffler approaching. Roscoe emitted a low growl. Rebecca glanced up. She sucked in her breath as she recognized the black VW Beetle. *Dalton*, she thought anxiously, *What's he doing here?*

The car slowed to a crawl as it passed in front of Animal Friends. She could see Dalton glaring at her through the driver's side window. A slow, evil grin spread across his face. Slowly, he mouthed the words, "You're dead" as he lifted his hand and mimicked firing a pistol at her. Then he hit the gas and sped down the street.

Rebecca's pulse was racing. She felt a shiver flow through her body and at the same time sweat break out on her upper lip. Her hands were shaking, and she felt weak in the knees. She took a few shaky steps toward the clinic and slid down the wall. She sat in the grass with her back pressed against the building for support. Roscoe whimpered and nudged her in the shoulder. Rebecca absently reached out and stroked his shoulder. He placed a paw on her outstretched leg and looked at her with wide, worried eyes.

"I'm okay, boy," she whispered. "Just give me a minute." *Why did I let that scare me so badly?* she wondered as she fought to calm her fear. Her normal reaction to something like that would have been to flip the guy the bird, but there had been something in his face. It hadn't seemed like an empty threat. The look on his face had been pure hatred.

She slipped her hand into the pocket of her jeans and pulled out her cell phone. She knew that Derrick was at the hospital, so she dialed Mitch's number.

"Hi, Rebecca, is everything okay?"

"Could you come to Animal Friends?" she asked in a shaky voice.

"What happened?" Mitch asked.

"Dalton just drove by. He threatened me." As she said the words, she suddenly felt foolish for reacting so strongly.

"I'm sorry, Mitch. I shouldn't have bothered you. I got scared and overreacted. I'm embarrassed that I called."

"Don't be an idiot, Rebecca. You did exactly what you should have done. I'll be right there. I'm getting in my car and heading your way. I'm only a few blocks from you, so I should be there within a few minutes. Then you can tell me exactly what happened."

Rebecca ended the call. She drew in a deep breath and released it slowly. She felt her heart rate slow as she drew in another big breath. She slowly pushed to her feet.

"Let's go back inside," she told Roscoe.

Only a few minutes had passed, when she heard a car pull into the parking lot. She peeked through the window blinds and felt a wave of relief wash through her as Mitch stepped out of his car. She pulled the door open and watched him stride purposefully toward her. As soon as he reached her, he pulled her into a quick hug.

He stepped back. His eyes quickly scanned her face. "You're pale as a ghost," he commented.

"Yeah, well, I just got the life scared out of me," Rebecca commented dryly.

"Tell me what he did to threaten you," Mitch commanded. He wore a serious expression that was very different from his usual teasing one. His eyes had a hard edge and his jaw was set firmly.

He's in cop mode now, Rebecca thought. *I bet he can be pretty intimidating when he uses that expression on bad guys.*

"I was walking Roscoe outside. We were in that grassy area on the east side of the clinic. I heard a really loud muffler, so I looked toward the street. Dalton was driving very slowly in front of the clinic. He mouthed, 'you're dead' and raised his hand and pretended to shoot me. Then he hit the gas and drove away. Like I said, it was stupid of me to react the way I did. It's not like he pointed a real gun or anything."

"It was a threat and we should take it seriously, Rebecca. How did he even know you were here? He must have been following you. Maybe he just meant to scare you, but we know the guy is capable of violence. I don't want to take any chances."

Rebecca felt fear creeping back into her mind. "What are you suggesting?"

"Well, for one, you shouldn't come here by yourself anymore until we have him safely behind bars."

Rebecca's eyes widened. She shook her head in denial. "I have to come here to check on my patients. There's no reason for me to drag someone else along every time I come."

"It won't be for long. His trial is scheduled for a week from Monday. I'm sure that between Derrick and me, one of us will be able to come with you."

Rebecca met his gaze. She could see the determined glint in his eyes. She sighed. "All right, Derrick told me that he's working today. I'll call him tonight and ask him what days he's free. I'll call you and let you know what days he isn't available."

"When did you talk to Derrick?" Mitch asked curiously.

Rebecca hadn't realized that Mitch didn't know about their date the previous evening. She blushed slightly and said, "We had a date last night."

Mitch's face relaxed into a grin. He looked more like the easy-going Mitch she was used to. "It's about time. I'm guessing things went well."

Rebecca felt more heat rush into her cheeks. "Yes," she replied. Bringing the subject back to the problem at hand, she said, "Is there anything else I should do about Dalton?"

"Just make sure to keep your door locked and your eyes open. If you hear or see anything suspicious around your house, call me immediately."

Rebecca nodded. "I will," she promised. "I'll be glad when this whole thing is over."

"Were you almost done here?" Mitch asked.

"Yes, I just need to feed Roscoe and then take him back outside one more time before I leave," Rebecca replied.

Mitch glanced down at the dog who stood silently at Rebecca's side. "What's up with his skin?"

"He had a bad case of mange. Animal Control brought him in on Monday. He's doing much better now."

Mitch's eyebrows rose. "If this it better, I'd hate to have seen what he looked like before."

Rebecca chuckled. "He looked pretty hideous, but soon he'll be as handsome as he is sweet."

A half-hour later, Rebecca was ready to leave.

"What time are you coming back tonight?" Mitch asked.

"I'll come back twice, once around 4:00 to feed him and again around 9:00 to let him out one more time."

"I'll pick you up at your house at a quarter to 4:00. Derrick should be able to come back with you tonight."

"Okay," Rebecca replied. "I'll see you this afternoon."

~

Except for the few hours she and Captain spent at the hospital, Rebecca was a ball of nerves all afternoon. She had hoped to run into Derrick at the hospital, but she hadn't seen him when she peeked into the ER as she and Captain passed by. Mitch showed up right on time to go with her to Animal Friends to feed Roscoe. She still felt like having an escort was going a bit overboard, but it did make her feel better to have him there.

As soon as Mitch dropped her off, she called Derrick.

"Hello, Rebecca. I didn't expect to hear from you today."

"I had an incident at the clinic," she said.

"What kind of incident?" Derrick asked. His voice had taken on a hard edge.

Rebecca proceeded to tell him about what had happened earlier that morning.

"That son-of-a-bitch," Derrick growled into the phone. "He better pray I don't get my hands on him."

Rebecca's heart did a little somersault at the protective tone of Derrick's voice. "Mitch made me promise to have one of you with me each time I go into the clinic during non-business hours. I'm planning on going back tonight around 9:00. Would you be available to go with me?"

"I'll be there in 15 minutes," Derrick answered.

Rebecca checked her watch. "It's only 5:30. There's no reason for you to come now. I know you've been working all day."

"I don't like the idea of you being there by yourself, Rebecca. I'm coming over," Derrick answered curtly.

"Captain's here. He'll make sure no one bothers me."

"I said I'll be there in 15 minutes. Stop arguing. It won't do you any good." Derrick said, ending the call.

Rebecca sighed and leaned back against the sofa cushions. Her body hummed in anticipation of seeing Derrick again. Her heart warmed with the thought that he was so worried about her. As much as she didn't think it could be possible, it appeared as if everyone was right. Derrick Peterson did have feelings for her.

It seemed like only a few minutes had passed before she heard a car pull into her drive. Captain gave a quick bark and jumped off the sofa.

"It's okay, boy. It's just Derrick," Rebecca soothed.

She stood and started moving toward the front door. Suddenly, the window beside the door exploded. Rebecca screamed. She threw her arms up in front of her face. A brick bounced across the floor and came to rest at her feet. Captain barked furiously. Rebecca heard the sound of tires squealing as the car sped away from her house.

She was shaking violently. She stared down at the brick. It took a moment for her mind to process what had just happened. Captain stood beside her with hackles raised and teeth bared. He growled low in his throat.

"It's okay, Captain. It's all over," she said softly, reaching out to place her hand on his head. Her heart continued to pound in her chest.

A moment later, she heard a car pull into her drive. Panic flashed through her brain. She glanced out the broken window and almost collapsed with relief when she saw that it was Derrick. She threw open her front door and hurried outside. Captain followed on her heels.

Derrick saw Rebecca's terror-stricken face and leaped out of the car. He sprinted around the hood. His guts contracted into a tight knot.

"What's going on?" he asked as he reached her.

Rebecca stepped into him and wrapped her arms around his waist. He pulled her to him. He could feel her trembling.

"Rebecca, tell me what happened," he urged.

"Someone just threw a brick through my window. I'm sure it was Dalton. I heard a car pull up to the house. I thought it was you. Then the window exploded."

Derrick felt a shiver move through her. He rubbed her arms briskly. He tilted her head up, so that he could see her face. Her skin was ashen, and her cheeks were wet with tears. His blood boiled with rage. He wanted to kill the bastard for frightening Rebecca like that.

"Let's go inside," he said gruffly.

She nodded and turned toward the house. Derrick kept her firmly tucked against him as they walked. Glass crunched beneath their feet as they stepped over the threshold.

"I need to clean that up before Captain cuts his paw," Rebecca said softly.

Derrick went to pick up the brick that still lay on the floor. He turned it over and pulled out the piece of paper that was attached by a rubber band. "Watch your back, bitch," he read aloud.

Rebecca sucked in her breath. She knew that Dalton had to have been the one who'd thrown the brick, but the words still shocked her.

Derrick stepped back over to her and wrapped her in another hug. "You go get settled on the sofa. I'll clean this up. Just point me toward the broom."

Rebecca started to protest. "No arguing, Rebecca," Derrick said firmly.

"The broom and dustpan are in the pantry in the kitchen," she replied.

Derrick nodded. He released her and stepped toward the kitchen. Rebecca collapsed onto the sofa and Captain curled up beside her. She gently stroked his side. She could feel his muscles relax beneath her hand. She felt some of the tension leave her body in conjunction with his.

Rebecca watched as Derrick swept the broken glass into the dustpan. *It's a good thing I don't have that ugly shag carpet anymore,* she thought, grateful that Brian's crew had finished the floors before she'd fired them. It would have been a nightmare to get the glass out of it. She swiped at the tears that continued to roll down her cheeks. She hated that she had cried in front of Derrick, but she was very glad he was there.

A few minutes later, he stepped up to the sofa. "Move over," he commanded.

Rebecca pushed at Captain and scooted away from the arm of the sofa. Derrick sat down beside her. He put an arm around her shoulders and drew her into his side. Rebecca sighed as she felt herself relax against him.

"I'm glad you're here."

He kissed the top of her head. "Me, too."

He reached into his pocket and pulled out his cell phone. "I need to call Mitch and let him know what happened. They'll need to send someone out to look around."

"I guess you talked to Rebecca," Mitch said in greeting.

"I'm at her place now. Someone just threw a brick through her window," Derrick replied.

"Was it Dalton?" Mitch asked.

"She didn't see who did it, but you and I both know that he's the only logical choice."

"I'll call it in. There should be an officer there within a few minutes to take her statement. Can I talk to her?"

Derrick handed Rebecca the phone.

"Hi, Mitch," she greeted.

"Hi, Rebecca. How're you holding up?"

"I'm fine. He just scared me. This was even worse than this morning."

"Did you see anything that could help us pin this to Dalton?" Mitch asked.

"No, I didn't see anything."

"Hopefully, one of your neighbors saw something that will help us. His car is pretty distinct."

"Now that you mention it, the car that pulled up to the house wasn't Dalton's. The muffler was too quiet, but it had to be him," Rebecca replied.

"It was him. We just have to find a way to prove it. I'm on my way to interview a suspect in that robbery case I've been working on. Officers should be there within a few minutes. I'll have them fill me in on anything they find out from the neighbors."

"Okay. Thanks, Mitch." Rebecca handed the phone back to Derrick.

"We need to take this guy's threats seriously. I plan to drag him in for questioning and to try to persuade him that harassing Rebecca will be seriously dangerous to his health. In the meantime, I don't like the idea of her being alone. You're going to stay with her, right?" Mitch asked.

Derrick looked down at Rebecca's upturned face. "Yes," he replied tersely.

"Good. I'll let you know as soon as I find out anything."

Five minutes later, two uniformed police officers arrived. They introduced themselves as Officers Green and Travis. Rebecca told them everything that happened. They took the brick and note as evidence and left to question the neighbors.

Rebecca and Derrick sat together on the sofa. The television was on, but Rebecca was having a hard time focusing on anything they were saying. The day's events had stretched her nerves to the breaking point. She was anxious to hear whether or not one of her neighbors could identify who had thrown the brick.

About an hour later, the officers returned. "I'm sorry ma'am," Officer Green said apologetically, "but none of your neighbors saw anything that can help us. Maybe we'll get lucky and whoever it was left some evidence on the brick or note."

"Thank you," Rebecca replied.

The officers nodded and turned to leave. Rebecca closed the door behind them. She turned to Derrick. Her shoulders slumped in defeat.

"They're not going to find any fingerprints. Our only hope is that someone saw something," she said dejectedly.

"I want you to go pack a bag. You're going to come stay at my house until he's no longer a threat to you."

"What?" Rebecca asked incredulously.

"You heard me. There's no way in hell that I'm letting you stay here alone. The guy doesn't know where I live. You'll be safer at my place."

Rebecca crossed her arms and glared at Derrick defiantly. She didn't like the idea of him telling her what to do. She also didn't want to act like a coward and go into hiding. Derrick's face remained passive, but his eyes burned with intensity. Several tense moments of silence passed. Finally, Rebecca heaved a huge sigh and threw her hands up in defeat.

"All right," she relented. Then she stomped angrily down the hallway to her bedroom.

Derrick grinned. He was glad to see that she had her spunkiness back.

Several minutes later, Rebecca emerged from her bedroom carrying a suitcase. Derrick and Captain were lounging on the sofa watching television.

"It'll just take me a minute to get Captain's things together," she mumbled. She set her bag on the floor and moved into the kitchen.

"What can I help you with?" Derrick asked.

Rebecca swung around to see him leaning against the door jam. She hadn't realized he had followed her. During the time it had taken her to pack her bag, her anger at being ordered about had dissipated. She realized that he was right. It would be safer for her at his place. Besides, she would get to spend more time with him. Her stomach tightened at the thought of spending the night in his house.

"It just occurred to me that we need to board up the window. There's some plywood in the back left over from Brian's construction crew. If you grab the wood, I'll get a hammer and nails."

"No problem," Derrick replied.

Within minutes, Derrick had the board nailed across the window.

"I'll call that contractor I told you about tomorrow and see how soon he can get someone out here to replace the window," Derrick stated.

"Thank you," Rebecca replied.

They loaded her and Captain's things into Derrick's car and headed toward his house.

CHAPTER 20

As they drove toward Derrick's, Rebecca suddenly remembered Roscoe.

"Can we swing by Animal Friends, so that I can let Roscoe out to take care of business?" she asked.

"I forgot all about him," Derrick replied. "Should we drop Captain off at my place first?"

"No, I want to keep him with me. He was pretty terrified by what happened earlier. I don't want to drop him in a strange place and then turn around and leave him."

Derrick glanced sideways. "You've got a heart as big as Texas, you know that? Most people wouldn't have thought of that. Hell, after what you just went through, most people wouldn't be taking the time to go let a dog out to take a crap. They'd just let him do it in his cage and worry about it in the morning."

"I'd like to argue with you, but I've had enough first-hand experience with how most people treat animals to know that you're probably right," she acknowledged. "I think animals are a blessing and should be treated that way."

He grinned. "See, heart as big as Texas."

Rebecca rolled her eyes. "Well, I certainly wouldn't go that far."

They grew silent as they continued toward Animal Friends. Rebecca felt her eyes getting heavy. The adrenaline rush from the evening's excitement had finally worn off. She'd drifted into a light sleep by the time they reached the clinic. She opened her eyes when she felt the car come to a stop.

"Why don't you just stay here and rest. I can run in and get the dog," Derrick suggested.

Rebecca shook her head. "No, Roscoe is a sweetheart, but he's still a little nervous around strangers. I need to be the one to get him. Why don't you walk Captain?"

She got out of the car and opened the back door for Captain. He leaped out and stood next to her. He wagged his tail slowly. Every other time he'd come with her to the clinic, he'd danced with excitement and wagged his tail so hard his whole body shook. Rebecca knew that he was still fearful after the evening's scare.

She bent and gave him a reassuring hug. "I'm sorry, Captain. The night's almost over," she whispered in his ear. He gave a slight whimper. Rebecca stood and handed the end of his leash to Derrick. Then she pulled the keys to the clinic out of the pocket of her jeans and let them inside.

She flipped on the lights in the waiting room. "Wait here. I'll go get Roscoe," she instructed.

When she opened the ICU door, she stopped short. Roscoe stood in the middle of the room on top of a large pile of dog food. Apparently, he'd managed to escape his kennel and overturn the trash can they used to store the dog food. He glanced up at her and then went back to happily devouring the pile.

"How in the world did you get out of your kennel?" she asked, shaking her head in dismay.

She walked over to the cage and examined the latch. It didn't appear to be damaged. *I must not have closed it properly.*

She grabbed a leash of the hook that was just inside the ICU door and went to loop it around Roscoe's neck. "Come on, you big glutton. Let's go for a walk."

A few moments later, she returned to the waiting room with Roscoe in tow.

"That's one ugly dog," Derrick commented dryly.

Rebecca chuckled. "You shouldn't be so quick to judge. He may not be much to look at, but he's smart. He apparently figured out how to open his kennel. I found him back there blissfully eating food he'd spilled out of a trash can. Besides, once all his hair grows back, he'll be very handsome."

Derrick and Captain followed Rebecca and Roscoe outside. As they walked the dogs around the yard, Derrick thought about how much his impressions of Rebecca had changed since he'd first met her a few months ago. He'd thought she was plain and a little nuts. Now, he thought she was caring, smart, and sexy as hell. She was right, he shouldn't be so quick to judge. Maybe if he hadn't judged her so harshly in the beginning, it wouldn't have taken him so long to recognize how wonderful she was.

They walked the dogs around for about 15 minutes. Then Rebecca declared that Roscoe had had enough exercise to make it until morning.

When they got back inside, she heaved a big sigh. "Now to clean up the mess," she said wearily. "Put Captain in one of the exam rooms while I put Roscoe back in his kennel. Then we can scoop up all the food he spilled," she instructed.

Between the two of them, they made short work of the cleanup. By the time they loaded back into Derrick's car and resumed the trip to his place, Rebecca was completely exhausted.

A few minutes later, they pulled up to the curb in front of Derrick's house. As they walked up the porch steps, they could hear Trouble barking from inside the house.

"Speaking of dogs who need to be let out," he mumbled as he inserted a key into the lock.

As soon as he stepped into the house, Trouble jumped up and placed her paws on his chest. "Hi, girl," he greeted as he gave her an affectionate ear rub and then pushed her back down on all four paws.

Rebecca smiled when she observed this affectionate exchange. She was glad to see that Derrick and Trouble had bonded so well. She shouldn't be surprised, Derrick had a big heart, even if he tried to hide it. Apparently, Trouble had spotted it right away.

Trouble moved to Captain. The two dogs greeted each other with tails wagging. Within moments, they had decided they were friends. They began to dance playfully around each other.

"Come on," Derrick said. "Let's put them in the backyard, so they can get some of their first meeting excitement out of their systems."

Rebecca chuckled. "Good idea."

She and the dogs followed Derrick through the kitchen. Rebecca was impressed. The countertops were made of black granite, and the cabinets were a deep mahogany. An island stood in the middle of the kitchen with a rack of gourmet pans hanging above it. Rebecca noted that other than a few dishes resting in the sink, the kitchen was very tidy.

"Beautiful kitchen," she remarked.

Derrick glanced back. He lifted a shoulder in a half shrug. "I love to cook. It helps ease the tension after a long day at work."

Rebecca chuckled. "I usually take a long bath and then order takeout."

Derrick laughed and reached to open the back door. As soon as the door was wide enough for them to squeeze through, the dogs darted past him and began playfully chasing each other around the yard. Derrick and Rebecca stepped out onto a large wooden deck. They moved to lean against the railing. Rebecca stared into the darkness. The moon offered enough light for her to see the dogs' shadowed figures moving around the yard. She was happy to see that Captain seemed to have forgotten all about the events that occurred earlier that evening. She let out a tired sigh.

Derrick glanced toward her. Looking at her standing there bathed in soft moonlight, he suddenly felt the urge to hold her. He reached out and placed an arm around her waist. Then he lifted her chin to tilt her head back. He slowly bent and placed a gentle kiss on her lips. He felt the stirrings of desire and marveled at the fact that such a simple act could affect him so strongly.

He pulled back a few inches. Rebecca blinked and looked up at him. Her eyelids drooped with exhaustion. She leaned heavily against him. "You're about ready to collapse. Let me show you to the guest room."

She nodded in agreement. Her last remaining vestiges of energy seemed to be quickly evaporating. Derrick whistled for the dogs, and they stampeded onto the porch. Rebecca shuffled along beside him as he took her back inside. She barely noticed the rest of the house as Derrick led her down a hallway and into a bedroom. He moved her to the edge of the bed and pulled back the bedding. He gave her a light push, and she sat abruptly down. She was only half aware of him bending to take off her shoes. Then she felt him lift her legs and swing them onto the bed.

"Thank you," she mumbled as he pulled a blanket over her. Captain leaped onto the bed to join her. Within seconds, she was asleep.

Derrick stood at the edge of the bed staring down at her. He felt his heart swell with protectiveness. She looked so frail and innocent lying there. He reached out and brushed a strand of hair away from her face. Her eyelids fluttered, but they didn't open. He bent and placed a kiss on her forehead. Then he turned and strode out of the room.

He dialed Mitch's number.

"Well, did you find the bastard?" Derrick asked as soon as Mitch answered.

"Yeah, we found him. We tracked him down at his brother's apartment. He swears he was there all evening, and of course, everyone there backed him up. I threatened him, but I'm not sure I got through. The guy's an arrogant asshole. I'm not sure he's smart enough to know that he should be worried. He seems to think the law can't touch him."

Derrick cursed. "How dangerous do you think he really is?"

"Well, we already know he doesn't mind beating up women. I also suspect that he and his brother are mixed up in some illegal activities. I'm digging around to see if I can find out how they could come up with his bail money so quickly," Mitch answered. "How's Rebecca doing? Is she with you?"

"She's asleep in the guest room," Derrick answered.

"Good. Dalton's trial is scheduled for a week from Monday. Rebecca will be safe once he's behind bars."

~

The next morning, Rebecca sat up and looked around the unfamiliar bedroom in confusion. It took her a few moments to remember where she was. As the fog of sleep lifted, her stomach growled. She became aware of a delicious aroma filling the room. She inhaled deeply. *Mmm. Sausage, eggs, and coffee,* she thought as she identified the mixture of smells.

She swung her legs over the side of the bed. Captain leaped off and ran to the door.

"I'm coming," Rebecca said with a yawn. "Hold your horses."

She shuffled toward the door and pulled it open. Captain raced down the hallway. She heard Derrick greet him and then let him outside. When Rebecca came around the corner, he looked up from the stove.

As he took in her disheveled appearance, his mouth spread into a wide smile. "Good morning," he greeted warmly.

"Morning," she answered groggily. "The food smells delicious."

"It's almost ready. Help yourself to a cup of coffee," he said, nodding toward the coffee maker. "Mugs are in the cabinet directly above the pot. Sugar and creamer are on the table."

"I like it black," she replied. Rebecca walked over to the cabinet, pulled out a mug, and filled it with coffee. Then she took a seat on one of the barstools pushed up against the island. Derrick stood with his back to her. He wore a pair of worn jeans and a black T-shirt. *Not only is the man brilliant, he's got a great ass,* she thought admiringly. A few seconds later, he turned toward her holding a plate in each hand. He placed one in front of her and slid onto the seat next to her.

Rebecca looked down at the plate and groaned hungrily at the sight of the fluffy omelet and golden-brown sausage links.

"Did you sleep okay?" he asked.

"Like a rock," she answered around a mouthful of sausage.

"Good," he answered. "So, do you have anything planned for today?"

Rebecca nodded. She swallowed and answered, "I'm meeting my mom, June, and Marilyn at a bakery to taste some cakes. June's got to pick one today, so they have time to make it before the wedding on Saturday. It's the last thing on the list. I can't believe we're going to pull this off. It usually takes months to plan a wedding, and we're getting it done in three weeks."

She took a bite of omelet. "My goodness, this is the best omelet I've ever tasted," she said, genuinely impressed. *Add great cook to his list of attributes,* she thought.

Derrick grinned. "I'm glad you like it. What time are you supposed to be at the bakery?"

"10:00," she answered.

"You'd better get a move on. It's after 9:00."

"What? Really?" she asked in shock. She couldn't remember the last time she'd slept past 7:00. She glanced at the clock on the microwave. "Crap, I still need to go feed Roscoe." She hurriedly finished eating the rest of her breakfast and then rushed back to the spare bedroom to change and freshen up.

Derrick cleaned up the dishes and then fed the dogs while Rebecca got ready to go. Within a few minutes, she returned to the kitchen.

"After we go by the clinic, you can just drop me off at the bakery. One of the girls will bring me back after we're done. You won't need to stay. I'm sure you can think of better ways to spend a Sunday morning."

"Okay," Derrick agreed. "The only thing on my agenda today is to mow the lawn. I'll be here whenever you finish up."

When they got to the vet clinic, Roscoe was waiting just inside the door. "You ornery dog," Rebecca chuckled, coming down on her knees to give him an ear rub. "I don't know how you're getting out. It's a good thing I secured the food last night."

She went back to the ICU to grab a leash. She checked the kennel, but she still couldn't see how Roscoe was managing to escape. She took him for a quick walk and then placed him back inside the kennel. This time she shut the ICU door, so that if he got out again, he wouldn't have the run of the clinic. She didn't want him getting into something that could harm him. By the time she'd finished, it was after 10:00.

"We'd better hurry. If I'm too late, my mom will call in the cavalry."

Derrick chuckled. "We should be there in about 10 minutes. Should you call her?"

Rebecca shook her head. "No, that would lead to a series of questions that it will be better to answer in person."

Derrick nodded. "I see your point."

She was 15 minutes late by the time they reached the bakery.

"I'll see you in a couple of hours," she said as she got out of his car. She turned toward the bakery and saw three familiar faces staring at her through the big store window. She squared her shoulders and steeled herself in preparation for the barrage of questions she was about to be bombarded with.

As soon as she stepped through the door, Barbara asked, "Was that Derrick?"

Rebecca nodded.

"Did you spend the night with him?" Marilyn asked with excitement.

"Yes, but not in the way you mean. I slept in his guest room."

"What on earth for?" Barbara asked incredulously.

"It's a really long story. Can we help June pick a cake and then finish the 20 questions?"

"No," all three women answered in unison.

"We couldn't possibly concentrate on picking a cake until we've had our curiosity satisfied," Barbara said.

"All right. Can we at least sit down?" Rebecca asked.

"Of course," answered June. "That's our table over there." She gestured toward a large round table covered with an assortment of small cakes.

After they were seated, Rebecca told them about the events of the previous day and why she was temporarily living in Derrick's guest room.

"I'm absolutely furious with you," Barbara said tersely. "Why didn't you call me? I'm your mother. If someone threatens you, I should not find out about it the next day."

Rebecca dropped her eyes to the table. "I'm sorry, Mom. You're right. I should have called you. By the time I got to Derrick's, I was so exhausted I was barely functioning."

"I want to know what Mitch is doing about this," Marilyn put in.

"There isn't much he can do. There weren't any witnesses to either event. It's just my word against his."

"How do you feel about all this?" June asked.

"I'll admit, yesterday, I was badly shaken. Nothing like that has ever happened to me before. But honestly, I think he was just making empty threats. I'm sure everything's going to be fine."

"I agree with Derrick and Mitch. You need to have someone with you at all times until he's locked up. It's better to be overly cautious," Barbara commented.

"I agree. I don't like it, but you're right," Rebecca replied. "Now, can we get on with the cake tasting?"

They spent the next hour choosing a cake. After trying several different flavors, they settled for a simple chocolate cake with almond buttercream frosting.

Marilyn insisted on being the one to drive Rebecca back to Derrick's. She was dying with curiosity to see where he lived. "So, how are things between you and Mr. Hunk?" Marilyn asked on the drive.

"We had a great date Friday night. He was incredibly sweet last night. Then this morning he made me the best omelet I've ever eaten. So, I guess things are going well. With everything that happened this weekend, it's hard to think about romance." Rebecca answered.

"Well, you're going to get to know him pretty well if you're going to be living with him for a week."

Rebecca chuckled. "There's nothing like diving right into the fire."

A few minutes later, they pulled up to Derrick's house. Marilyn let out a low whistle. "Hubba, Hubba," she said appreciatively.

Derrick was mowing his front lawn. He was shirtless. His chest and arm muscles rippled with strength as he pushed the lawn mower. Sweat glistened across his tanned skin. Rebecca's mouth went dry. Blood pounded in her ears. She fought to catch her breath. *He's magnificent*, she thought.

He spotted the car and cut the lawn mower's engine. He lifted his arm and waved. He turned and grabbed a shirt off a nearby bush, quickly pulled it over his head, and jogged toward them.

"Too bad," Marilyn commented.

When he reached the car, he opened Rebecca's door. He offered her a hand and helped her out of the car.

"Hi, Marilyn. Thanks for bringing her back. Would you like to come inside for a glass of lemonade?"

"No thanks. I've got to get home. I promised Emma some afternoon mother-daughter time."

"Maybe next time," Derrick commented as he swung the door closed.

Rebecca was grateful for the exchange between Derrick and Marilyn. It gave her time to compose herself. She had her racing heart back under control by the time Derrick turned to her and asked, "So, were you successful?"

It took her a moment to comprehend the question. "Oh, yeah, we settled on chocolate," she finally answered.

Derrick grinned. "Do you mind if I finish up out here?" he asked.

She shook her head. "By all means, don't mind me."

"Feel free to help yourself to some lemonade. It's in the fridge."

"Thanks. It's such a beautiful day. I think I'll drink it out on your deck."

"I should be done here in a few minutes. Then I'll shower and join you."

CHAPTER 21

Derrick dropped into the chair next to Rebecca. "I called Terry Olson, the contractor, while you were cake testing. He said he could stop by your house on Monday to take a look at the window and see what needs to be done to finish up your kitchen. He seemed like a good guy."

"What time did he want to meet?"

"He said he could be there at 6:30 tomorrow night. I figured that would give me enough time to pick you up at the clinic and drive you over there. Does that work for you?"

In the past, when anyone had tried to step in and take over things in her life, she'd become angry and defensive, feeling as if they were saying that she couldn't handle it on her own. Being independent and self-reliant had always been very important to her. She was surprised to find that she only felt gratitude towards Derrick. She smiled. "Sounds good. Thank you for calling him."

Derrick returned her smile. "No problem. Glad to do it. Now, about dinner, I hope you're not too full of cake, because I also stopped by the store and picked up some steaks to cook for us tonight."

"If you cook steak as well as you make an omelet, then I'll make room."

Derrick chuckled. "I'll do my best not to disappoint."

They spent the afternoon sitting on the porch in quiet conversation. Rebecca learned that Derrick and Mitch had been the starting guards on Spring Valley's state winning basketball team. They discovered that Rebecca had been in the eighth grade that year. Mitch and Derrick had been seniors. They laughed about the way Mr. Snider, the history teacher, had fallen asleep every day in class and about how, Ms. Tillman, the literature teacher had the habit of snorting loudly when she laughed. Rebecca told Derrick about how she'd missed her senior prom because she'd come down with a bad case of mono. He told her that Mitch had insisted that he go to the prom. They'd double dated with two cheerleaders. Mitch had been crowned Prom King, which, Derrick said, only inflated his already overly large ego.

Finally, Derrick announced that it was time for him to start preparing dinner. He declined Rebecca's offer to help, so she grabbed a couple of tennis balls and went out into the yard to play fetch with the dogs.

Derrick disappeared into the house. Several minutes later, he returned to the porch to light the grill. He heard Rebecca laugh joyfully. He glanced into the yard and felt a warm glow ignite in his heart at the sight of her interacting with the dogs. He'd always rejected the idea of joining his life with someone else's, but as he stood there watching Rebecca, he couldn't believe how right it felt to have her there with him.

When dinner was ready, Derrick called Rebecca inside. He'd prepared a spinach salad, steamed broccoli, steak, and Italian bread.

"It smells wonderful," Rebecca commented as she stepped inside.

"What would you like to drink? I've got beer, soda, lemonade, or water."

"Beer, please," Rebecca responded as she took a seat on one of the barstools.

Derrick reached into the refrigerator and pulled out two beers. He handed one to Rebecca and then slid onto the barstool next to her.

Rebecca took her first bite of steak. "Okay, it's official. You're an incredible cook."

Derrick grinned. He'd been complimented for his culinary skills before, but it was especially gratifying to hear it from Rebecca. "I'm glad you think so," he replied.

When they'd finished their meal, Rebecca said, "I need to go check on Roscoe one last time."

They quickly cleaned up the kitchen and then headed toward Animal Friends. When Rebecca opened the door to the ICU, Roscoe leaped up on her.

"Out again, are you?" Rebecca chuckled as she reached for a leash and slipped it around his neck. He half dragged her to the front door in his eagerness to get outside.

"Apparently, he really needs to go," Rebecca called over her shoulder as she and Roscoe hurried past Derrick. He laughed softly and followed them outside.

They walked Roscoe around for about 15 minutes and then returned to Derrick's house. When they got inside, they moved to the sofa to watch some TV. Derrick sat on one end and Rebecca sat pressed against him. Captain immediately leaped up and settled next to Rebecca. Trouble placed a paw on Derrick's knee and let out a soft whimper. She looked up at Derrick with pleading eyes. Her spot had been taken by Rebecca.

Derrick chuckled and said, "Guess we should shift down and give her some room."

Rebecca grinned and pushed Captain further down the length of the sofa. As soon as there was an inch of available space, Trouble jumped up and squeezed herself onto the other side of Derrick. It was a tight fit, but they made it work. The four of them snuggled cozily on the sofa for the next hour. Derrick was struck again at how much he was enjoying having Rebecca there with him. Usually, he couldn't wait for whatever woman he'd had over to leave. He had certainly never cuddled with any of them on the sofa.

He felt Rebecca's weight shift slightly. He glanced down and saw that she'd fallen asleep. He studied her face. Her nose was slightly upturned at the end. A row of tiny freckles marched across the bridge. Even in sleep, there was a stubborn set to her jaw. The warm glow he'd felt in his heart when he'd watched her earlier burned a little brighter. He realized that he was precariously close to losing his heart altogether.

He slid an arm around her back and another under her knees. He stood, effortlessly lifting her with him. Her eyes fluttered open. They widened in surprise. "Did I fall asleep?" she asked.

"Yep," he replied.

"Why didn't you just wake me up?"

"Because this is more fun. I told you once before how much guys like to carry pretty girls around in their arms."

He started moving down the hallway. He slowed slightly as they passed by the door to his room. He briefly thought about taking her to his bed. Then he quickly dismissed the idea. It was too soon. They'd only just begun to get to know each other. He didn't want to rush things.

Rebecca felt his steps slow. Her eyes flew to his face. She saw his indecision. She also knew the moment he'd made up his mind. She felt an odd mixture of relief and disappointment when he continued down the hall.

He carried her into her room. He released her legs, so that she could stand, but he didn't let go of her. He gazed down into her face. She could see the passion burning in his eyes. His eyes dropped to her lips. They parted slightly as she sucked in a quick breath. Her heart fluttered in her chest. She wanted him to kiss her more than she'd ever wanted anything. The memory of the last kiss they'd shared flashed through her mind, and she suddenly felt like she was on fire.

Slowly, he lowered his mouth to hers. She moaned with pleasure as soon as their lips met. She felt her knees go weak. She grabbed his arms for support. He slipped his arms around her and pulled her tightly against him. Her fingers tingled with the desire to touch him. She slid her hands under his T-shirt. She felt his muscles tighten as her hands made contact with his skin. She softly ran her hands up his back, loving the feel of his firm muscles beneath her fingertips.

Suddenly, he broke off the kiss. They leaned into each other, both breathing hard. It was tough to tell if the pounding she heard in her ear was his heart or hers.

He gave a soft chuckle, "Much more of that, and I wouldn't have been able to stop."

"I'm not sure I wanted you to," Rebecca answered.

He groaned. "This is all really new to me, Rebecca. I've never felt like this before. I'm a love 'em and leave 'em man. But with you, it's different. I don't want to mess it up by moving too fast."

"I understand," she said.

He chuckled. "Do you? I'm not sure I do."

She pulled back and rose up on her toes to place a chaste kiss on his cheek. "Good night, Derrick."

He dropped his arms to his sides. "Good night," he replied. He turned on his heel and strode from the room, closing the door softly behind him.

A moment later, she heard Captain scratch at the door. Rebecca sighed and went to let him in. He ran across the room and leaped onto the bed. She shook her head. *Not quite the same as having Derrick there, but at least I won't be sleeping alone*, she thought wryly.

Derrick went into his room and took a cold shower. It only mildly cooled the desire coursing through him. As he lay in bed, images of Rebecca's naked body lying beneath his kept flashing through his mind. No matter how hard he tried to turn the images off, they refused to leave. Several times, he fought the urge to return to her room. He barely slept. He was relieved when morning finally arrived.

"Good morning," he greeted Rebecca when she shuffled into the kitchen. By the size of the bags under her eyes, it appeared as if she hadn't slept any better than he had.

"Morning," she mumbled.

"Hope you like French toast," he said, turning back to the skillet.

"I adore it," she answered as she went to the coffee pot and poured herself a steaming cup. She sat on one of the barstools and carefully sipped at the coffee. She could feel herself reviving as the warm liquid made its way into her stomach. She sighed.

"Better?" he asked in an amused tone.

Rebecca glanced up to find Derrick grinning at her. "Much," she answered. "Thanks to you I could barely sleep a wink last night."

Derrick was surprised by her bluntness. "If it makes you feel any better, I didn't sleep much myself."

"Well, I say we don't kiss like that again until we're ready to close the deal," she said.

He chuckled. "Close the deal? You make it sound like a real estate transaction."

She blushed. Now that she was more awake, she was completely embarrassed by the conversation. "Oh, you know what I mean."

Derrick was completely charmed by her. One minute she's blaming him for getting her too aroused for sleep and the next she's blushing like a school girl.

After they'd eaten breakfast, Derrick drove Rebecca to Animal Friends. He walked her inside and stayed until June arrived.

"I get off at 5:00. I'll come straight here to get you. I'll call if I get hung up. June, will you make sure and stay with her until I can get here?" he asked.

"No problem," June replied.

As soon as he left, June asked, "So, how's living with Derrick going?"

"I just saw you yesterday. Nothing's changed since then," Rebecca replied.

"You haven't slept with him yet?"

"No," Rebecca said with a slight edge to her voice.

"Do I detect a little frustration on that point?" June asked in amusement.

Rebecca sighed. "He wants to take it slow. Usually, that's my line. Part of me agrees with him, but another part of me wishes he would rip my clothes off and have his way with me."

June threw her head back and laughed. "I'm sure he won't be able to resist you for much longer."

Jimmy sauntered into the waiting area. "What's so funny?" he asked.

Rebecca blushed. "Nothing," she said quickly. She flashed June a 'don't you dare' look. June raised her eyebrows and placed a hand on her chest in a 'who me?' gesture. Rebecca sighed with relief.

"Sounded like something to me," Jimmy responded, glancing back and forth between the two women. Seeing that they weren't going to enlighten him, he turned around and went back into the treatment area.

The day passed quickly. It was a typically busy Monday. She performed several routine surgeries and gave a ton of vaccines. She also had to euthanize one of her long-time patients, which always left her feeling melancholy.

A little after 5:00, her cell phone rang. It was Derrick.

"Hi," she answered.

"I'm sorry, but I'm going to have to pull another half a shift. Dr. Shumaker's wife is having an emergency c-section. I called Mitch, and he said he could be at the clinic by 6:00. I told him about the contractor, so he knows you need to swing by your place."

Rebecca felt a little disappointed that they wouldn't be spending the evening together. "What time do you think you'll get home?"

"It will be close to midnight," he said.

"Okay, I guess I'll see you in the morning, then."

"Yeah. I'll still plan on taking you to work."

After she ended the call, she turned to June. "Derrick's pulling another half shift at the hospital. Mitch'll be here around 6:00 to pick me up. I really don't think you need to stay. I'd only be by myself for about half an hour."

"I told Derrick that I'd stay. It won't bother me in the least to hang around a few extra minutes."

Rebecca was giving Roscoe his evening walk when Mitch pulled into the parking lot. He jumped out of the car and strode toward her. His mouth was stretched into a wide grin.

"Looks like I get to be the lucky man to spend the evening with you tonight," he said in greeting.

"Yep. Can you cook as well as Derrick?" she asked playfully.

"Not even close. How about Chinese takeout?"

"Perfect," she answered.

He glanced down at Roscoe. "It's only been two days since I last saw him, but it looks like he's grown back more of his hair. He doesn't look nearly as ugly."

Rebecca bent and gave Roscoe a hug. "Don't listen to him, Roscoe. You're a great looking dog."

Mitch leaned down and rubbed Roscoe on the ear. "Sorry, buddy. I didn't know you were one of those sensitive types."

Rebecca chuckled and straightened back up. "Let me put him up and tell June she doesn't have to play babysitter any longer."

Mitch followed her into the clinic. "Hi, beautiful," Mitch greeted June.

"Hello, you handsome devil," June replied.

"Are you all set for the big day?" Mitch asked.

"Yep, everything's done but the 'I do's'."

"Now that your relief is here, you're free to go," Rebecca cut in.

June shook her head. "You always act like it's such a big chore for anyone to do you a favor, Rebecca. Your friends care about you, and we really don't mind doing things for you."

Rebecca smiled. "I know. I just don't like putting anyone out on my account. Thank you for staying. I'll see you tomorrow." She moved to put Roscoe back in his cage.

June grabbed her purse and came around the counter. As she passed Mitch, she paused and said, "Take good care of her, Mitch. She's priceless."

Mitch nodded. "I know," he replied.

When Rebecca joined him, he said, "Derrick mentioned that you had a contractor who was meeting you at 6:30. If we're going to make it on time, we'd better get a move on."

They pulled into her drive at 6:35. A beat-up blue Nissan pickup was parked in front of her house. A burly, silver-haired man wearing scuffed work boots, faded jeans, and a stained red T-shirt stepped out of the truck. He walked across the lawn to meet them.

"Rebecca Miller?" he asked as soon as she exited Mitch's car.

"Yes, and you must be Terry Olson."

He nodded.

"This is Mitch Holt," she said, gesturing toward Mitch.

He and Mitch exchanged a brief handshake. Then he turned his gaze back to Rebecca. "I hear you had a little trouble a few days ago and need a window replaced."

"That's right. I also have a kitchen renovation job that's half finished."

"Let me take a look," Terry responded.

They walked up to the porch. Terry stopped in front of the boarded window. "I can put the new window in the day after tomorrow. I can stop by and do it before I head out to the job I'm working on," he stated.

Rebecca grinned. "Great!" She unlocked the door and led them inside.

Terry walked into the kitchen and slowly looked over what had been done. "The workmanship is good," he commented. "At least you weren't getting cheated."

"No, not as far as the work was concerned anyway," Rebecca said dryly.

Terry gave her a quizzical glance, but didn't try to get her to elaborate. "It'll be about two weeks before I can get to the kitchen, but I could definitely finish it for you. I can take some measurements when I put in the window. Then I can give you an estimate on how much it will cost to finish the job. Most of the work's been done already."

Rebecca nodded. "That sounds wonderful."

"Will 6:30 Wednesday morning be too early for you?" Terry asked.

"No, that will be perfect," Rebecca answered.

After she and Mitch left her house, they stopped in and grabbed some Chinese takeout.

"How are we going to get into Derrick's house?" Rebecca asked.

Mitch grinned mischievously. "I'm a cop. You don't think I know a thing or two about breaking into homes?"

Rebecca laughed. "Seriously?" she asked.

"No," he replied. "I have a key. Derrick and I exchanged them years ago."

A few minutes later, they arrived at Derrick's. Sure enough, Mitch had a key and was able to let them in. Rebecca released Trouble and Captain into the yard.

"Those two seem to have adjusted quickly to living together. Have you and Derrick been able to make a similarly fast transition?"

"It's been surprisingly easy. Neither one of us has experience living with someone else, but we seem to have settled in pretty well. It's only been a couple of days. We're bound to step on each other's toes at some point."

Mitch smiled. "I'm glad things are going well. You're good for him, you know."

"You think so?" Rebecca asked.

He nodded. "I do."

Just then, Mitch's phone rang. Rebecca began setting out the food while he took the call. He moved into the living room. She could hear his muffled voice, but couldn't understand what he was saying.

A few minutes later, he walked back into the kitchen. "Dalton's been arrested," he said.

"What?!" she asked incredulously.

"When Dalton and his brother came up with his bail money so fast, I arranged for some surveillance on them. I had a suspicion that they were into something illegal. I thought they might even be involved in the robberies that I've been investigating. It turns out, they were running a chop shop. My guys spotted them stealing a car and followed them to an abandoned warehouse. When they raided the building, Dalton and his brother opened fire. Dalton's brother was shot and killed. Dalton surrendered. There won't be any bail this time."

Rebecca slid onto a barstool. "Wow, that's a lot to take in," she said. "I'm glad that this mess is over. I'm especially happy that Kara won't need to keep looking over her shoulder. I assume you need to go take care of this."

He nodded. "Do you want me to call Derrick?" he asked.

She shook her head. "No, I can call him. Now that Dalton's off the streets, there's really no reason for me to stay here. Would you have time to drop me at my house on your way to the station? I can get my car and then come back here to collect Captain and my things."

"Sure," he replied. "It's on the way, but I'm sure Derrick won't mind if you stay here one more night."

"No, this way he won't have to get up so early in the morning to take me to work. This will be much better. Let me just put the food in the fridge, and I'll be ready to go."

CHAPTER 22

As soon as Rebecca got home, she tried calling Derrick. She was disappointed when he didn't answer his cell phone. She guessed that he must be tied up with patients. She left a voicemail telling him that Dalton had been arrested, and she had moved back to her house. She asked him to call when he got the message.

She decided to deliver the news to Kara and Jimmy personally. She knew they'd both been worried sick that Dalton would try to come after Kara. She drove to their apartment and climbed the stairs to the third floor. She was slightly winded by the time she stopped in front of their door. She'd never been inside the apartment before, but she'd given Jimmy a ride home a few months ago when his car had refused to start.

She looked around for a doorbell. Not seeing one, she raised her hand and knocked sharply on the door. She could hear voices inside the apartment. A few minutes later, the door opened enough to allow the person on the other side to peer through a crack. A heavy chain secured the door.

"Dr. Miller! What are you doing here?" Jimmy asked in stunned amazement.

Rebecca smiled in amusement at the surprised look on his face. "May I come in?" she asked.

"Oh, sure," Jimmy answered. He pushed the door closed, and Rebecca could hear the chain slide away. Then a moment later, he swung the door wide.

A small head covered in dark curly hair popped out from behind Jimmy's legs. A young boy was using Jimmy as a shield. Rebecca smiled down at him. He buried his face in the backs of Jimmy's knees.

"It's okay, Trevor. This is my boss, Dr. Miller. She's nice," Jimmy said to the boy. Then he glanced back up at Rebecca. "Trevor's Kara's son. He's three."

Rebecca nodded. "Hi, Trevor," she said, grinning down at him. Then she looked back up and asked, "Is Kara here?"

"Yeah. She's already gone to bed. She hasn't been sleeping well. She kept fallin' asleep on the couch, and I finally told her to go on to bed, and I'd take care of getting Trevor down for the night. We were just about to read a bedtime story." He paused. Cocking his head to the side, he asked quizzically, "So, what's goin' on, Doc? Do you have some news for us?"

Rebecca nodded.

"If it couldn't wait until tomorrow at work, it must be serious," Jimmy guessed. "Let me go get Kara."

"Please do," Rebecca replied. "She's going to want to hear this."

Jimmy scooped Trevor into his arms and disappeared into the kitchen. Rebecca heard him knock on a door followed by a muffled reply. She looked around the meager apartment. She stood in a small living room. The furniture consisted of a worn sofa and mismatched recliner. A small TV sat on a stack of milk crates that were being used as a makeshift entertainment center. A card table and four folding chairs took up one corner of the living room. Rebecca guessed they served as the dining set. The kitchen was separated from the living room by an open entryway. Most of the kitchen was blocked from view. Although the space was small, it was tidy.

A few moments later, she heard Jimmy's footsteps returning to the living room.

"Make yourself comfortable," he said, gesturing toward the sofa. "Want anything to drink?" he asked.

"No, thank you, Jimmy. I won't take up much of your time. I just knew you would want to hear this news in person."

Kara appeared in the kitchen doorway. Dark circles ringed her eyes. She looked like she'd lost several pounds. Her hair was no longer spiked like it had been when Rebecca first met her. It was now cut into a short bob. Her face was also clear of any makeup or piercings. Rebecca noted that she was really a very pretty girl.

Kara stood stiffly with her arms crossed over her chest in a defensive posture. She appeared as apprehensive as a cornered cat. She eyed Rebecca warily.

Wanting to ease Kara's obvious anxiety, Rebecca blurted out, "Dalton's been arrested."

"What?!" Jimmy asked. "What did he do?"

Rebecca saw Kara's muscles relax as she sagged against the door jam. Rebecca smiled. "Why don't we sit down, and I'll tell you all about it," she suggested.

Rebecca sat on the sofa. Kara walked across the room and joined her. Jimmy pulled up one of the folding chairs and quickly sat. Rebecca spent the next few minutes explaining how Dalton and his brother had been caught operating a chop shop. She told them about the shootout and that Dalton's brother had been killed.

"I knew Dalton had to be into something illegal," Kara said. "He was constantly sneaking out at night and was always really secretive about where he was goin'."

"Apparently, my friend, Mitch, thought so too. That's why he had them under surveillance," Rebecca replied.

Suddenly, Jimmy let out a loud whoop and pumped his fist into the air. "I hope they throw away the key," he said, his voice full of excitement.

Rebecca grinned. "I'm with you on that one."

"Do you really think it's over?" Kara asked in a stunned whisper.

Rebecca nodded. "Yes. They shot a police officer. He'll be locked away for a long time."

Kara's eyes began to sparkle. Then tears started streaming down her face. Rebecca enveloped her in a warm hug. She held her for several minutes. Finally, Kara pulled back and said, "Thank you for letting us know, Dr. Miller. I don't know how to thank you for everything you've done for me. You've been great."

Rebecca wiped at the moisture in her own eyes. "I'm just glad it's over," she said. "I won't keep you guys any longer. I've got to go let Roscoe out for his nightly walk. I'll see you at work tomorrow, Jimmy."

~

Mitch spent almost three hours interviewing Dalton. He discovered that Dalton's older brother had been the mastermind behind their chop shop operation. He found buyers for the parts they got after disassembling the stolen vehicles. Dalton's job was simple; find a nice car, steal it, bring it to the shop, and scrap it. He couldn't really tell Mitch much about who the buyers were or how his brother contacted them. Initially, Mitch thought that Dalton was lying about not having any useful information, but the more he talked with him, the more convinced he became that Dalton was telling the truth. He was too stupid to be trusted with any of the business details.

As Mitch exited the interview room, he wearily ran a hand over his face. Then he checked his watch. It was a little after 9:00. The three hours he'd spent with Dalton had been exhausting. Between Dalton's lack of intelligence and his periodic breakdowns over the loss of his brother, the interview had pushed Mitch's patience to the breaking point. However, he was extremely relieved that Rebecca wouldn't need to worry about Dalton any longer. The officer who had been shot was in stable condition and should make a full recovery. Add shooting a police officer to Dalton's list of crimes and the man was going to be put away for a long time.

~

Rebecca was two blocks away from Animal Friends when suddenly, she heard a loud pop. Her car jumped and then pulled to the right. This was followed by a terrible grinding noise. She slowed the car to a crawl and pulled into the parking lot of a dental office. It was well after the office's business hours, so the lot was empty. She got out and slowly walked around the car searching for the source of the problem.

"Well, crap," she muttered when she saw that her right front tire had been shredded. "Guess I'm changing a tire."

The streetlights offered plenty of illumination. She walked to the back of the car and popped the trunk. She lifted the carpet and plywood off the spare tire. It took her a few minutes to loosen the screws that secured the tire to the trunk. Then she pulled the tire out of the car. As soon as it hit the pavement, she knew it was going to be of no use to her. It was completely flat.

"Double crap," she growled in frustration. Heaving an exasperated sigh, she tossed the tire back into the trunk. She decided to walk to Animal Friends and call her mom to come get her. She'd worry about having the tire repaired in the morning.

She started walking and called her mom.

"Rebecca, is everything all right?" Barbara asked, concern in her voice.

"Yes. I'm fine, but my car's got a flat. The spare's flat, too."

"Where are you?"

"I'm on my way to the clinic to take Roscoe for a walk. I was only a few blocks away when the tire blew, so I'm just walking the rest of the way. Could you come pick me up?"

"Sure, but isn't Derrick with you?"

Rebecca had forgotten that she hadn't told her mom the news.

"Derrick had to pull an extra shift at the hospital, so Mitch came to stay with me. A few minutes after he got there, he got a call telling him that Dalton had been arrested."

"That's great!" Barbara exclaimed. "I've been so worried about you."

"To be honest, I was a little worried myself," Rebecca replied. "We can talk about it more when you get to the clinic."

"Okay, I'm on my way."

A few minutes later, Rebecca arrived at Animal Friends. She walked across the parking lot and pulled her keys out of her pocket. As she unlocked the door, she heard a thud come from inside. *Roscoe must be out again*, she thought ruefully. A second later, Roscoe started barking hysterically. *Wonder why he's so upset*, she thought as she stepped into the clinic.

She flipped on the waiting room lights and hurried toward the ICU. Roscoe continued to bark furiously.

"It's okay, Roscoe. I'm coming," she called, feeling uneasy about his unusual behavior.

Her apprehension intensified as she walked into the treatment area. Roscoe was snarling and slamming his body against the closed ICU door. Suddenly, she was jerked backwards as someone grabbed her from behind. She started to scream, but a gloved hand quickly covered her mouth. Another arm snaked around her waist holding both arms to her sides in a strong grip. Rebecca twisted against the restraining arms.

Her heart pounded in her ears. She fought for breath as the hand pressed tightly against her mouth. She felt herself begin to panic. Her movements became frantic. One of her arms slipped free. She quickly jabbed an elbow into her assailant's midsection. She felt a spurt of satisfaction when she heard the man grunt. She slammed her heel down hard on his booted foot. He took a small jump sideways, but didn't break his hold on her. She quickly brought both feet up off the ground, planted them on the side of the treatment table, and shoved with all her might.

The man stumbled backwards, slamming into a counter. Rebecca felt his arms loosen their hold. She threw herself against the loosened arms and slipped from his grasp. She let out a sharp cry of pain as she was suddenly jerked backwards by her hair. Her hands flew up to claw at the hand who held her in its grip. Tears sprang into her eyes as the man savagely twisted her hair.

She flailed her arms wildly, blindly reaching for anything that might help her. Her arm skimmed across the top of the treatment counter. She felt a moment of elation as her hand closed around a pair of scissors.

She gripped the scissors tightly and shoved her arm backwards. She felt the scissors sink into flesh. The man howled in pain. He let go of her hair as he grabbed at the scissors embedded in his thigh.

"I'm gonna kill you for that, bitch," he growled.

Rebecca scrambled away as the man pulled the scissors out of his leg. Roscoe continued to throw himself against the ICU door. *If I can just reach the door and let him out,* she thought desperately.

She lunged toward the door. Her hand closed around the doorknob. As she started to twist, a heavy weight slammed into her back, knocking her to the floor. Her head stuck the tiled surface. She felt bile rise in her throat as pain exploded behind her eyes. The man pushed himself off her. He kicked her in the ribs. Rebecca felt them crack as blinding pain burst through her. Then he brought his foot up and stomped down on her back.

After delivering a few more kicks, he flipped her over and came down to straddle her midsection. He started ruthlessly punching her in the face. She bucked against him, but he was too heavy for her movements to have any effect. Her vision blurred as the punches kept coming. She felt herself losing consciousness.

Suddenly, she heard a fierce growl, followed shortly by the man's cry of pain. She felt his weight leave her. She blinked rapidly, trying to clear the fog from her brain. Her vision cleared enough for her to see Roscoe sink his teeth deeply into the man's left forearm. *Take that asshole,* Rebecca thought triumphantly.

The man cursed violently as he drew back his right arm and slammed it down on Roscoe's neck. Roscoe yelped and released his grip. He fell to the floor, but quickly righted himself. He flew at the man again. This time, he sunk his teeth into the man's already injured thigh. The man let out another cry of pain.

Rebecca tried to move, but she couldn't get her body to respond to her urging. She desperately clung to consciousness as she watched Roscoe viciously attack the man. *Good boy, Roscoe. Get the son-of-a-bitch,* she thought as she felt herself slipping into the beckoning darkness.

~

Barbara pulled up in front of the clinic. As she stepped out of her car, she could hear a dog barking inside. She felt a cold shiver run up her spine. She was suddenly gripped with fear. *Don't be silly,* she chided herself. *I'm sure everything's fine.*

She hurried toward the door. As soon as she entered, Roscoe ran from the back. Barbara's heart flew into her throat. The dog's muzzle was covered in blood.

"Oh my God," she whispered. "Rebecca!" she called. "Where are you?!"

Roscoe turned and disappeared into the back. Barbara rushed after him. As soon as she rounded the corner, she spotted Rebecca lying on the floor. A pool of blood surrounded her. Another trail of blood led to the back door. Roscoe sat near Rebecca's shoulder. He whimpered softly.

Barbara flew to Rebecca's side. Blood covered her face. Her eyes were swollen shut. Her lips were split and bleeding. A large laceration ran from above her right temple disappearing into her hairline. There were no bite marks on her. For a moment, she had thought that the blood on Roscoe's muzzle might have belonged to Rebecca. It must belong to whoever did this to her.

Barbara stretched out a shaky hand and pressed it to Rebecca's neck. She breathed a sigh of relief as she felt a pulse beat beneath her fingers. She quickly pulled her purse from her shoulder. She reached inside, pulled out her cell phone, and dialed 911.

"911, what's your emergency?" a voice answered.

"There's been a break-in at Animal Friends Veterinary Hospital. Please hurry, Dr. Miller's badly injured. She needs an ambulance."

"Is the intruder still there, ma'am?" the voice asked.

"No," Barbara answered. "He was gone by the time I arrived."

Barbara stayed on the line long enough to give the dispatcher her name and as much information as she could about Rebecca's condition and the state of the clinic.

Within minutes of hanging up, she heard sirens approaching. Rebecca hadn't regained consciousness. Her breathing was shallow, but steady. Silent tears streamed down Barbara's face as she sat beside her daughter, gently holding her hand. *Please hurry,* she thought. *My baby needs you.*

Roscoe gently nudged Barbara's shoulder. She glanced at him. She'd forgotten he was there.

"I think you saved her life," she said, reaching out to put an arm around the dog's shoulders. He glanced at her, then turned worried eyes back to Rebecca. "She's going to be all right," Barbara said firmly.

~

Mitch was on his way home when the call came over the radio reporting the break-in at Animal Friends and injuries on the scene. "What?!" he yelled.

His tires squealed as he executed a quick U-turn. He knew this was the time that Rebecca usually went to make one last check on the animals. His heart pounded in his chest as he raced toward the clinic. His guts clenched in fear as he thought about what might have happened to Rebecca.

He flew into the parking lot and slammed his brakes. A police cruiser and ambulance were already on the scene. He leaped out of his car and ran into the building. He met the EMTs as they wheeled Rebecca out of the back. Barbara saw him and hurried over.

"What happened?" he asked.

"I'm not sure. Someone must have broken in and attacked her. She was unconscious when I got here." Her voice broke on the last word.

Mitch reached out and put an arm around her shoulders. "Did you see anyone?"

Barbara shook her head. "No. I think the dog attacked him. He was loose when I came in, and his muzzle was covered with blood. There's blood everywhere back there. It's not all Rebecca's," she answered shakily.

Roscoe stood next to the gurney. Mitch could see dried blood on his muzzle and shoulders. The dog watched anxiously as the EMTs finished loading Rebecca into the ambulance. "You go ahead with them. I'll find out what I can here and then I'll meet you at the hospital." He gave Barbara a gentle squeeze. "Your daughter's a tough woman. She's going to be okay."

Barbara nodded. Her throat constricted as fresh tears streamed down her face. She hurried to climb into the ambulance.

Mitch moved over to grab Roscoe as he tried to follow Barbara into the ambulance. "Sorry, buddy. They won't let you go," he said softly.

Roscoe whimpered as they watched the ambulance drive away. "Come on, Roscoe," Mitch said, leading him back inside the clinic.

As he entered the treatment area, he stopped to survey the room. He saw blood-stained scissors on the floor near the treatment counter. A smeared blood trail went from the treatment counter to just in front of the ICU door. A moderate amount of blood was focused in that area. Another trail of blood droplets led to the back door.

Officers Sanders and Michaels came over to talk with him.

"Hello, Detective," Sanders greeted.

"Sanders. Michaels," Mitch responded with a slight nod toward each man. "What do we know?"

"The back door's lock is busted, but according to the victim's mother, the front door was unlocked. So, it looks like the perp must have already been inside when the victim arrived. He attacked her. There was a struggle. The dog must have gotten out of his kennel and attacked the perp. Then the guy split," answered Michaels.

"Okay, so we need to monitor the hospital and doctors' offices for anyone seeking treatment for dog bites," Mitch answered. "Did you see any evidence that Dr. Miller had been stabbed with those scissors?"

"No, sir," Sanders answered.

"All right, then the perp will also have a stab wound. That should make it pretty easy to pick him up if he tries to seek treatment."

"The forensic team's on its way to collect DNA and fingerprints. We'll get the guy. You think he's part of the gang that's been robbing all the pharmacies?" asked Sanders

Mitch nodded. "That would be my first instinct."

"I heard you talking to the victim's mother," Michaels commented. "Do you know them?"

"Yes, Rebecca Miller is the woman who was hurt. She owns this clinic. She's a close friend of mine. I'm going to go to the hospital to check on her. Call me if anything pops on this guy tonight."

The officers nodded in agreement.

Mitch looked down at Roscoe, who was sitting at his feet. "What am I going to do with you?" he asked. It seemed cruel to just leave him there after what the dog had been through. He decided to take him by his place on his way to the hospital. He grabbed a couple of dog dishes and some food. Then he loaded the dog into his car.

Mitch's thoughts turned to Rebecca as he drove toward home. Then he thought about Derrick working the ICU.

"Shit," he cursed as he pictured how his friend was going to respond to seeing Rebecca wheeled in on a gurney. Rebecca was supposed to have been his responsibility tonight. Derrick would never forgive him if she didn't recover from this.

CHAPTER 23

Derrick rubbed his temples as he leaned against the nurses' station.

"Are you okay, Dr. Peterson?" asked Sharon, an older nurse who liked to mother everyone who worked in the ER.

"I'm fine. It's just been a long day," Derrick answered. "Since we seem to have a lull, I think I'll go lie down for a few minutes."

Sharon nodded. "We'll page you if we need you," she answered.

Derrick turned and started to move away. The sound of an approaching ambulance stopped his movement. He sighed heavily. Sharon smiled sympathetically and reached out to pat his arm.

He watched as the EMTs opened the back of the ambulance and pulled out a gurney. His eyes widened in shock as he saw Barbara Miller exit the ambulance. He felt his heart jump into his throat. His stomach clenched into a tight knot. His legs felt like lead as he started moving toward the ER entrance. *Rebecca!* his mind screamed as panic built within him.

Barbara spotted him and hurried in his direction. Derrick's attention was entirely focused on the gurney. The EMTs turned it, so that it faced the ER door. Derrick got his first glimpse of Rebecca's severely battered face. He let out an anguished roar as white-hot rage ripped through him.

He felt someone grab his arm. He jerked it away. "Derrick!" a voice cried urgently. Something in the tone of the voice penetrated his pain-filled mind. He glanced down into the tear-stained face of Rebecca's mother.

"Did Dalton do that to her?" he asked through clenched teeth.

Barbara shook her head quickly. "No. She was attacked at the vet clinic. I'll explain it all later. Right now, you've got to get hold of yourself. She needs you."

Derrick hesitated only briefly. With great effort, he pushed his fear aside and regained control of his emotions. He hurried toward the gurney. The EMTs relayed Rebecca's vitals as they moved her onto a waiting bed.

She was in shock. Her blood pressure was dropping. Her breathing was very shallow.

Derrick quickly examined her. His anger at whoever had done this to her threatened to consume him. He wanted to beat the bastard to a bloody pulp. He struggled to maintain his composure as he barked out orders to the nurses. "Call the OR. She needs surgery now. She's bleeding internally."

Within minutes, she was being wheeled out of the ER and into the surgery ward. Derrick felt helpless as he watched her being taken away. Part of him wanted to scrub in for the surgery, but he was still rational enough to know that the surgeon would be better able to perform his job if he didn't have Derrick hovering over his shoulder.

He went to find Barbara. She was standing in the corner of the ER waiting room, her arms wrapped around her stomach. Her eyes were red-rimmed and swollen. When she saw him enter the room, she hurried toward him.

"How is she?" she asked anxiously.

"She's bleeding internally. They've taken her into surgery. She's also got several broken ribs. She hasn't regained consciousness. We won't be able to determine the extent of the head injury until she does."

Barbara nodded. "She's going to be okay, isn't she?"

"Yes, dammit," he growled. "The bastard beat her to within an inch of life, but Rebecca won't give up. She won't let him win."

Barbara laid her hand on his arm. He took a deep breath. Barbara felt a faint shutter course through him. They walked down the hallway to the surgery waiting room and moved to sit in two of the chairs.

Derrick leaned forward and braced his elbows on his knees. "Tell me what happened," he said softly.

Barbara told him about the phone call she'd received from Rebecca. She told him that Rebecca had informed her that Dalton had been arrested, and that was why she was going to the clinic alone. Then Barbara described the scene at the clinic when she arrived.

Derrick let out an angry growl when Barbara described what Rebecca had looked like when she found her.

"Mitch will be here soon. He'll be able to tell us more about who did this," she said as she finished filling him in.

Just then, Barbara spotted June hurrying toward them. She'd called her and Marilyn while she'd been in the ER waiting room. She stood and moved to meet her. The two women embraced.

"How is she?" June asked anxiously.

"She's in surgery," Barbara answered. "Derrick says she's bleeding internally and has a head wound. That's really all we know."

June glanced past Barbara. Derrick sat in a chair across the room. He was leaning forward with his forearms resting on his knees. He was staring at the floor. His face was set in a stony mask.

"He doesn't look like he's taking it very well," June whispered.

Barbara glanced over her shoulder, then turned back to June. "You should have heard the sound he made when he first saw Rebecca. It was heart breaking."

"Did she look that bad?" June asked.

Barbara nodded. "Her face was almost unrecognizable."

As the women approached Derrick, he glanced up. June sucked in a quick breath at the mixture of pain and rage that danced in his eyes. She sat next to him and placed an arm across his broad shoulders.

"She's going to be okay," June said confidently.

Derrick nodded, but didn't answer.

~

Mitch sped toward the hospital. It took him longer than he'd planned to get Roscoe settled. He'd felt compelled to give the dog a quick bath. He just couldn't leave him covered in blood. Roscoe shivered fearfully throughout the entire bath. When he finished, Mitch spent a few minutes trying to soothe the obviously frightened animal. He'd left him curled up on the couch. He hoped that his house wasn't shredded by the time he got home.

He'd also called the precinct to check on the status of the hunt for the man who'd attacked Rebecca. So far, there were no suspects. Mitch was confident the guy would show up. From the amount of blood on the clinic floor, he was sure that Roscoe had wounded him badly.

Half an hour later, Mitch arrived at the hospital. He checked in at the information desk and was directed to the surgery ward.

Derrick spotted Mitch moving toward them. He felt rage bubble up inside him. He'd left Rebecca in Mitch's care and now she was fighting for her life. He jumped up and turned to face Mitch.

Mitch's steps faltered as he read the anger on his friend's face. He knew Derrick needed someone to take his fear and anger out on. He squared his shoulders and continued walking toward him.

Angry sparks flew from Derrick's eyes. He stood ramrod straight. His hands were clenched into fists at his side. "You were supposed to be watching her," he bit out furiously.

"I got a call telling me that Dalton had been arrested. I needed to go handle that. There was no reason for me to stay with her," Mitch explained.

"Obviously, there was a reason. She's lying in a hospital bed fighting for her life!" Derrick said angrily.

"You have no idea how much I regret that," Mitch replied, his voice filled with regret. "There was no way for me to know she was still in danger."

Mitch watched as Derrick struggled to gain control of his emotions. Every muscle in his body was hard as stone. He was taking quick, shallow breaths. A pulse pounded in his temple.

Barbara watched the exchange between the two men. She wasn't sure whether or not she should step in or let them work it out. She didn't want to witness any more violence.

Just then, Marilyn rounded the corner. She saw the two men squared off, looking like they were ready to attack each other.

"How's Rebecca?" she called out, breaking the strained silence.

Both men turned toward her. Barbara purposefully walked between the two men on her way to meet Marilyn. June jumped up to join them.

"She's still in surgery," Barbara answered.

A moment later, the doors to the OR opened and Dr. Johnson hurried through them. Derrick's anger turned to fear as he saw the worried look on his face.

"Mrs. Miller?"

Barbara nodded.

"I'm Dr. Johnson. I've just finished the surgery on your daughter. She's in recovery. Her spleen had ruptured. We had to remove it. Her liver and both her kidneys are severely bruised, they should heal, given time and rest. She's got a severe concussion with quite a bit of swelling around the brain tissue. Her nose and both of her cheekbones have also been fractured."

With each injury Dr. Johnson named, Derrick felt like he was receiving a blow to that area. Pain ripped through him at the thought of the beating Rebecca had suffered at the hands of her attacker. He wanted more than anything to cause the man the same pain he'd caused Rebecca.

"When can I see her?" Barbara asked.

"She's being moved into ICU. Once she's settled, you'll be able to see her. With her head injury, we're not sure when she'll wake up. We've placed a drain to help relieve the swelling. She'll be able to have visitors, but only one at a time and no one will be able to stay for more than a few minutes. The next 24 hours are critical."

"Thank you, Doctor," Barbara said softly.

Dr. Johnson nodded. Then he turned on his heel and disappeared through the surgery doors.

Barbara moved to sink into a chair. Marilyn and June sat on either side of her.

Mitch and Derrick still stood facing each other. Derrick nodded toward the door and turned to walk toward it. Mitch followed him out.

"Who did it, Mitch?" Derrick asked, his voice still held a note of anger.

Mitch shook his head. "I don't know. I'm pretty sure it's a member of the gang that's been stealing prescription drugs. I think Rebecca must have walked in on him robbing the clinic. That dog, Roscoe, attacked the man, and it looks like Rebecca stabbed him, so we're contacting all the medical treatment facilities. When he goes in to have those wounds treated, we'll get him."

Derrick let out a sigh and leaned back against the wall. He closed his eyes. "I almost lost her, Mitch," he said softly. He opened his eyes and met Mitch's gaze. Mitch had never seen his friend look so scared. "I could still lose her."

"You're not going to lose her," Mitch said confidently. "Rebecca's one of the toughest women I've ever met. She'll pull through this."

They remained silent for a few moments. Each man lost in thoughts of Rebecca. They both cared very deeply for her.

Derrick broke the silence. "What happened to the dog?" he asked. "Rebecca will want to know as soon as she wakes up."

Mitch grinned. He knew the question was Derrick's way of saying things were okay between them. "You're right. That's probably the first question she'll ask. He's at my place."

Derrick gave a quick nod. "Good."

~

Derrick sat in a chair next to Rebecca's hospital bed. It was close to dawn. He'd been in to see her several times throughout the night. He'd had to share the rotation with Barbara, June, and Marilyn, so his visits had been few and far between. Rebecca had not regained consciousness, but her vitals were strong and steady.

Mitch had left after being assured that Rebecca was in stable condition. He'd made Derrick promise to call him if she woke. His main objective was to find the man who had done this to her.

Derrick gazed at Rebecca's swollen features. His guts twisted painfully each time he looked at her. Her recovery was going to be slow and painful. He wanted to take the pain away. Being the person sitting beside the bed filled with fear, felt so different from being the doctor looking at the patient through detached eyes. He hated the feeling of helplessness.

Derrick reached out and gently took Rebecca's hand. "It's time to wake up now, Rebecca," he commanded gruffly.

He felt a slight movement in her fingers. His eyes flew to her face. She let out a soft groan.

"I know it's painful, sweetheart, but you need to wake up," he said softly.

Her eyelids fluttered. Then her eyes opened to slits. The swelling prevented Rebecca from opening them fully.

"Derrick?" she croaked.

"Yeah, it's me," he answered around the lump in his throat. "You gave us all quite a scare."

"Roscoe?" she whispered.

Derrick chuckled. "Mitch and I knew that would be the first thing you asked about. You were brutally attacked, and your initial thought is for the dog. He's fine. Mitch took him home with him."

"Good," Rebecca said softly. "He saved me."

"Yes, he did," Derrick agreed. "I need to go let everyone know you're awake." He stood and gazed lovingly down at her. "I'm glad you came back to me, Rebecca," he said softly as he leaned down and gently brushed his lips across her forehead. He straightened and left to let the others know she was finally awake.

He stopped by the nurses' station. "Rebecca Miller is awake," he informed Stacy, the nurse on duty. She jumped up and hurried into Rebecca's room.

Derrick went out into the waiting room. Three sets of tired eyes swung his direction.

He grinned at the three women. "She's awake," he said simply.

Barbara leaped to her feet and ran to him. She threw her arms around his waist. The next thing he knew all three women were embracing him. He was at a loss. He stood there awkwardly as they squeezed him from three sides.

Finally, Marilyn broke away and began to dance a jig. Barbara and June joined her. They were all three laughing as tears ran freely down their faces. Derrick watched the women in stunned amazement. He'd never witnessed such unabashed joy before. He felt the weight that had been crushing down on his heart lift. Relief washed over him. He found himself grinning foolishly at the three women as they danced around him.

A moment later, the doctor on duty stepped into the waiting room.

"I just finished examining Rebecca. She remembers everything. Her reflexes are normal. Her vitals are strong. It doesn't look like there is any brain damage."

"Woohoo!" the three women chorused.

"Can I see her now?" Barbara asked, grinning from ear to ear.

"Yes," the doctor replied, returning her grin.

"I'll be quick," she told June and Marilyn. "I'm sure she'll want to see you, too."

Derrick stepped outside to call Mitch.

"Is she awake?" Mitch asked groggily, sitting up in bed.

"Yeah, and we were right. The first thing she asked about was that dog."

Mitch chuckled and looked over at Roscoe, who was stretched out on the other side of his bed. The dog lifted his head and thumped his tail. "Be sure and tell her he's made himself right at home. When do you think she'll be ready to talk to me?"

"The ladies are taking turns visiting her now. Then she'll probably need to rest. Maybe she'll feel up to it in a couple of hours."

Mitch glanced at the clock on his nightstand. "It's 6:30 now. I'll have some breakfast. Then go check in at the station. I'll head to the hospital around 9:00. I need to get her statement as soon as possible."

"Still no sign of the guy?" Derrick asked, frustration in his tone.

"No, but I'm sure he'll turn up soon," Mitch replied. "Why don't you go grab a couple of hours of sleep, Derrick? You can meet me at the hospital. I'm sure you'll want to be there when I question her. She'll need your support."

Derrick had been up for 36 hours. He was completely exhausted. "Okay, I'll see you at 9:00."

He went back into the waiting room and told Barbara about his conversation with Mitch. "You should think about getting some rest, too," he suggested.

She nodded. "Rebecca's going to need us even more now that she's awake," Barbara agreed.

CHAPTER 24

On the way home, Derrick thought about Captain. The poor dog had been home alone all night. He groaned with fatigue and turned his car to make a detour to Rebecca's house. When he arrived, he realized that he didn't have a key. Then he remembered that Rebecca had told him her neighbor had a key, so he could let Captain out on the nights she got stuck in the clinic. Derrick walked over to the neighbor's and rang the doorbell. It was 7:00 Tuesday morning. He hoped they hadn't already left for work.

Within moments, a tall, lean man with short gray hair answered the door.

"May I help you?" he asked politely.

"I'm Derrick Peterson. I'm a friend of Rebecca's. She's been in an accident and is in the hospital. Her dog's been home alone all night. She told me that you have a key to her place. Would you mind letting me in, so that I can get the dog?"

The man eyed Derrick warily. "How do I know you're a friend of hers?" he asked.

"Look, this is not some elaborate scheme designed to steal Captain." Derrick said, trying to remain calm and not let his temper flare.

The man continued to hesitate. Derrick realized that he probably looked like a bum. He hadn't slept, shaved, or showered in two days. He sighed heavily and tried again to reason with the man.

"I appreciate you being cautious, especially given the fact that someone threw a brick through Rebecca's window a few days ago, but I assure you, I'm only here to take care of the dog. I'm obviously not a stranger if I know the dog's name," he reasoned.

The man finally relented. "Okay, I'll let you in. You're right, there would be easier ways to steal a dog. What kind of accident? Did it have to do with the man who threw the brick?"

"Someone broke into her vet clinic. It wasn't the same person who threw the brick," Derrick answered wearily.

"Is she okay?" the man asked.

"She's in the ICU at Saint Luke's, but it looks like she's going to be okay," Derrick answered. "I don't mean to be rude, but I'm really in a hurry."

The man nodded in understanding. "Just let me get the key," he said, disappearing back into his house.

Derrick turned and walked over to Rebecca's. He waited impatiently for the man to bring the key. He felt anger wash over him as he stood on the porch staring at the boarded up window. Rebecca had been through hell the last few days. He vowed to make sure she never had to go through anything like it again.

The neighbor finally arrived with the key. When they stepped through the door, Captain ran and leaped up onto Derrick. Then he turned and raced toward the back door.

The neighbor chuckled. "He obviously knows you. I'll leave you now."

Derrick nodded and then followed Captain to the back. He opened the door and stepped outside. He watched as Captain quickly ran into the yard and relieved himself. As soon as he finished, Captain ran back up onto the porch and sat at Derrick's feet. He looked up and gave a soft whimper.

Derrick bent down and rubbed his ears. "She's hurt, boy, but she's going to be okay. I'll take you back to my place. You can play with Trouble until Rebecca's ready to come home."

By the time he got home, it was after 7:30. He took a quick shower and then grabbed an hour of sleep. Being a doctor, he was used to going long stretches with little sleep. He was eager to get back to the hospital and check on Rebecca. He didn't want her to relive what had happened to her without him being there. He'd kill Mitch if he didn't wait for him.

When he arrived at the hospital, he was informed that Rebecca had been moved out of the ICU and into a regular room. When he got to her room, he found Barbara snoozing in a chair next to the bed. She apparently hadn't taken his advice to go home to get some rest. Rebecca was also sleeping. Barbara opened her eyes as he moved further into the room.

"How is she?" he asked softly.

"She's in a lot of pain, but she's stable. They moved us up here about 30 minutes ago. She's been sleeping since we got here."

"I thought you were going to go home and get some rest," Derrick chided softly.

"I didn't want to leave her alone. I can go now that you're here," Barbara answered.

Derrick was relieved to hear her say that. He was hoping that Mitch would be able to question Rebecca without Barbara needing to hear it. He was sure that Rebecca would tell her about it eventually, but he thought it would be better for Barbara if she had some time to recover from the horror of last night before hearing it.

Barbara slowly unfolded herself from the chair. "I'll be back in a few hours. Call me if she needs me," she whispered.

"I will," he answered.

As the door closed behind her, Derrick took a seat in the chair she'd just vacated. His eyes slowly wandered over Rebecca's swollen and bruised face. He felt moisture fill his eyes. Last night, his fear and anger kept the pain at bay.

Now as he sat there looking at her, he felt the pain rip at his heart. Her soft, beautiful features were puffy and covered with dark bruises.

Rebecca opened her eyes and saw Derrick sitting beside her. She was shocked to see the tears streaming down his face.

"Do I really look that bad?" she asked.

"No, you look beautiful," he said softly.

She gave a soft laugh. "You're a terrible liar."

He reached for her hand. "You do look beautiful to me." He paused. Then said, "Last night, when I thought I might lose you, I didn't know how to handle it. I've never felt that kind of pain in my life. You've opened my heart, Rebecca. I'm not sure I like it. I don't like feeling so vulnerable. I've never cried for anyone before."

Rebecca gave his hand a gentle squeeze. She didn't know what to say. A large lump formed in her throat. She felt her heart swell with love for him. She couldn't believe that this big, strong, brilliant, wonderful man had just admitted something like that to her.

Derrick dipped his head and placed a soft kiss on her hand. Then he rested his forehead against it. He let out a heavy sigh.

"Ahem," Mitch cleared his throat from the doorway.

Derrick jerked his head up and turned toward the door. He felt his face flush with embarrassment. Mitch sauntered into the room. He ignored Derrick as he went around to the other side of the bed and smiled down at Rebecca. He pulled a stuffed dog out from behind his back.

"I know it's not the real deal, but it will have to do for a while," he said, handing the dog to Rebecca.

She cracked a slight smile. It was all she could manage with her swollen lips. "Thank you, Mitch. It's great."

Then she let out a loud groan.

"What is it?" Derrick asked worriedly.

"Captain. He's been home by himself all this time," she answered, her voice filled with remorse.

Derrick sighed with relief. "I went to get him first thing this morning. He's busy playing with Trouble."

Rebecca squeezed his hand gratefully. "Thank you," she sighed. "How did you get in?" she asked quizzically.

"I asked the neighbor to use the key you gave him," Derrick answered.

"Rebecca, I hate to have to put you through this, but I really need to hear about what happened last night," Mitch said. "Do you feel up to it?"

She nodded. "Yes, I know it's important to tell you." Her face had gone very pale.

"Take your time," Derrick said. He still held her hand in his.

"I went to let Roscoe out. On my way, I had a flat tire, so I walked the rest of the way to the clinic. I knew something was wrong as soon as I got there. I could hear him barking. He never does that." She paused and took a deep breath. She knew she needed to tell Mitch everything that had happened, but the terror she'd felt during the attack threatened to overwhelm her as the images floated through her mind.

"As soon as I walked into the back, a man jumped me from behind. We fought. Roscoe kept throwing himself against the ICU door. I knew that if I could get to him, he'd help me fight the guy off. I reached the door, but before I could get it open, the guy knocked me to the ground and started kicking and punching me." She paused again. She closed her eyes, trying to hold the terror at bay. Derrick gave her hand an encouraging squeeze. She opened her eyes and glanced at him. His face was a stony mask.

She took another deep breath and continued, "The next thing I knew, Roscoe was attacking the guy. I'm not sure how he managed to get out of the room. I must have cracked the door open just enough for him to get out. Then everything went black."

"What can you tell me about the guy? Did you get a look at his face?" Mitch asked.

"No, he was wearing a mask. He was big, probably close to six feet. He was also muscular. I could feel his muscles bulging as he held me to him."

"There were bloody scissors on the clinic floor. Did you stab him?"

"Yes, in his left thigh," she answered.

Mitch grinned. "That's my girl. Did he say anything to you that might give us a clue as to who he is?"

Rebecca shook her head. "No. The only thing he said was 'I'm gonna kill you for that, bitch' after I stabbed him."

"Was there anything distinctive about his clothes?"

Rebecca thought about that for a moment. "No. I'm sorry. All I remember is they were black."

Mitch smiled down at her. "You did great, Rebecca. Between the stab wound and whatever wounds Roscoe gave him, we should be able to identify him."

"How's Roscoe?" Rebecca asked.

"He's fine. He slept with me last night," Mitch answered.

Rebecca smiled slightly. "Thank you for taking him home with you. I told you he was a great dog."

"After what he did to save you, you won't get any argument from me. He's welcome to stay with me as long as he likes." He bent down and placed a chaste kiss on the top of her head. "Last night gave us all quite a scare. I promise to catch the guy who did this to you."

"I know you will," Rebecca answered as he straightened.

Mitch nodded and said, "I'll keep you informed of our progress." Then he turned and left the room.

Rebecca watched him leave and then turned her head to look at Derrick. He'd remained silent while she'd talked. His eyes were intense as they looked into hers.

He cleared his throat and said, "It kills me that you had to go through that alone. I wish like hell I'd been there."

She lifted her hand and cupped the side of his face. He placed his hand on top of hers, then turned slightly and brushed his lips against her palm. Rebecca felt a tingling sensation run up the length of her arm.

"I love you, Rebecca," he said simply.

Rebecca's breath caught in her throat. Her heart pounded hard in her chest. Her eyes locked with Derrick's. The gold flecks in his eyes glowed with a bright intensity as they bore into hers.

She struggled to speak around the large lump in her throat. Finally, she answered softly, "I love you, too."

Derrick's mouth tilted into a sexy grin as they continued to stare into each other's eyes. The spell was broken when a nurse opened the door to her room and hurried inside.

"I'm sorry, but I need to check her," she said to Derrick. "You can come back in about 15 minutes."

Derrick nodded. He stood and leaned to place a gentle kiss on her swollen lips.

"I'll be back," he promised as he straightened away.

As soon as he left the room, the nurse commented, "That is one fine-looking man."

"Yes, he is," Rebecca agreed.

~

The rest of the day passed in a foggy haze. The medications they were giving her were making it difficult for Rebecca to stay awake. Barbara and Derrick had both been steady fixtures in the room throughout the day. Marilyn also stopped by to see her.

Late in the afternoon, June walked into her room.

"Hi, kiddo," she greeted. "How do you feel?"

"Probably a lot like you did after your car accident," Rebecca answered. "They have me on some good drugs. I'm having a hard time staying awake."

"Well, don't even try. You need the sleep," June answered.

"That's what Derrick and I have been telling her," Barbara said.

Derrick had left about an hour previously to check on the dogs, so Barbara was the only one currently in the room.

"I tell you what, that man looked like he was going through hell last night," June said. "He loves you, you know."

"Yes," Rebecca agreed. "He told me earlier today."

"What?!" Barbara said in shock. "And you waited until now to tell me?"

"I haven't had a chance to tell you before now," Rebecca answered.

June moved to sit in a chair near Rebecca's bed. "That's wonderful, Rebecca. I've known he was crazy about you for a long time, but I wasn't sure if he was ever going to admit it. I guess almost losing you was enough to make him realize how he felt about you."

Rebecca nodded. Her throat suddenly went very dry. She grabbed the large cup of water on the table beside her bed and tilted the straw to take a long swallow. She felt weak as a kitten. She couldn't believe how much effort it took to hold the water.

She returned the water to the table and took a deep breath. When she could talk, she said, "Speaking of love, I'm sorry I'm not going to be able to make it to your wedding Saturday. The doctor says I'll be here for at least a week. They have me on dialysis until my liver and kidneys start working right again."

"Are you kidding me?" June asked. "You think I would have the wedding without my maid of honor?"

"You can't cancel your wedding because of me," Rebecca protested.

"I don't plan on canceling it. They have a chapel in this hospital, don't they?"

"Oh, June, you don't want to get married in a hospital," Rebecca said.

"Why not?" June asked. "I'll still be married. Walter and I don't care where it happens."

Rebecca felt tears sting her eyes. She couldn't believe what June was suggesting. She reached out and squeezed June's hand.

"Thank you, June. It will mean the world to me to be there."

"Good. It's all settled. Barbara and I can go talk with the hospital. You close your eyes and get some rest."

"Before you go, tell me what's happening with Animal Friends."

"The police have it all taped up. They let me in long enough to grab the appointment book, but only after I called Mitch and he told them to do it. Anyway, I've called all the clients we had scheduled for the next month and told them that the clinic was temporarily closed. I also changed the voice-mail message."

Rebecca sighed. "Thank you, June. I knew you'd take care of things." Then she bit out angrily, "This is such bullshit. I can't believe someone did this to me, and for what, drugs?"

Barbara placed a hand on her shoulder. "You have a right to be angry, honey."

"I hope the wounds Roscoe gave him are hurting like hell," Rebecca muttered.

CHAPTER 25

The next morning, Derrick brought Captain to visit Rebecca. When they arrived, she was sleeping. They stopped next to her bed. Derrick's mind was filled with marvel at the fact that this small, feisty woman had stolen his heart. Now that he'd admitted his feelings for her, he felt almost overwhelmed with the need to keep telling her how much she meant to him. It was as if he'd been living under a dark cloud his entire life, and now it had been replaced by sunshine.

Captain let out a soft whimper.

"It's okay, boy," Derrick whispered. "She's going to be fine. She'll be very happy to see you."

Captain thumped his tail. His eyes were fixed on Rebecca.

Rebecca slowly opened her eyes. Her face lit up when she spotted Captain.

"You brought Captain!" she said in delight.

Derrick didn't bother to answer as all her attention was focused on her beloved dog. He'd placed his paws on the side of her bed, and Rebecca was showering the top of his head with kisses. Captain was groaning with pleasure. His tail was waving so hard, Derrick could feel the breeze.

A moment later, Mitch sauntered into the room.

Rebecca glanced up. Her eyes sparkled with happiness. "Hi, Mitch."

Mitch smiled. "Hi, hot stuff. I see you've been reunited with your favorite guy."

Rebecca chuckled. "Well, he's certainly one of them." She met Derrick's eyes, and her heart fluttered at the love she saw shining in his.

Mitch saw the look that passed between his friends. "Don't tell me that this guy finally came to his senses and told you how he feels," he said in exaggerated surprise.

"As a matter of fact, I did," Derrick answered. "I'm in love with this exceptional woman and the crazy thing is, she loves me back."

"What in the world do you see in this guy?" Mitch teased.

Rebecca grinned. "I think you have that backwards. What could a guy like him possibly see in me?"

"Are you kidding? You're perfect. He's the one with all the problems."

"Hey, watch it," Derrick growled in mock anger.

"Do you have any news?" Derrick asked seriously.

Mitch shook his head. "Nothing, so far. We've alerted all the medical treatment facilities, but he hasn't showed. I'm thinking someone must have patched him up. If he's part of the gang that's been robbing pharmacies, they probably have all the supplies they would need. We know that most of the other break-ins have been done in pairs. I'm not sure why this guy was alone last night. Maybe, he's not part of the same group or maybe something happened to his partner."

Derrick frowned. "You don't have any other leads?"

"No. They hit ten places over the last three months, and we've got nothing," Mitch bit out in frustration.

"I know you'll catch him," Rebecca said confidently.

"So, tell me more about you," Mitch said. "How long are they going to keep you?"

"I'm not sure. I'm hoping not more than a week. It depends on how long it takes my kidneys to start working to the point that I don't need dialysis, and how long they have to keep this drain in my head," Rebecca replied, pointing to the long tube coming out of the left side of her forehead.

"Isn't June's wedding Saturday?" Mitch asked.

"Yes, but she's decided to have the wedding in the hospital chapel, so I can be there."

Mitch chuckled. "I didn't even know you could get married in a hospital."

Rebecca grinned. "Well, it's not ideal, but the hospital gave her permission. She's set on getting married on Saturday, and she's determined to have me there."

Mitch stayed for a few more minutes and then announced that he'd better get back to work. He assured them that he'd let them know as soon as they got any solid leads.

~

Later that evening, Mitch decided he needed some fresh air. He grabbed a leash. Roscoe started dancing around his legs in excitement. Mitch chuckled at the dog's antics.

"I guess you'd like some fresh air, too," he commented.

Woof!

"All right, then," Mitch said as he attached the leash to Roscoe's shiny new leather collar. He'd made a trip to the pet store earlier that day to buy dog supplies. He'd concluded that whether he liked it or not, he was stuck with Roscoe for the foreseeable future. He didn't really mind. Roscoe was a good dog.

They set out on a brisk walk. It was dusk. The sky was slightly overcast, so it was darker than usual at this time of night. Mitch was lost in thought as they walked. He wasn't paying too much attention to where they were going. It just felt good to get out and get the blood pumping. *The guy's got to show up somewhere,* he thought, as frustrated anger coursed through his system.

They'd been walking for about an hour when Roscoe suddenly growled low in his throat. Mitch's attention snapped back into focus. He looked down at Roscoe. The dog's hackles were raised.

"What is it, boy?" Mitch asked warily. He glanced into the darkness that surrounded them. They were in a run-down neighborhood. The few working streetlights cast everything into shadow. The street and sidewalks were empty. Mitch couldn't see what was upsetting Roscoe.

Roscoe continued to growl. He was staring straight ahead. He'd gone very still, every muscle in his body tensed.

Mitch peered into the darkness ahead of them. His heartbeat quickened. His senses were on high alert.

Roscoe caught Mitch off-guard when he suddenly lunged, jerking the leash from Mitch's grasp. Then he took off at a sprint down the sidewalk. Mitch ran after him.

A man in a dark shirt and jeans appeared out of nowhere several yards ahead of Roscoe. He saw the dog and turned to run. The man stumbled. He ran with a pronounced limp, almost dragging his left leg. Roscoe was closing fast. Mitch could hear the dog snarling viciously. He pulled his gun.

"Stop!" he yelled. "Spring Valley PD!"

The man continued to move frantically away from them. A few seconds later, Roscoe launched himself into the air. He slammed into the man's back, knocking him to the ground.

"Get him off me!" the man screamed, his voice filled with terror.

Mitch sprinted toward them. He reached down and grabbed Roscoe's leash and tugged him off the fallen man. Roscoe continued to snarl as he took a few steps away from the man.

Mitch saw a bandage on the man's right arm. He also saw blood on his left pant leg.

"I think he knows you," Mitch said.

"I don't know him. I was just minding my own business," the man said in a shaky voice.

"What happened to your leg?" Mitch asked.

"I was in a car accident," the man replied.

"Sure you were," Mitch responded wryly. "How about we go down to the station and have a talk about how you really got those wounds?"

"Man, I ain't done nothin'," the man complained. "Can I get up now?" He was still lying face down on the pavement.

"Sit up nice and slow," Mitch commanded as he reached into his pocket and pulled out his cell phone. He called the station and requested they send a couple of cars.

The man sullenly glared at Mitch and Roscoe while they waited for the patrol cars. A few minutes later, they heard approaching sirens.

Officers Sanders and Michaels got out of the first car. Officers Bolton and Montgomery got out of the second.

"What's going on, Detective?" Officer Sanders asked as they approached him.

"Roscoe and I were taking a walk. He took off after this guy. I'm certain he's the asshole who broke into Animal Friends. We're going to need a doctor to confirm that his wounds are from dog bites and a stabbing. We're also going to need to collect some DNA to compare it to the DNA collected at the crime scene, but I'd bet my badge that he's our guy."

Officer Michaels bent down and rubbed Roscoe on the head. "Good boy, Roscoe," he praised. Then he straightened and walked over to the man staring belligerently up at him from the ground. He reached down and jerked the man to his feet.

He held the man firmly by the elbow as he walked him over to the waiting car. While they walked, Michaels read the man his rights. He opened the back door and shoved the man inside.

"I'm going to have Bolton and Montgomery take me by my house, so I can drop off Roscoe. I'll meet you at the station in a few minutes. Just put him in one of the interview rooms and call a doctor."

"You got it," Sanders said as he and Michaels climbed into their car and pulled away.

~

Early the next morning, Derrick heard his cell phone ringing just as he stepped out of a hot shower. His throat constricted with fear as he hurried to pull his phone from the pocket of the jeans he'd been wearing earlier that day. He checked the caller ID.

"What's going on, Mitch?" he asked gruffly.

"We got him," Mitch declared triumphantly.

"The bastard who attacked Rebecca?" Derrick asked.

"Yep. We brought him in last night. He spilled his guts to us. We know the whole story. Apparently, he and his girlfriend had been pulling the robberies. They were selling the drugs to a gang over in Beacher. His girlfriend left him last week, but he decided to keep doing the jobs without her. We picked her up a few hours ago. We called the Beacher PD and gave them the information on the buyers."

"How did you find the son-of-a-bitch?" Derrick asked.

"Roscoe found him," Mitch replied. He proceeded to tell Derrick everything that had happened the previous evening.

"I want you to go home and feed that dog a steak," Derrick commented.

Mitch chuckled. "Sure thing, he deserves it."

After he ended the call, Derrick hurriedly dressed. He couldn't wait to give Rebecca the good news.

Half an hour later, he arrived at the hospital. When he got to her room, he found June, Barbara, and Marilyn huddled around Rebecca's bed.

"Hi, Derrick," Marilyn greeted, when he strode into the room.

"Hi, Marilyn, what brings you ladies out so early in the morning?" he asked curiously.

"June's wedding is in two days. We're here to get everything finalized," Barbara answered.

"What's going on with you?" Marilyn asked. "You look like you've got something on your mind."

All four women gave him their full attention. He met Rebecca's gaze. She looked at him questioningly.

"Mitch called me this morning. They caught the guy," he said simply.

Barbara sucked in her breath. Rebecca's eyes went wide. June and Marilyn gave each other high fives.

"When? How?" Rebecca whispered.

Derrick related the story to the women. They listened with rapt attention.

"I wish Roscoe were here. I'd give him a great big hug," Rebecca choked as tears started to stream down her face.

"I told Mitch to feed him a steak," Derrick replied. He moved past the three women who were hugging each other in their happiness. He stopped beside Rebecca's bed.

"It's over, sweetheart," he whispered as he bent and lightly touched his lips to hers. "Now all you have to do is get strong enough to get out of this place."

"Amen to that," Barbara said. "We'll leave you two alone while we go down and take a look at the chapel."

The other two women nodded in agreement and turned to follow Barbara out.

"I almost can't believe it," Rebecca said, after they'd gone.

"I know. It seems a little surreal to me, too," Derrick replied.

~

Two days later, Marilyn and Barbara were helping Rebecca dress for the wedding. She absolutely refused to attend June's wedding wearing a hospital gown. All three women were in high spirits. The room was full of chatter and giggles as they struggled to get Rebecca into her dress.

Rebecca was recovering quickly from her wounds. Her kidneys had regained most of their functions. The doctor thought she'd be set to go home within the week. She still felt weak as a kitten, and it would take her several more weeks to be ready to return to work, but she was feeling good about her recovery.

Derrick had taken the week off from work and had spent almost every waking moment with her. Her love for him grew with each passing day. She'd never expected to fall so hard for anyone. She was overwhelmed by the fact that he loved her in return.

As soon as Rebecca was dressed, she sank down into a wheelchair. Marilyn pushed her out of the room. Derrick was waiting in the hallway. He pushed himself away from the wall when Rebecca's door opened. She sucked in her breath at the sight of him.

He wore a black tuxedo. The white shirt contrasted sharply to his deeply tanned skin. He grinned down at her.

"You look amazing," Rebecca whispered.

"And you look beautiful," he replied.

"Thank you for saying it, even if it isn't true," Rebecca commented dryly.

"It is true. You will always look beautiful to me. May I have the honor?" he asked, moving to take Marilyn's place.

They walked down the hallway and took the elevator down to the first floor. Several people cast curious glances their way as they moved toward the chapel.

"There's a small room just down the hall where June is getting ready," Marilyn told Derrick. "I'll take Rebecca the rest of the way. You can go on inside the chapel."

Derrick nodded and then bent to give Rebecca a kiss.

As he walked away, Marilyn bent and whispered in Rebecca's ear, "I almost swooned when I saw him. He's gorgeous in a tuxedo. You are one lucky woman."

Rebecca nodded. "I know. I still can't believe out of all the women he could have, he picked me."

"He's lucky to have you, and he knows it," Marilyn responded.

Barbara pulled the door open to the room June was getting ready in. June turned toward them.

"Wow, you look great, June, even better than when you tried it on. I think it must be the glow of happiness on your face," Barbara said, smiling widely.

"I just need someone to zip me up, and I think I'm all ready," June replied.

Barbara hurried into the room and stepped behind June.

"How are you feeling, Rebecca?" June asked.

"I'm feeling fine. Don't worry about me. Just enjoy your day," Rebecca replied.

Marilyn pushed her into the room. Barbara handed her a bouquet of white roses.

"I'll come get you when the music starts," Marilyn told Rebecca. "Then once we're at the chapel, I'll hand you off to Walter's son."

Ten minutes later, Marilyn stepped back into the room.

"Ready?" she asked June.

"Definitely," June replied.

Marilyn wheeled Rebecca into the hallway. When they reached the chapel, Walter's son, Matthew, stepped in to take her place. Marilyn hurried into the chapel and took a seat next to Derrick. Rebecca's eyes met his as she passed by him. She could feel her cheeks grow warm at the intensity of his gaze. Her heart fluttered in her chest as she saw his love for her shining in his eyes. She pulled her gaze away and looked down the aisle. Walter stood next to Reverend Stevens. He wore a black tuxedo. His normally unruly hair was slicked down on his head. His mouth was stretched into a huge, happy smile.

Barbara, June, and Marilyn had spent the morning decorating the little chapel. They'd placed white bows on the ends of each pew. Several baskets of colorful flowers were scattered around the front of the room.

Matthew wheeled Rebecca into her spot, and he moved to take his place near his dad. A moment later, *The Wedding March* filled the small chapel. June was escorted down the aisle by Walter's other son, Jonathon. Her eyes sparkled with happiness as she made her way toward Walter.

Tears sprang into Rebecca's eyes as Reverend Stevens began the ceremony. Rebecca turned to glance out at the audience. Her eyes passed over Kara, Jimmy, and his girlfriend, Amy. Kara looked very pretty sitting there in a simple blue cotton dress. Jimmy and Amy were exchanging loving looks. Next, she turned her gaze to her mother. Tears were streaming down her face. Rebecca smiled at her mother's emotional display. Mitch was sitting next to Barbara. He gave her a charming grin and an exaggerated wink. Her gazed wandered to Marilyn. Her friend caught her glance and smiled.

Finally, her eyes came to rest on Derrick. He was staring at her. He mouthed, "I love you."

Rebecca felt heat rush into her cheeks. "I love you, too," she mouthed back.

She turned her eyes back to June and Walter. June's face was radiant as she looked into Walter's eyes.

Reverend Stevens pronounced Walter and June, man and wife.

Rebecca smiled as the couple embraced for their first kiss as husband and wife. *Mom's right*, she thought, *dogs are wonderful companions who give unconditional love, but there's something amazing about loving a man.*

ABOUT THE AUTHOR

Dr. Billi Tiner graduated from Oklahoma State University's College of Veterinary Medicine in 1999. She has worked in a variety of veterinary fields including small animal practice and shelter animal practice. She currently lives with her husband, two children, three dogs, and three cats in Missouri. Dr. Tiner is the author of four middle-grade fiction novels (*Welcome Home, Friends for Life, The Rescue Team,* and *Heart of a Hero*). Each of her middle-grade novels have animals as their main character and are told from the animal's point of view. She is also the author of the young adult western series, *Bounty Hunter*.

For more information about Dr. Billi Tiner and her books visit www.tinerbooks.blogspot.com.

31666072R00152

Made in the USA
Charleston, SC
24 July 2014